D0054136

WHAT NIGEL KNEW

WHAT NIGEL KNEW

Evan Field

CLARKSON N. POTTER, INC/Publishers
Distributed by Crown Publishers, Inc.

New York

The characters portrayed in this novel are fictional. Any resemblance to persons living or dead is purely coincidental.

Inquiries should be addressed to Clarkson N. Potter, Inc., One Park Avenue, New York, New York 10016

Printed in the United States of America

Published simultaneously in Canada by General Publishing Company Limited

Library of Congress Cataloging in Publication Data

Field, Evan.
What Nigel knew.

I. Title.
PS3556.I374W5 1981 813'.54 81-5844
ISBN: 0-517-544687 AACR2

Designed by Dennis J. Grastorf
Art by Edward Gorey

10 9 8 7 6 5 4 3 2 1
FIRST EDITION

For Mother.
For Dad.
With much love.

Thursday

WHAT NIGEL KNOWS

Tinseltown Tidbits and Tattle

by Nigel Whitty

FILM FOPS TAKE NOTE: The New York Film Festival is coming to town, and with it the international film crowd. That is, all the Jean-Lucs and Jean-Pauls, Hanses and Klauses, Leonardos and Michelangelos whose pretentious porn and amorous angst have been passing too long as movie Art. Ah, just think what you can get away with when a Tit talks Italian or a Boob goes to Berlitz! But the American-made movie, *Subway*, is another matter altogether. Talking native turkey all the way, its gobble is unmistakable. In fact, when old Nigel heard that this disaster would be the Festival's Opening Night selection, he couldn't help wondering just who or what the movie's matinee-idol-turned-director, Danny Blue, has been bribing or bedding? More about Blueboy next time. As for his *Subway*, suffice it to say that the New York transit system should sue. . . . NEWS OF THE CONTRALTO: Having sneaked a peek at the Festival's other American selection, a remake of that 1944 musical cult classic, *Allergic to Love*, Nigel can only report that on seeing its star newcomer, Becky Luna—she of the frog eyes and Jiminy Cricket lips—trying to chirp a tune, he has developed a violent aversion. Is there any cure? Doubtful, even among Becky's notorious supply of pharmaceuticals. . . . MYSTERY OF THE MOMENT: What chic celebrity, having slowly chomped on the feminist chestnut that it's a woman's world, has decided with a vengeance to cut off all her old acquaintances? And yes, I mean you, cookie. For readers remaining in the dark, further clues to come. Nigel has it all down in his little black book. . . . ★

1

NIGEL WHITTY loved watching them squirm. As he sat by the edge of the fountain in the plaza of Lincoln Center, sipping from a container of coffee and reading over his column in the morning *Tribune*, it struck him how much he really relished his work. How he loved raking over those cretinous celebrities—media whores who scratched after fame like ravenous dogs a buried bone. *There's no people like show people, all right*, he thought, no people so worthy of punishment and humiliation. When you made a public spectacle of yourself, you deserved public scorn.

What an irony it was that ten years ago when Nigel had first been offered the chance to be a Grand Inquisitor, a national inquirer, he had been reluctant. Nigel Whitty, a gossip columnist! After all, he had been, and still was, a film critic noted for his intellect and rigorous standards. But all the standards in the world didn't pay the rent. They certainly didn't pay for the vintage French wines, the custom-made Italian shirts, or the English cashmeres which were, to Nigel, no mere luxuries, but appurtenances befitting his stature in life. Nigel had early on decided he was to the manner born, and he was determined to live up to his own great expectations, whatever the cost.

And so if the gossip column at first seemed to call his dignity into question, it had other compensations. Among these was celebrity. Today Nigel, both as daily columnist and weekly critic, was syndicated in over three hundred newspapers. Everybody who was anybody read "What Nigel Knows," while Nigel himself was a frequent guest on the "Tonight Show," a regular denizen of the world of the Beautiful People, and a worthy item in gossip columns other than his own.

More important, though, Nigel believed that over the long haul his inimitable brilliance would transform plebeian chatter into an authentic art form—a Boswellian diary of contemporary culture and mores. That was in his lighter moments. In his darker ones he saw himself as a one-man fury, a self-appointed avenger, torturing guilty consciences and making the foolish and feckless suffer.

It amused him that most of his readers hated him for this; yet this was also precisely why they read him. The razored edge of his column had brought him fame, and better, power. For years, when he had concentrated solely on serious criticism, none of those fools had paid attention. But now they paid attention all right. Now, in fact, they paid. He had them by the balls—that is, he snickered, if they had any.

Nigel finished his coffee and, crumpling the empty cup, looked about for a receptacle. Finding none, he impatiently tossed the container into the splashing fountain. The morning was cool and clear, and he took a long, deep drink of the fresh September air. He felt good, and the world looked good to him as well, with the bluish sunlight redefining the edges of the buildings, giving New York City a sharp new radiance. Even Lincoln Center—that mammoth granite shopping mall of the arts—had a special brightness. In any case, what a relief to come here in the morning rather than at night when the entire complex was filled with all those revolting suburban culture-vultures, with their false eyelashes and equally false appreciation. At this hour there was hardly a person around to interrupt the crisp, clean structural patterns of the city. Only one eyesore offended him. A rotund and filthy figure was curled up in the entryway of the Metropolitan Opera House under the Chagall windows, her shopping bags at her feet. One of those homeless creatures whose useless presence littered the city. She'd be better off incinerated, Nigel thought.

As if to put her out of his vision, Nigel got up and walked briskly across the plaza. Unfortunately, he had a screening to attend. If only the New York Film Festival didn't intrude so on this beautiful morning and on his time in general. What an absurdity to bring twenty-five new films into town at once and force critics to see them all within the space of two weeks. What a tedious business! But not so tedious, Nigel speculated, as seeing so much of one's colleagues.

Nigel sauntered down the steps to Sixty-fifth Street and then crossed over to the small plaza in front of Alice Tully Hall.

"Well, Nigel Whitty!" A familiar nasal voice accosted him.

It was Sammy Nachman, that aggressive little flack who telephoned Nigel at least twice a week with items of singular insignificance: Goldie Hawn's new brand of toothpaste; Robert Redford's latest ski bindings; Burt Reynolds's recipe for chicken soup.

"Well, well," Nachman persisted, shaking the remains of a box of Good 'n' Plenty into his mouth. "Look who the cat dragged in!"

"Congratulations, Nachman. You can always be counted on to come through with an idiotic comment, even if it's only a salutation. May I point out to you that the cat couldn't have dragged anyone *in*, since you and I, my friend, happen to be *outside* on this wretchedly beautiful morning."

Nachman giggled, crinkling the two little brown dots that were his eyes, and which gained a peculiar prominence by being set in a face totally without any other contrasts. "You're too much, Nigel, just too much, too much. But as long as you can come through with an ad quote for

Alan Savory's new musical, you can even throw a pie in my face."

"*Allergic to Love?* Are you mad? Didn't you see 'What Nigel Knows' this morning?"

Sammy Nachman shook his head sheepishly.

"I publicly denounced its bubonic star, Becky Luna," Nigel glowered, "and on Saturday I'll be denouncing the film itself. But if you want me to slaughter it now, how about: 'Sleeper of the year! A yawn a minute! The greatest thing for insomniacs since the invention of Nytol!'"

"'The greatest,'" Sammy brightened. "Can I quote you on that?"

"Don't you ever learn, Nachman? We've been through this before."

"Oh, come on, Nigel, come on. I was only kidding. I mean, it's a good movie. What more do you want than Becky Luna singing 'The Polonaise' and Gyorgii Gdansk dancing to 'I'm a Lonesome Polecat'?"

"Sounds like little more than a Polish joke, Nachman," Nigel said and promptly took his leave. But he wasn't to enjoy his solitude for long.

"Hi, Nigel—" a bright pink smile greeted him. "What a nice tie."

What did this twit know about ties, he wondered. And who was she anyway?

"Saw your item on *Subway* this morning." She moistened her lips as punctuation. "It was brilliant, Nigel. So original." The pink smile expanded to reveal large, glistening white teeth.

She looked familiar, but her name escaped him. She was probably another one of those bright young things working the Festival each year, trying to break into what they thought was the big, glamorous world of movie criticism. In any case, at this moment she was trying to break into the big, glamorous world of Nigel Whitty.

"I really love your work," pink lips was saying. Her tongue worked its way across her lips again.

Nigel would have none of it. Last night had really done him in. That little piece he'd picked up in front of Bloomingdale's—who looked just like a teenage boy—had been absurd, making a scene so distasteful that he literally had to throw her out of the apartment, along with her clothes and shopping bag. By now he should know better than to sniff around those ridiculous tarts with their stiletto boots and stenciled lips. But he had a weakness for them. They all looked the way Rio once did. Still, as hip as they pretended to be, they were always too dense. They could never get the hang of the games *he* loved to play.

"Hope you like the movie," pink lips persisted.

"We'll see." Nigel threw her a morsel. Then he strolled on toward the hall, catching a glimpse of his reflection in the glass doors. Not bad. In fact, quite good, he thought, for forty-five. He did see, didn't he, a touch of Sean Connery around the smile? A bit of Errol Flynn about the mustache? Something of Paul Newman in the blue-gray eyes? People had always told him he should have been on the screen rather than watching it, but actors, actors were such mindless fools! Such vain, childlike, whimpering creatures! Besides, Nigel loved the distinction of being attractive in a profession where attractiveness was so rare.

Good God! he thought, looking about now at his colleagues as they made their way through the sleek modern lobby with its bronze fixtures and wine-colored velvet decor. What moles they were! Pallid and puerile, these pusillanimous creatures lived in the dark, and that was where they all belonged. Fenton Farnabee, for example, that presumptuous little dandy in his precious pastel suits, who had dared to trespass on Nigel's territory with a gossip column of his own. Some column, Nigel snorted to himself, fag trash! Then he smiled. He'd had that bitchy little tattletale up against the wall before, and he'd have him there again.

And Vernon and Beatrix Leakey. What a pompous pair they were, and how strangely well matched in being so completely mismatched. He the five-foot-five mindless academic, she the six-foot-tall talentless poetess whose embarrassingly autobiographical verse was laden like a cornucopia with fruit-and-vegetable imagery. Nigel had always suspected she'd married Vernon in part for his name. For the two had nothing whatever in common—except, that is, their lack of talent and their shared passion for the bottle.

A buzzer rang—the five-minute signal indicating that the screening was about to begin. Nigel glanced at his Piaget watch and then back toward the entrance. He felt a twinge of annoyance about Sara Nightingale. *Where was she?* Dammit! When he'd hired that girl to assist him, he'd warned her that if there was anything he found irritating, it was lateness. And in this instance, especially, after he'd gone out of his way to arrange a pass for her. She'd been dying to see *Le Dernier Souffle*, and so he'd agreed to take her with him. He smiled as he thought about this girl, this Sara Nightingale. Despite her disarray, there was something quite irresistible about her, with her coppery red hair, bright blue eyes, and freckles like snowflakes alighting on her nose. She had a quality more exciting than simple beauty: character, spunk. Even Whitty was at a loss for a word to confine her.

There was the buzzer again—the final warning. Where was she? Among other things, he would have liked to have made his entrance into the auditorium with her—he always enjoyed having a pretty girl on his arm.

He looked impatiently toward the door again, only to see not Sara, but TV interview hostess Elizabeth Salt rush in together with *Subway*'s director, Danny Blue. He noticed that pudgy little Lizzie was looking at him as though he'd just killed her mother, but that was typical. You could count on Lizzie to overreact. As for Danny Blue, he tipped his tweed jockey's cap at Nigel.

"*Loved* that item in this morning's column," he called out. "I wouldn't take the subway for the next few weeks, if I were you, pal."

"And I wouldn't read my column if I were *you*," Nigel retorted menacingly as all three made their way into the already darkened screening room and then parted company.

Nigel settled back in his usual seat in the next-to-last row. The row was empty, but that was the point. Nigel detested being too near his colleagues. While the screen itself remained black, a tubercular cough erupted from the amplifiers, filling the hall with its phlegmy assault. Oh, these imbecilic French films! *Le Dernier Souffle, The Last Gasp!* And what, indeed, could he expect from Jean-Paul Pauljean, that anorexic little Frenchman who'd grown famous on a series of esoteric short films about corners—corners of windowsills, corners of rooms, corners of napkins. He had even gone so far as to direct a feature film about corners, something called *90° and Wake Up! Variety* had dubbed it "brainy, but tough sell at box office." To Nigel, it seemed instead merely a tough sit.

And so, too, *The Last Gasp*, Pauljean's "triumphant transition to commercial moviemaking," according to the Festival's press release. Nigel vowed that it would be the director's last gasp if it was the last thing he ever did.

The movie seemed interminable, but after all, what kind of action could you invent for a romantic comedy about two hospital patients who fell in love when their iron lungs were positioned catty-cornered to each other? For a while Nigel busied himself with watching a couple some ten rows ahead of him who seemed to be kissing and hugging madly. It must have been Danny Blue and Elizabeth Salt. It certainly couldn't have been Beatrix and Vernon Leakey since both of them could be heard snoring even louder than usual. In between their snores, scattered yawns and whispers completed the concerto of boredom, and Nigel found himself looking at his watch as frequently as he looked at the screen. It was obvious that Sara Nightingale had forgotten about the film altogether or had found something better to do.

It occurred to him that he might as well catch a few

minutes of sleep himself, since he'd been up with that dopey teenage tart half the night. His eyes began to close, and he allowed himself to enjoy the thick twilight zone between waking and sleeping. He was about to surrender himself to the pleasures of slumber when suddenly he was jerked awake. It was something around his neck. A thin, silky ribbon of some sort. Who was joking? Sara? He tried to turn and see, but he couldn't. The ribbon was just too tight. And it kept growing tighter and tighter. It hurt. Badly. He was losing breath and losing strength. He began to choke, to gasp. Oh, God, no!

He tried to cry out, but he couldn't make a sound. Everything was blurring, fading, and Nigel found himself sinking. The screen, the room itself, began to disappear. But something else was happening as well. He felt an intense throbbing in his groin; he was growing hard and stiff. His excitement mounted in a crescendo of excruciating sensation. Oh, God, yes! He could hardly see, and he could hardly hear. But there was a voice. . . . What was it that voice was saying now? It was so close to his ear that he could feel the warm breath brushing his skin. . . . What was it again? Who was it? He strained to understand.

"You scorpion." Was someone calling him a scorpion?

A hiss. "May you sizzle in the fires of hell, you prick."

What? What nonsense! But suddenly his body began to shudder. . . .

Then, for the very last time in Nigel Whitty's life, the screen faded to black.

2

SARA NIGHTINGALE was frantic. Whitty would be furious, she thought, as she stood on the corner of 45th and Madison, searching for a cab. It was eleven-thirty, which not only meant that every taxi in sight was filled with people trying to squeeze in a last morning appointment or rushing off to an early lunch, but that the screening had started over an hour ago. She was so late, later than usual, which even Sara Nightingale knew was very late indeed.

"Taxi!" she called out at the top of her lungs. Instead of a yellow cab, a small van labeled Polar Bear Air Conditioning pulled to a halt at her corner. The driver, a young man wearing lightly tinted aviator glasses and a very broad smile, winked at her and whistled. "Want a lift, Red?"

Should she hop in and ask him to drive her to Lincoln Center, she wondered? Why not? Nothing could possibly happen to her at midday on 45th and Madison.

"Sure," she called back. The driver leaned over, slipped the door lock, and Sara quickly climbed into the van. "Sixty-fifth and Broadway, if you don't mind." She smiled.

"Whatever you say, Red." He winked, inching the van into the cross street and totally blocking the cross-town traffic. Cars honked madly, drivers shouted, but the young man paid no attention. Instead, he looked over at Sara and grinned. "I'd take you to the moon, Red, if you get what I mean," he said, reaching down and unzipping his fly.

Sara's eyes were riveted. "Is that all you've got to say for yourself," she snapped, and hastily climbed out of the van, slamming the door behind her. Better late than raped. Better Whitty should have her head than this guy her blue lace underpants. But what to do now? There still wasn't an empty cab in sight. And dammit all, the day had begun so well. She hadn't slept through the alarm. She hadn't scalded the coffee. She hadn't dropped a contact lens on the bathroom floor. And by eight o'clock she'd been seated at the desk in her tiny living room, typing with a speed and efficiency that astonished even herself. And all the more so in that cleaning up a Whitty article was no mean task. Not that she was supposed to be editing, but what else could she do? So many errors of fact (How could he have thought Berlioz wrote that score! Or that it was the *Hindenburg* which hit an iceberg!) And his spelling! Unbelievable. As it was turning out, the formidable Nigel Whitty had an Achilles' heel or two.

But what had really held Sara up this morning was Richard Singer-Murray, Nigel's editor at the *Tribune*. As instructed, she had dropped off the copy she'd been working on only to have Singer-Murray insist on going over it then and there. Sara had tried to explain that she was supposed to meet Nigel at the Film Festival, but Singer-Murray worked according to his schedule and nobody else's. In his midthirties, of midheight, with wire-rimmed glasses perched on a face of middling character, he was one of those young men whose unassuming, vaguely esthetic features promised intelligence and sensitivity. Singer-Murray was also slightly awesome, wielding the power he did as cultural editor of the *Trib*. And so, as she sat with him poring over Nigel Whitty's copy—not only the review she'd been working on this morning and which would run next week, but also the gossip column for tomorrow—Sara couldn't help but steal a glance or two at his pale eyes and wonder what secret tendernesses lay behind them or think about what it would be like to take a walk with him through Central Park or by the East River or across the Brooklyn Bridge at sunset.

At long last, an empty cab pulled up.

"Lincoln Center, Alice Tully Hall," she told the driver as she climbed in. "As quickly as possible. I'm carrying a spear in the opera, and my cue is in ten minutes."

Sara really had no idea why she'd said this, except that whenever she got into a cab, she always made up some story or other just to entertain the driver. It struck her that driving around all day must be excruciatingly boring. But as it turned out, this particular cabbie—a beefy, middle-aged man with a chunk of wet cigar between his teeth—hardly needed any distraction. His taxi was a home away from home, filled with all kinds of entertainment. Hanging from the rearview mirror was a small mechanical bird whose yellow beak kept flapping open and whose wings waved up and down, while on the dashboard standing firm on a pair of suction cups was a six-inch Hawaiian lady whose hips and breasts undulated with the rhythm of the traffic. Next to her was a small blue-and-white plastic madonna, and behind her was a small gallery of photographs: babies, brides and grooms; little girls in white dresses; and an aerial shot of the Vatican. Below this gallery and on a specially built shelf sat a small black-and-white television set which was turned up at a volume to rival the blare of the traffic. Sara couldn't believe her eyes. Today, she was really getting the winners!

"Opera? Spear? Figured you were an actress," said the cabbie whose name, his license revealed, was Luigi L. Lippi. "Haven't I seen you on TV? In that after-shave commercial?"

"I don't shave," Sara said sharply. "And I wish you wouldn't watch commercials or anything else while I'm in this cab, Mr. Lippi."

"Just call me Louie the Lip. All my friends do."

Whether it was Lippi, Louie the Lip, or even Fra Lippo Lippi, Sara wondered if she shouldn't get out of this car, too. How could this man watch TV and the traffic at the same time? Certainly, if she was better off late than raped, she was also better off late than dead.

"TV's good for the nerves," said Louie the Lip. "Lean back. Relax. Let the opera start without you. Besides, this is a good program. The 'Elizabeth Salt Hour.'"

Despite herself, Sara couldn't resist looking at the screen. After all, Elizabeth Salt was a regular item in Nigel Whitty's column; he was always taking stabs at the brilliant and brittle TV personality who was so popular that her evening interviews were rerun the next day at noon. It was then that housewives, and apparently cabbies, too, could catch her chats with movie stars, powerful political leaders, and movie stars who'd become powerful political leaders, all of whom divulged intimacies to her that they gave to nobody else.

"Get a load of that!" Louie the Lip exclaimed, pointing the wet stub of his cigar toward the TV. "That" was a palatial Hollywood bedroom in which Elizabeth Salt now sat interviewing the room's owner, actor-director and national heartthrob—and who knew, Elizabeth Salt inserted, possibly one day United States President—Danny Blue.

"This is quite a room, Danny," the small, chubby blonde commented.

"You can say that again!" Louie muttered.

"And quite a ceiling!" Elizabeth Salt continued, as the camera tilted up to reveal the wall-to-wall mirrors and then tilted down to focus on a handsome young man with full, sensuous lips who now lay flung across the pale satin spread of his huge bed.

"Don't you think that ceiling is a bit much, Danny?" Elizabeth Salt asked with a chuckle.

"*I* sure do." Louie whistled.

Danny Blue looked at Elizabeth Salt seductively. His glance made Sara uncomfortable—among other reasons because Elizabeth Salt was old enough to be Danny Blue's mother. "Too much? Not really, Lizzie, babe," he said. "It makes me happy. This way, the first thing I see when I wake up in the morning is some cat I love."

Elizabeth Salt's reply was drowned out by a sudden chorus of blaring car horns and screaming voices. Sara glanced at her watch. Twelve-fifteen. Nigel would really wring her neck. By now, the movie might even be over.

"Can't you do anything?" she asked Louie. "Please. This is really important."

The cabbie shook his head. "Can't grow wings, lady. Sorry." He stuck his cigar stub back into his mouth and began to suck on it. "Relax," he advised. "You want me to change the channel?"

"I'd like you to turn the whole thing off," Sara said wearily.

This time, Louie didn't argue. "All you young girls, you're all so frazzled. Take it easy, take the long view. Meditate," he suggested, mashing the cigar in his mouth. "Meditate. I got this yogi. And I chant. It's good for the nerves." And then and there Luigi L. Lippi proceeded to chant right through his cigar.

"Do you *mind?*" Sara reprimanded him in her best schoolmarm tone.

She could see him eyeing her through the rearview mirror.

"Red hair, huh?" he teased. "I see you got a big temper, too."

"Only when I'm late," she said irritably.

"Well, I better watch out then, because lemme tell ya, the traffic ain't moving." And he began to chant again.

Sara looked about her. Manhattan at midday was a nightmare of buses, trucks, limousines, taxis, exhaust fumes, and honking horns. The streets looked impossible to negotiate. Should she get out and walk? Or shouldn't she? Whichever, the outcome seemed hopeless.

Damn! She'd really wanted to see that movie! *Le Dernier Souffle* had been directed by Jean-Paul Pauljean, who was a friend of Claude Bitran, the Turkish cinematographer she'd lived with all last year, mostly in Paris. But then again, *Le Dernier Souffle* was probably awful, just as pretentious as all the rest of Pauljean's movies, or "exercises in structural-conceptual communication," as he called them.

How could Bitran have thought she was the least bit

interested in that creep? She sighed with weariness at the thought of the scene he'd made that night at the Deux Magots, punching Pauljean in the nose; of the scene he'd made almost every night and at almost every café they'd been in. He was the most jealous man she'd ever met, and how she'd taken his hysteria for an entire year was beyond her. Of course, he hadn't been quite so bad at the beginning. She remembered back to when she'd first met him. She'd left her passport at the Banque Montparnasse, and he'd picked it up and brought it to her hotel room off the Boulevard St. Michel. She'd found him so romantic, so Byronic, so exotic back then. She'd come to Paris to find passion, adventure, possibility, and here it all was, standing at her door with a green passport in its hand, magnificent green eyes, and a green turban to match.

Of course, she'd hoped for a Modigliani-like painter or a Hemingway-type writer, but a dark, handsome, deeply intellectual Turkish cinematographer wasn't too bad a stand-in. Besides, the world he'd brought her into was an exciting one whose constant motion and change were perfectly suited to Sara's temperament. Above all, it suited the restlessness that had led her to leave Mount Holyoke in the midst of her junior year—in spite of her straight-A average and the fury of her straight-laced lawyer father back in Grosse Pointe, Michigan. It was her restlessness too that had led her first to join a research party studying bat life in Madagascar, and then to sign on an expedition which, sailing from Lima to Sydney, hoped to prove that Australian aborigines were really Incas. The Spam and saltines finally got to her, though, and rather than sail back with the crew, she took a plane to Europe where for a while she led *son et lumière* tours through Florence and Rome and then, when she tired of groups like the Dallas Opera League and the Boise Boy Scout Leaders, she got a job writing copy for the American Tourist Bureau in Paris. But nothing, she learned, excited her as much as the constantly shifting sets and fantasies of movies.

She'd gone with Bitran on location to a small town outside Madrid, to a village in Holland, to the coast of Yugoslavia, to the mountains of Italy, loving the family feeling of a movie crew, the gypsylike movement, even the chatter about film—its nature, its images, its stories, its stars. She'd assisted Bitran and the other cameramen; she'd worked on sound; she'd written English dialogue; and she'd even worked as an extra, doing an underwater nude scene in a futuristic science-fiction fantasy called *La Planète des Simiens Nus (Planet of the Naked Apes)*. Bitran had been absolutely furious, a raving madman in fact, when he saw her doing that scene, swimming around in nothing but seed pearls and fins.

She couldn't understand it, she told him. He hadn't gone crazy, she reminded him, when the two of them had gone to that nude beach in Yugoslavia, or when he'd encouraged her to go topless in Saint-Tropez.

That was different, he'd explained.

She didn't see how. He was so backward, she'd screamed at him, so atavistic. Claude Bitran, the Ataturk, she dubbed him. Who else would have accused her of holding a stranger's hand in the movies one night? Who else would have slapped her face when a man brushed up against her in the Metro? Did he want her to wear a veil, go into purdah? But, she had to admit, even the Ataturk had had just cause for fury the time she went off for a weekend to ski in Cortina with Berto Balducci, the Olympic ski champion-turned-actor who was starring in the biblical extravaganza Bitran had been shooting in Rome. It was the only time in that whole year she'd been unfaithful to him. Although adventurous and daring and restless enough to try anything once, Sara was still at heart essentially a monogamist. But she'd been sick of Bitran's possessiveness and temper and had found Berto so warm and funny. Besides, the ski report had been fantastic that weekend.

Even if she did have to live through wild scenes with the

violent Ataturk, it was all somehow worth it since Sara emerged from that year with a greater sense of vocation than she'd ever had before. Not that she knew exactly what she wanted to do. Maybe screenwriting, maybe directing, maybe even criticism. But at least she knew the world in which she wanted to travel—the world of movies.

And so, shortly after she came back to the States, when her old college roommate Mimi MacIntosh told her that the prestigious film critic, Nigel Whitty, was looking for an assistant, she thought, why not give it a try? Mimi, who had been kind enough to put her up for a few weeks in spite of the fact that her apartment was the size of a peanut shell, was a trainee at the *Trib.* She had gotten wind of the job opening through Nigel's editor and had given Sara the columnist's unlisted number. It took her four phone calls before Whitty and not his machine answered. And he didn't exactly jump to set up an appointment.

"Send me a résumé along with three references," Nigel Whitty had growled into the phone. "And I'll get back to you."

She'd sent what he'd asked for that very day, including two unpublished essays on the Paris film scene she'd written months ago when she'd been living with Bitran. But it took three weeks for Whitty to call and arrange an interview.

Sara was pleased and nervous. She had spent a great deal of the interim reading the works of Nigel Whitty, and she was impressed. Yes, he was as brilliant as he was reputed to be. His book on film esthetics, *Cinema Clarified,* was marvelous. And his critical essays—many of them already collected in bound volumes—were right on the mark. Sara's curiosity was also kindled by having seen Nigel a few years ago on the "Today Show," cutting up the Academy Awards presentation with his acid wit. He was an interesting-looking man, not really handsome, but definitely sexy. More than that, even, there was something so electric about him, so immediately controversial. This incredibly talented man who was also so incredibly cruel! And here Sara came face to face with the fact that there were really two Nigel Whittys: on the one hand, an extraordinary man of letters who wrote brilliant critical essays and, on the other, the repellent and vulgar tattletale who authored a cheap little gossip column. She couldn't seem to put these two disparate people together, and so she simply ended up dismissing that distasteful aspect of him to the eccentricities of genius.

She looked forward to meeting him, yet it was with some trepidation that she approached the interview. It started off badly.

Nigel Whitty had forgotten all about her. When she arrived at his midtown apartment, situated in a huge Gothic-looking building in the West Fifties, he was still in his maroon silk pajamas, although it was eleven o'clock in the morning. He had apologized, but not quite profusely enough, for her money. And to make matters worse, he had asked her to come back, not today or tomorrow, but next week.

But she'd pressed to see him right then and there, and he'd softened, though he had still kept her waiting another three-quarters of an hour. She had sat in his dark, elegant living room, one which had obviously been put together for its esthetics rather than its comfort. The chairs were stiff-backed antiques. The brown velvet couch was angular and thinly cushioned. The books behind the glass-enclosed bookcases were bound in leather and seemed untouchable. And everything appeared so ordered that, were a single porcelain *bibelot* to have been moved, the balance of this coldly perfect room would have been thrown out of kilter. Here, clearly, one did not set drinks down on coffee tables without coasters, or flick cigarettes into ashtrays without first asking permission. It gave Sara an almost uncontrollable desire to make a mess.

The phone kept ringing. The typewriter clacked away. She wondered what Nigel Whitty was doing in that room on the other side of the foyer which was either his office, his bedroom, or both combined. She couldn't quite figure out the layout of the apartment, but she was afraid to explore lest she be caught in the act. So she contented herself with sitting on the velvet sofa, arranging and rearranging the folds of the white silk shirtwaist she had bought especially for this occasion.

He finally emerged, dressed now in a beige Pierre Cardin summer suit, and sat down on a taupe silk chair facing her. "Well, Miss Nightingale, or is it *Ms.*—? Consider your answer carefully. Your fate may depend on it."

This Sara could handle. "Just call me Sara."

He raised an eyebrow a bit menacingly, and she thought she saw his lip curl beneath his mustache. Sara recoiled despite herself. There was something about this man that was chillng and as forbidding as the room in which he now sat. Yet at the same time he was charged with a bizarre magnetism. It struck her that this was precisely the kind of effect which Count Dracula must have had on women and as Whitty talked she kept imagining his canines growing longer and longer. The image must have delighted her more than she realized because suddenly she heard Whitty's voice:

"All right, *Sara* Nightingale," he interrupted her reverie, "would you be so kind as to tell me why that idiotic grin is plastered across your otherwise attractive visage? I consider myself a man of great wit and humor, but the formalities of an interview have yet to send me, or any other being of reasonable intelligence, rolling in the aisle. So might you do me the courtesy of telling me just what is so funny?"

"Nothing," Sara answered. She was furious with herself for being caught looking so foolish.

"Nothing?" he barked. She could see that she was losing him. Dammit, she had to think fast.

"Well, actually this is kind of embarrassing," she said hesitantly, tossing her head so that her hair fell demurely over her shoulders, "but I suppose I was smiling because I was just amazed by how much you look like, well, Sean Connery."

Nigel Whitty melted like snow in summer. He puffed out his chest and smiled benignly. "Yes, others have remarked on that before. But now," his voice grew sterner, "let's get down to business. Your experience seems very haphazard, your education sketchy, but I was very impressed, let me tell you, with those essays you sent me. But be assured, there's nothing creative about this job. You may find it very boring."

"No, I won't."

"Well, then, can you type?"

"Like a whiz."

"Are you good at proofreading?"

"I have an eagle eye and my grammar and spelling are, if you'll allow me, impeccable."

"What about research?"

"I'm an absolute Sherlock Holmes."

"You're also very glib, very clever, and—" he paused for emphasis—"very pretty."

Sara felt herself blushing. Couldn't she find a better response?

"You could go far, you know," he said, "and I might be able to arrange that for you."

What a creep! Sara thought. He really does think he's Sean Connery!

"You and I will be working late a great deal, you know." His voice took on a seductive tone.

The nerve! Sara stood now and drew herself up to her full five foot seven. "You were right, Mr. Whitty. I just may be bored with this job, after all."

"Well, now." Nigel's lips curled upward in amusement. "I've frightened you, haven't I?"

"I beg your pardon."

"Intimidated you. Made you nervous."

"You flatter yourself, Mr. Whitty."

"Then why are you running away like a scared rabbit?"

"I'm not a rabbit. And I'm certainly not running away." Beneath Sara's indignation, she experienced a rush of pleasure. Sparring with Nigel Whitty made her feel good.

"Then I assume you're still interested in the job," he said, curtly now, "because I don't have all day."

Of course Sara had told him yes. How could she have said otherwise? Nigel Whitty was quite simply the most intriguing human being she had ever met. And the challenge he presented was irresistible.

Nigel Whitty's demands, his idiosyncrasies, were even greater than Sara had imagined. He was a stickler for punctuality, so much so that it was as if he had a time clock in his head. He was neat the way an old maid was neat. And he had a fetishistic concern with details. First-draft manuscripts had to be on yellow paper marked up with red pencil; second drafts on blue paper with black pen; he couldn't begin to work until the dictionary was on the left of the typewriter, the *Thesaurus* on the right. He insisted that his gold cigarette box had to be filled to the brim at all times, and only with Gitanes *filtre* that the French Film Office sent over each morning; and Sara was required to place on the right-hand corner of his desk the basket of flowers that inevitably arrived each day from one movie company or another.

As many things as she was required to do, there were an equal number she was forbidden to do. She was never to open any mail *ever*, not even those items which were clearly coupons, ads, and requests for donations. She was never allowed to answer his unlisted phone line or take messages off his machine. She was allowed to go into his filing cabinets *only* when he was in the room. And each day she was instructed precisely what to do. Nigel flew into a rage when she did less; he became like a madman when she did more.

However, sometimes she couldn't see how she could do anymore—he was so demanding. It never occurred to

Nigel that she might want to have a personal life, and he kept her at work until all hours. She hadn't even had time to settle into her new Greenwich Village apartment, or to make up an extra set of keys before she lost the first.

There was one nice thing, however. More and more, Nigel counted on Sara's little insights and opinions, a gesture that flattered her immensely. But he also criticized her endlessly. And it was exhausting to have to deal with his moods; you never knew which way his wind was blowing. Would Nigel bark at her like a vicious animal who had lost his senses? Would he demolish her with his wit like a savage genius? Or praise her lavishly, a generous man of reason? The experience of working for him was draining. Still, she remained fascinated.

And now he would have her head! The taxi pulled up at 65th and Broadway. It was twelve forty-five. Not only had she missed *Le Dernier Souffle*, she just may have missed Nigel as well. Sara hurriedly handed the cabbie a five-dollar bill and told him to keep the change. "You're a sport, Red, even if you don't shave," Louie the Lip saluted her with his wet cigar stump.

She waved back at him as she ran toward the entrance to Alice Tully Hall.

"Peace," he called. Then he jumped a red light and sped down Broadway.

The sidewalk in front of the hall was jammed. There must have been fifty or sixty people milling about. As Sara began to push her way toward the doors, she suddenly noticed a police barricade. Four uniformed officers were guarding the entryway, and a line of squad cars was parked in the side street. What was going on?

She pushed through the barricade and went up to one of the policemen, a young man whose face was so pink and whiskerless that, were it not for his size, you'd think he was a kid dressing up in his father's clothes. "Look, I have to get through," she told him. "Someone's waiting for me."

"Sorry, miss. I can't let you in."

"But I have a pass. Inside, there's a pass waiting for me."

"Sorry, sweetheart, I can't help you."

"But you don't understand. I'm supposed to meet someone very important."

"I don't care if you're supposed to meet the Mayor himself. There's a stiff in there, and you can't go in."

"Stiff? What do you mean, stiff?" Sara heard her own voice climbing.

"You know—dead, lady."

"Someone had a heart attack?"

"No, sweetheart. Someone got bumped off."

"You mean murdered?" What was wrong with her? For some reason, her brain was short-circuiting; she wasn't making connections.

"Right, sweetheart. Murdered." The pink, whiskerless face smiled now. "This one's a pip. Some guy got it. Some critic. Watching a movie, of all things."

3

CORNED BEEF AND CABBAGE. Always corned beef and cabbage. At least once a month Detective Lieutenant Michael Connelly tried to make it his business—barring blackouts, transit strikes, or psychopathic snipers—to head down to his mother's for lunch. And each and every time, Bridget Connelly would serve him corned beef and cabbage. Michael smiled to himself. He *hated* corned beef and cabbage; no, that was too mild a word—*despised* seemed more apt. But what was the point of telling her? Bridget Connelly was one of those sweetly dotty ladies who heard only what she wanted to hear. It was her favorite dish. It had been her husband's favorite dish. And so it had to be her son's.

In any case, corned beef and cabbage was definitely Father Fitzgerald's favorite dish. And more often than not, whenever Michael was there, so was Father Fitzgerald. Michael enjoyed him and, among other reasons, Michael always used to joke, because the Father had always been like an uncle to him. He was a rotund little man with a red nose and playful dimples, and he was almost as short as Bridget herself, who stood just five feet tall. As priest of the Church of Our Lady, Queen of Martyrs, around the corner from the Connellys' apartment in the Bay Ridge section of Brooklyn, he had baptized all four of Bridget's sons, taught them their catechism, and seen them through their first communion. And in the twenty years since Bridget's husband had died, Father Fitzgerald had been a regular caller at the Connelly household. By now he was an institution. And so, too, were the flirtatious little exchanges between Bridget and this man of the cloth.

"You're looking lovely as a four-leaf clover, Bridget," Father Fitzgerald would always begin.

"Oh, now, Father, go on with you. You're a wicked old flatterer," Bridget would return, placing one hand on her chubby waist and, with the other, smoothing back a few wisps of fine white hair that had escaped from her carefully arranged bun. At that moment she would look like nothing so much as a proud little hen.

"No, truly it amazes me how every week you grow younger and younger. Why, you look like the sister of your four strapping lads!" After which Father Fitzgerald would help himself to a shot glass of whisky to celebrate Bridget Connelly's eternal youth, and then another to toast her cooking.

And then he would turn to Michael. "I pray to the good Lord, my boy, that you will find a woman who can boil up a corned beef and cabbage as tasty as your ma's."

And inevitably Bridget Connelly would answer, "Ah, Father Fitzgerald, you're full of the blarney today."

Full of the blarney, Michael would think. It was his *mother* who was full of the blarney, or at least susceptible to it. He had never known anyone so touched with Irish whimsy, so easily carried away on endless flights of fancy. A mere song could send her to moonlit places; simple magazine serials could transport her to steamy climes. But her greatest romance was with the movies, for they carried her farthest, and with a vividness and clarity her imagination could not supply.

But if Bridget Connelly's head was often in the clouds, her feet, Michael had to admit, were planted firmly on the ground. For where her sons were concerned, she was hard-nosed and realistic. Michael was amazed that she had somehow rallied what little practicality she had to insure that her sons absorb a lot of it. Bridget had raised all her boys not to be dreamers, but to be sensible and responsible family men like their father—the kind who might tell tales and tipple now and then, but who found his way home every night and gave a paycheck to his wife every Friday. Her own Will had been a model of such high fidelity. As a bus driver for the city, a worker with insurance and a good pension, he had even managed to provide for his family after his death. Bridget had encouraged all her boys to follow in his footsteps and work for the city, too. Will, Jr., had become a sanitation engineer, Eammon a fireman, and the two youngest, Patrick and Michael, policemen. Bridget was proud of her sons because, aside from being steady, they were also, God be praised, big handsome fellows like their dad. Black Irish every one of them, with thick, straight dark hair and eyes as green as the Emerald Isle itself. All except Michael, whose sandy hair fell in soft waves, whose eyes were a baby blue, and who, at five foot nine, was the runt of the litter.

But Michael made up in smarts for what he lacked in height. He was smart as a whip at school, a smart aleck at play and, according to Bridget Connelly, too smart for his own good, in general. Still, she was as proud as a peacock when he made detective lieutenant, and then when he was made commander of his squad. Now all she asked was that, like his brothers, he marry a good Irish Catholic girl and add to her already burgeoning brood of grandchildren.

"Mick, you're thirty-three, you're not getting any younger, y'know," she'd always say. "And neither am I. It's high time you settled down."

"I'm looking, Ma," he'd tell her. "A good woman is hard to find."

"Not as hard as you're making it, Mick," she'd always reply.

For both of them knew that Michael wasn't really looking at all. He liked his freedom too much, and one lunch a month at his mother's was enough domesticity to last him from visit to visit. Besides, he had an eye for pretty girls, and pretty girls, in return, seemed to have an eye for him. Bridget, however, had a fish-eye for the whole business. And whenever she referred to Michael's women and what possibly went on in his bachelor apartment way uptown in Yorkville, she would cross herself and mutter a silent prayer.

At this point, Father Fitzgerald would inevitably save the day. He would get up right in the middle of the meal and walk over to the small color television set that sat on the kitchen counter and which was her pride and joy. "Now what movie could we be missing on the TV?" he'd say, turning up the set, just as he did at this very moment.

"Oh, look, Mick," Bridget Connelly exclaimed. "Look what's on. Oh, Father," she said, turning to Father Fitzgerald, "you must have known!" She ladled second helpings of corned beef and cabbage onto their plates and then sat down to watch.

"But, Ma, it's *White Heat*. I've seen it two hundred times."

"Then close your mouth, Mick, and see it two hundred and one." She sat mesmerized, as usual.

Unbelievable. Michael shook his head. Bridget Connelly and TV. It was her constant companion and she kept it on all the time, even when visitors arrived. Everyone who knew Bridget knew her weakness: old movies, morning movies, afternoon movies. Then evening and late night movies. Her favorites were those pictures with a touch of the Irish about them, and featuring Irish stars. Best of all were the movies she had shared with Will during their courtship. He'd taken her to *Public Enemy* on their first date, and she'd had a soft spot in her heart for James Cagney ever since. In fact, she prided herself on her twenty-seven Jimmy Cagney scrapbooks and her charter membership in the Irish Eyes for Cagney Fan Club, which she had helped found back in 1943. Her proudest possession was a pair of tap shoes, size 7, which Cagney had ostensibly worn in *Yankee Doodle Dandy*, and for which she'd traded a rare set of color photographs from the

"Shanghai Lil" tap dance number in *Footlight Parade.* These she'd obtained from an Australian collector for an exorbitant sum, her household money for a week. (That was the memorable week they ate tuna casserole seven nights in a row.) But it wasn't really Cagney, the dancer, whom she loved. It was Cagney the tough guy, the mean, rotten Cagney who'd shoved the grapefruit into Mae Clarke's face. It was he who appealed the most.

Incredible, Michael thought. Nearly every dream in her life, nearly every waking fantasy and bit of romance seemed to flow from the movies and back into them again. And it wasn't just that the world of glamorous painted backdrops made her own shabby surroundings—the cracked linoleum on the floors, the peeling paper on the walls, the threadworn covers on the chair—more bearable. It was that it made them, and her own life as well, absolutely insignificant. A long time ago, in the midst of one of those Saturday afternoon triple features she used to make all the children suffer through, he vowed he wasn't going to live his life vicariously. He was going to live it. And really live it. Adventure—that was what he wanted! And it was probably why, more than anything else, he had become a policeman. It was also why he hadn't married, he guessed. He wasn't going to live his life in a scrubbed, sorry kitchen stinking of cabbage and let the people in the little electronic box do his fighting and loving for him.

"That Cagney, Father," Bridget clucked, concentrating on the movie now, "what a good son. It touches my heart."

"Oh, Bridget." Father Fitzgerald patted her hand. "You're *all* heart. You'd forgive Judas himself." He allowed his hand to stay, resting lightly on hers.

She smiled shyly, like a young girl on her first date.

This, Michael thought, was the only real adventure in her life. And how much of it simply borrowed from *Going My Way, The Bells of St. Mary's,* or any of those Irish-Catholic fantasies of the forties she loved almost as much as movies starring Jimmy Cagney.

"Oh, this is it, Mick," she cried out. "Our favorite scene."

Now, on the screen before them, the message was going down the prison line: "Tell Cody his ma is dead. . . . Tell Cody his ma is dead."

"Now he's gonna get up, Mick, and stand on the table. Watch, oh, watch, he's gonna go crazy. . . ."

The phone rang.

"You get it, Mick." Bridget was annoyed. "And be quick, say we'll call back."

It was the precinct. A murder. Lincoln Center.

"Damn!" Michael muttered. It was his day off, after all. But on the other hand, he'd had enough corned beef, cabbage, and Cagney.

"Okay," he said into the phone, "it'll take me about half an hour to get up there. Who was it, by the way?"

"I dunno. Some writer. Some big-time Charlie."

Michael laughed as he hung up the receiver. He thought he was listening to another forties' movie.

He grabbed his coat and shook Father Fitzgerald's plump little hand. Then he kissed his mother goodbye.

She gave him a quick peck on the cheek. "Oh, Mick," she chirped, turning back to the television, "just look at that!"

Right before their eyes, Cagney went crazy.

Nigel Whitty's corpse sat slumped in its seat at Alice Tully Hall, precisely as usher Dwayne Jones had found it. It was Jones's job to check out the auditorium after each screening; usually the pimply-faced youth, who in his uniform might have been taken for a West Point cadet, found notebooks, wallets, felt-tipped pens, eyeglass cases, and mutilated morning newspapers from which the movie reviews had been clipped. On this Thursday noon, however, he'd found only Nigel Whitty, dead as yesterday's column and with a typewriter ribbon wrapped around his neck.

"A typewriter ribbon?" Lieutenant Michael Connelly questioned the medical examiner who was checking out the body.

"Yup, I think it's a first, Connelly. We've had shoelaces, belts, electric cords, jump ropes, but never a typewriter ribbon," the examiner replied, removing his rubber gloves.

Michael turned to the other members of the crime scene unit: the police photographer who was snapping pictures from every conceivable angle; the guy from forensics who was dusting for prints; and the curly-headed little man chalking off the area. "You guys almost finished?" Michael asked. "When you are, you can pack it in. Just remember to send me the reports first thing tomorrow."

Michael walked down the steps toward the nearest auditorium exit. "Where's that usher who found the body?" he asked one of his plainclothesmen who was standing at the door.

"In the press office," the man nodded, pointing up the stairs and to the right.

Michael waved a thank-you and headed in that direction.

The phones were ringing crazily as he entered the long narrow glass-enclosed office at the far end of the lobby. "Lieutenant Michael Connelly," he introduced himself over the din.

A tall, sleek brunette with horn-rimmed glasses and an air of great efficiency extended her hand. "I'm Lynn Ericson. I handle the press for the Film Festival," she said. "I simply can't believe this. It's a terrible tragedy. Terrible, terrible." As she spoke, water began pouring uncontrollably from her efficient-looking brown eyes.

"Here, lambchop, here, use my hanky," a sweet-faced, balding man with soft round features tried to comfort her. "Sammy Nachman—" he turned to Michael. Then he picked up an insistent phone. "No, no comment." His voice was brisk. "Nothing yet." He hung up the receiver, then took three more calls, exasperated, before the rings subsided. "Take the phones off the hook," he ordered

Dwayne Jones, who was patiently waiting to be questioned. Then he turned back to Michael. "What a kettle of fish! Who could have done such a horrible thing?" Sammy Nachman moaned.

"I'll let you know as soon as I find out," Michael returned. "Now you tell me something." He looked at both Nachman and Lynn Ericson. "Just who was this Nigel Whitty?"

"Whitty?" Nachman cried. "You don't know Whitty? Why, he was only the most brilliant critic alive. A genius!"

"A genius?" Lynn Ericson exclaimed through her tears. "He was a louse. A rat. The scum of the earth." And she sobbed even harder.

Why, then, Michael wanted to know, was she crying?

"Because that worm has ruined my beautiful festival."

"Nah, it's good publicity. Look at the bright side," Nachman suggested, "the party tomorrow night's gonna be the hottest ticket in town."

"It's not going to be a party. It's going to be a wake," Lynn Ericson moaned.

"Nah, you're wrong, lambchop, it's not gonna be a wake, it's gonna be a happening," Sammy Nachman corrected her and began munching on a peppermint. "We're gonna have headlines in every paper in this city—the *News*, the *Post*, the *Times*, the *Trib*, and even the *Wall Street Journal*."

"You really think so?" Lynn cocked her head. Her voice sounded hopeful.

Michael stared at these two creatures as though they were from outer space. A guy lay murdered a few yards away from them, and all these two jokers could think of was their goddamned movie festival and how much publicity they could get.

He turned to the usher. "You the guy who found him?"

Dwayne Jones nodded.

"Does it strike any of you three funny that no one else noticed the body?"

Lynn shook her head no. "Whitty used to sit in the back

of the screening room, all by himself, if possible. That was so he could sneak out without being seen."

"Even so, as people were leaving, wouldn't they have glanced up toward the back row?" Michael asked.

"What if they did?" Nachman shrugged his round, narrow shoulders. "They'd figure he was asleep. These critics are always snoozing. Believe me, I can give you a rundown of who snores, who doesn't, and just how loud. And I swear to God I never slept with any of them."

"Okay, then, how many people were in the auditorium with Whitty?"

"Only eleven others," Dwayne piped up. "I clicked them in on my machine."

"And all of them left after the screening, just like that?"

"All except me," Sammy Nachman said. "I went into the office to talk to Lynn."

"Does that situation strike you as usual?" Michael asked.

"Yes, of course," Lynn said. "Most of the time critics leave right after a screening and don't say a word to anyone."

"Now tell me this." Michael directed his question at Dwayne. "How easy would it have been for someone else to come in and out during the movie?"

"Impossible. The stage entrance was locked and bolted. And anyone coming into a screening needs a pass. Also, I was out front clicking everyone in."

"In other words," Lynn Ericson chimed in, "there was no way anyone could get into that auditorium without being seen."

"Couldn't someone have been here all night, waiting, hiding?"

"Impossible," Dwayne said with growing authority.

"Absolutely," Lynn agreed. "The place is checked out thoroughly at night."

"Okay." Michael nodded. "Now can you tell me who those other ten people were, besides Nachman."

"Certainly." Lynn Ericson took out her press list and

handed it to Michael. It was neatly typed and dated, and there was a check mark next to all of the names except one, indicating, Lynn explained, who had entered the auditorium.

Le Dernier Souffle 9/20 10:30 A.M.

√ *Danny Blue*
√ *Enzo Carbonare*
√ *Maria Cortese*
√ *Fenton Farnabee*
√ *Gyorgii Gdansk*
√ *Beatrix Leakey*
√ *Vernon Leakey*
√ *Becky Luna*
√ *Sammy Nachman*
Sara Nightingale
√ *Elizabeth Salt*
√ *Alan Savory*
√ *Nigel Whitty*

Only a few of these names were familiar to Michael: Danny Blue, some of whose movies he'd seen. Dancer Gyorgii Gdansk, whose face had been plastered all over the papers when he'd defected. Celebrity interviewer Elizabeth Salt whom he knew from TV. And gossip columnist Fenton Farnabee. Well, Michael didn't actually know him, but his name and testimonial were part of every movie ad he'd ever seen. "Wonderful! A roller coaster of a mystery!"—*Fenton Farnabee*. Or, "Fantastic! A cream puff of a tragedy!"—*Fenton Farnabee*. Besides, Michael had often heard Farnabee's radio show back in the days when he was on the nightshift.

"And what about these others?" he asked.

Lynn Ericson explained as Michael took notes. Alan Savory was the hottest producer in Hollywood, and his current film, *Allergic to Love*, starring Gyorgii Gdansk and newcomer Becky Luna, was going to be shown here at the Festival's Closing Night. Becky Luna, she reminded Michael, was the troublesome daughter of the legendary comedienne Billie Glover. As for Vernon Leakey, he was an extremely influential critic, while his wife, Beatrix, wrote feminist and vegetarian poetry. Enzo Carbonare was one of Italy's leading directors and was in New York for the American premiere at the Radio City Music Hall of his latest film, another Festival entry, *The Green Sky*. Maria Cortese, an Italian actress, was his constant companion and the movie's star.

"That's it?" Michael asked.

"That *couldn't* be it," Sammy said, his voice high and incredulous now. "None of these people could have done it. None of them."

Lynn Ericson stared at him. "What are you saying, Nachman? Are you crazy? *All* of them could have."

"We'll see." Sammy shook his head. "What a crumbcake business!" He reached into his pocket, took out a little brown package, and popped an M&M into his mouth.

"Do you have another copy of your list?" Michael asked Lynn.

"I have dozens," she returned.

"Give me phone numbers and addresses, too."

Lynn went to her Rolodex and scribbled the information down beside each name, then handed him the list.

Michael walked to the door of the press office, called out to one of his men, and gave him a piece of paper. "Here, Friedkin, get in touch with all these people. You and O'Reilly get them down to the station and get statements from them. And tell them not to leave town because I'll want to talk to them myself."

"Say, Lieutenant Connelly," Sammy Nachman offered eagerly as Michael walked back into the office and closed the door behind him, "they'll all be at the gala tomorrow night. Why don't you come and talk with them there."

"Thanks, but no thanks, Nachman." A party full of movie stars! Just what he needed after a lifetime with

Bridget Connelly and her scrapbooks. But then again it might not be a bad idea to see these characters in action. "On second thought, Nachman, where is this bash? I just might stop by and do a little observing."

"Oh, great," Lynn piped up. "And as long as you're going our way, we'd love to have you come to the premiere of *Subway*, Lieutenant. As our guest, of course."

Michael must have looked taken aback, for Lynn reached out and took his hand. "And we won't take no for an answer," she said firmly.

What the hell had he gotten himself into? But before he could come up with an answer, a knock on the glass pane of the press office door distracted him. It was one of the uniformed officers. "Hey, Lieutenant, there's this chick outside. Says she worked for the stiff. Says she was supposed to meet him here. She's driving me nuts. A real pain in the ass."

She could drive a lot of guys nuts, Michael thought when he walked into the lobby and got a glimpse of her sitting on one of the banquettes. She wasn't quite a 10, but she was up there, with those long legs and that wild red hair. And though she did make a lot of noise at first—letting out a stream of "I can't believe it's" and "It's all so horrible's"—when all was said and done, she seemed pretty cool for someone who had just been told that her boss had been strangled with a typewriter ribbon.

No, more than cool. At moments she seemed downright arrogant.

For example, when he let it slip that before today he'd never heard of Nigel Whitty, she looked at him as if he were retarded. "You didn't know about Nigel Whitty?" she practically gasped. "Have you lived your life under a rock or something? He's the most famous movie critic in America."

"So what's the big deal?" Michael baited her.

"To you, it may not be a big deal. To others, it is." Sara Nightingale's nostrils flared. *"Chacun à son goût."*

"What?" he asked.

"To each his own taste," she practically sneered.

This one was really a lulu. But there was something about her that got to him. And if he was going to be totally honest, his motives were probably just a little suspect when he called several hours later and asked her to meet him at Nigel Whitty's office/apartment.

"You really could be useful to me, Miss Nightingale," he said. "The apartment's been broken into and rifled and I thought you might be able to sort things out. That is, if it won't upset you too much, if you think you can handle it?"

"Don't worry," she answered, defiantly. "I can handle anything."

Lieutenant Michael Connelly thought he could detect just the slightest quiver in her voice. But he silently agreed that yes, she probably could. . . .

Had the meticulous Nigel Whitty seen his apartment, he would have died a second death, Sara Nightingale assured Michael when she arrived. Drawers had been opened, their contents spilled onto the floor. Shelves had been cleared and books violently tossed about. The room that served as Nigel's office had been particularly devastated. The file cabinets had been emptied, and the floor was carpeted with folders, manuscripts, and clippings. The forensic team had already been here searching for fingerprints, and a fine dust now covered everything.

"Any idea of what they were looking for, Miss Nightingale?" Michael asked, sitting down behind Nigel's desk.

Sara was quiet for a moment. "Money?" she began. "Jewelry? Clothes? Perhaps. Nigel had some rather expensive possessions."

"I'll say." Michael nodded as he picked up a cashmere sweater from the bedroom floor and examined the Gucci label. "But anything really worth killing him for?"

"I don't think so," Sara called to him as he walked into the bathroom and opened the medicine chest.

No drugs here not even an aspirin. Instead bottle upon bottle of men's cologne sat on every inch of space possible. Around each hung a little tag: compliments of the Four Seasons, compliments of Sardi's, compliments of GMG pictures.

"Your boss sure got a lot of presents," Michael said, walking back into Whitty's office.

"At least one a day. Sometimes as many as ten. Nigel called them his 'thank-you's' and his 'be-kind-to-me billet-doux.'"

"Billet-doux?" Michael asked.

"Love notes," Sara explained. "Nigel was being funny, in case you don't get it."

Michael didn't get any of it, but decided to ignore it. As his eyes skimmed the room, they were riveted to a large grouping of photographs hanging on one wall—photos of Nigel with various celebrities and at various festivals and parties. Something seemed to be unbalanced about the arrangement. Michael moved closer.

Of course, that was it! A clean rectangular patch stood out on the wall. "Look at this!" He motioned to Sara Nightingale. "You know what was here?"

Sara stood silently before the dust mark. "I can't remember," she said.

"Take your time."

Then suddenly she brightened up. "Oh, I know. It was an old photo of Nigel and two other people in front of this incredible flowering tree."

"Who were the others?"

"I'm not sure. There was a young boy who was gorgeous, he looked exactly like Montgomery Clift. And there was a woman, but I don't know who she was, her face was hidden by one of the branches of the tree." Sara turned to Michael. "Why would anyone want to steal a photo like that?"

"When we can answer that question, we may be able to answer a lot of others, too." His eyes roved the room once more. "Anything else seem to be missing besides this photo? Any information? Any papers?"

"Well, there was his little black book."

"What was that?"

"He always referred to it in his columns. It's the book where he kept all his information. All his sources and evidence."

"Well, we haven't found any little black book yet. Where'd he usually keep it?"

"I don't know. I never saw it."

"Never?"

Sara shook her head. "Look, I told you I only worked for Nigel Whitty for a few weeks. And he was very secretive."

"How so?"

"I was never allowed to open his mail. To go to his files without precise instructions. To pick up his private phone or take messages off his answering machine."

"Yes, I wanted to ask you about that," Michael said. "There are a few very strange messages on it which I'd like you to listen to." Michael turned on the Doro machine at his right, rewound the tape, and pressed the play button.

An angry masculine voice spoke out. *"Nigel, you pig,"* it began. *"You sadistic pig. I put my heart and soul, every penny I had, and two years of my life into that movie, man. Couldn't you have laid off it a couple of lousy days? Couldn't you have given me Opening Night you bastard?"* Click. Michael glanced at Sara.

"Danny Blue," she said. "I'd know that voice anywhere."

"What's it all about?" Michael asked.

"Blue directed his first film, *Subway*—it's opening the Festival. Nigel murdered it in his column this morning."

"I'd like to see the column. In fact, I'd like a copy of all his recent columns," Michael said as he turned on the machine again. *"Allo, Monsieur Whittee. Zees ees Marie from zee French Film Office. We would like you to come to a brunch Sunday morneeng een honeur of Jean-Paul Pauljean. Répondez, s'il vous pleez."*

Then a high-pitched Minnie-Mouse squeak. *"Listen, you old fart, you probably won't do this, but I left my pussypoppers in your apartment last night, and I blew all my bread at Bloomie's and can't afford no more. So what I want is for you to put the bottle into a shopping bag and leave it with your doorman."* Click.

"Now that sounds like a teenage voice to me," Michael said. "The question is, was Whitty into kids, pussypoppers, or both?"

"How should I know? And although I hesitate to ask you, Lieutenant Connelly, what in God's name are pussy-poppers?"

"My dear worldly Miss Nightingale, have you been living under a rock all your life? Pussypoppers, for your information, are a form of Butol nitrate. You inhale it—some people get a rush; others, a heart attack." He paused. *"Chacun à son goût."*

"Touché," she said. "You're learning fast."

"I'd like to learn even faster. That is, if you could explain a few more things to me. For instance, what do you know about this?" Michael handed Sara the receiver's stub of a check from Perdue Pictures made out to Nigel for $10,000. "I thought Whitty was a critic. Did he also do some freelancing for movie companies?"

"Ten thousand from Perdue Pictures?" Sara asked in astonishment. "Nigel would never take money from the studios. It would be a conflict of interest. I don't get it."

"Look at this list," Michael said, showing her his copy of Lynn Ericson's screening list. "Anyone here connected in any way with Perdue Pictures?"

"Well, *Allergic to Love* is their hot new movie, and it stars Becky Luna and Gyorgii Gdansk," Sara offered. "And

Alan Savory is Perdue's vice-president in charge of worldwide production. In fact, *Allergic* is his movie."

"Alan Savory, that's interesting," Michael said, picking a note out of the pile of papers before him. It was typed on beige stationery and dated almost two years ago. He passed it to Sara. *"Dear Nigel,"* the letter read. *"It's always best to know which side your bread is buttered on. From one gourmet to another. A."* The *A* stood for Alan, that is, Alan Savory, as the beautiful modern graphics of the letterhead made clear.

"Whitty obviously had a history with Savory. Had Savory been seeing Whitty lately?" Michael asked.

"I think they had dinner together last week. It was on Nigel's calendar. But he never spoke about it."

Michael handed Sara another note. This one was handwritten in a large childish scrawl on lilac-colored paper with a dainty flowered border. *"Nigel Whitty, how could you do this to me?"* it began. *"What do you mean, 'yellow cowslip cheeks' and 'cherry nose'? Who the hell are you to take offense at my body? And to say that I had no lips and looked like I had no teeth! Just let me tell you, my orthodontist is going to sue, and my shrink is going to talk to you personally. Oh, God, Mama was right, you* are *the meanest man in America. In the world! Because of you, I've cried myself to sleep every night for the past two weeks. I hate you, Nigel Whitty."* It was signed, *"Ms. Becky Luna."*

"Your boss was a real sweetheart, wasn't he?" Michael observed dryly.

"He had high standards."

Michael looked at her quizzically. "That's one way of putting it." He began to run his fingers across the top of a dark green leather cigarette box that sat on the desk. It was obviously old and had been used a great deal, since the gold Florentine tooling had been rubbed off at certain places. Absentmindedly, he opened the lid. A delicate, tinkling tune filled the room. What was it? It was so familiar.

"Isn't that funny," Sara said. "I never realized that was a music box."

Michael closed the lid and turned the box over. On its dark green underbelly were the remains of a gold inscription: . . . *igel fr* . . . *Rio.* He held it out to Sara.

"It must have said, 'To Nigel from Rio,'" she read, squinting.

"Good thinking, Watson." Michael smiled. "But who's this Rio?"

"I have no idea."

Sara crossed the room and sat down on the tufted black leather sofa where Nigel had done all his reading. "Look, Lieutenant, Nigel Whitty wasn't your run-of-the-mill human being. Sure, I suppose he had a cruel streak, but I guess you could also say it was his business to hurt people."

"One of them obviously wanted to hurt him back. The question is, which one?" As he spoke, Michael caught a glimpse of an engraved invitation. It was to the Film Festival's Opening Night events, the film and party that Lynn Ericson and Sammy Nachman had advised, no, insisted, he attend. He held the white card up to Sara. "Will any of the gang be here?"

"I'm sure most of them will attend," Sara answered.

"Good. Then so will we."

"We?"

"What's wrong with 'we,' Miss Nightingale? I was simply thinking that you might be helpful to me. Connect names with faces, things like that."

"Oh."

"Don't be hurt. I find you very attractive."

"I'm sorry to say, Lieutenant Connelly, the attraction is not mutual." And she began gathering herself up to leave.

This girl was a real wise guy, but something about her struck his funny bone. He smiled as he watched her long legs stride purposefully to the door, then, with somewhat less purpose, return to him.

"My purse?" she asked, a bit flustered. "I forgot my purse. Have you seen my purse?"

Michael let her sift through the papers and folders on Whitty's desk. Then he walked over to the typewriter on which she'd perched her large maroon bag, the kind of free-folding leather item which looked as though it might have contained horse feed, and which struck him as very hard to misplace. "Is this what you're looking for, Miss Nightingale?" He grinned, handing it to her.

She nodded. But suddenly, she wasn't looking at the bag at all. She was looking at the typewriter.

"Lieutenant Connelly," she whispered. "The ribbon. It's gone."

Michael lifted up the hood of the beautiful old Remington and stared at the barren spools. Sara was right—the ribbon had been removed. Christ Almighty! he thought. Somebody'd really gotten this bastard back in spades. They'd hung him by his own rope, strangled him with that thin black ribbon on which he'd banged out his venomous prose.

Friday

WHAT NIGEL KNOWS

Tinseltown Tidbits and Tattle

by Nigel Whitty

WORTH A HOT FLASH? More on Danny Blue, fabled Hollywood stud and self-proclaimed "director." For those waiting with bated breath, Danny's newest romance is menopausal million-dollar TV personality and queen of the suck-up-to-'em star interviews, Elizabeth Salt. The question is, does Blueboy's current crush on seven-times-married, seven-times-divorced Lizzie have to do with (1) some secret she knows and he wants her to keep; (2) her lush green bank account; (3) the fact that Lizzie pulls a lot of weight with the Film Festival; (4) that Daddy dearest is Chairman of the Board of T(elevision) C(orporation) of A(merica), or, last and certainly least, (5) the irresistible appeal of Lizzie's chubby pink thighs? And even more important, what does she see in Danny? Is he to be the eighth in a long list of dumbbell Adonises she has bedded and/or wedded? And why not since Lizzie, it seems, lives by the credo: "Mirror, mirror, tell me true/If my men are pretty, will I be, too?" . . . **SLEEPERS:** Was that heavy snoring we heard at a recent screening coming from no less a critic than Vernon Leakey, daddy of the school of filmophobic esthetics? And was that chorus of heavy hiccoughing beside him coming from his heavy-drinking better half, Beatrix? Tsk, tsk, it's getting so that we can't take filmdom's happiest couple anywhere anymore. . . . **MYSTERY OF THE MOMENT**: What Hollywood missus and former National Baton-Twirling Champ in the 21-and-Over Class has given up team sports and started sporting with teams instead, much to the dismay of her better half who's quite a sport himself? Name escape you? Just wait. Nigel has the answer down pat in his little black book. . . . ★

4

NIGEL WHITTY'S COLUMN was all the talk on the Film Festival's Opening Night. A whisper of malicious little "Did you hear about's," of patronizing "I suspected as much's," and of vindictive "That's just what they were asking for's" echoed from the first row to the last of Alice Tully Hall where Danny Blue's movie *Subway* was being premiered. And at Tavern-on-the-Green, where a party was held afterward, the buzz grew into a din as electric as the hundreds of lights ablaze in the theatrically illuminated Central Park restaurant.

"All the more power to her! But she sure as hell looks like his mother," a buxom blonde in a sequined gown murmured to a man who just might have been her father.

"I hear he flies in from the coast every month just to give her a mercy fuck," a crotchety octogenarian in a tuxedo nodded to a blue-haired matron wearing pince-nez.

Each remark that Sara Nightingale heard sent a vague stab of guilt through her conscience, a stab made even more acute when she saw Elizabeth Salt sweep into the restaurant on the arm of Danny Blue, her head held just a little too high, her laugh just a trifle too loud, her mascara a bit heavy. After all, Sara was an accessory to the crime, wasn't she? It was precisely this column that Sara had delivered to the *Trib* yesterday morning and which, together with Nigel's damning review of *Subway*, was among the materials she had gone over with Richard Singer-Murray.

But it wasn't only the gossip that made Sara uncomfortable. It was that here she was, just one day after Nigel's murder, at a glamorous party enjoying herself, and perhaps just a little too much. Poor Nigel! He didn't deserve to die—and not that way! Murder! People didn't get murdered in real life—only in movies and on the front page of the *New York Post.* What a waste! A tear came to Sara's eye. That brilliant mind gone and moldering in the grave. But she wasn't going to think about it tonight. Not now. After all, tomorrow was another day.

And, in any case, this place was irresistible. A diminutive crystal palace adorned with chandeliers and mirrors, with lavish bouquets of late-summer flowers and exotic potted trees, Tavern-on-the-Green swept you up in its romantically festive aura. Indeed, Sara thought as she stood under the softly hued Japanese lanterns in the restaurant's tiny garden, if she hadn't seen that smug and self-satisfied Lieutenant Michael Connelly lurking about, she might have forgotten Nigel's death altogether.

Sara didn't think she'd ever been in a place before where there were quite so many glamorous people in quite so many glittering costumes: Joan Fontaine in a white ballgown that looked exactly like the one she'd worn in *Rebecca*; Paul Newman wearing a blue shirt which was a perfect match for his eyes; Lauren Bacall in a snug-fitting gold lamé evening dress; Mick Jagger sporting a rust-colored raw silk antique smoking jacket; Truman Capote in a white linen suit; and Princess Lee Radziwill in a flowered Yves Saint-Laurent creation. Former Mayor John Lindsay was here, towering over the crowd. Dolly Parton wore iridescent purple jeans topped with an angora sweater. And John Travolta came in a huge and forbidding Claude Montana leather jacket. This film scene was certainly more opulent than the one she had known in either Paris or Rome. And it was more incandescent than the bat caves of Madagascar and splashier than her voyage across the Pacific.

Sara must have been thinking aloud, for Lieutenant

Michael Connelly suddenly interrupted her. "Gee, Miss Nightingale, aren't you sorry you left your autograph book at home?"

"I can't believe, Lieutenant, you're that far above it all. These people are everybody's fantasy figures, everybody's dreams," Sara returned.

"Not mine, sweetheart," he said curtly. "To me, this world looks as phony as a three-dollar bill."

What a superior-sounding prig, Sara thought. "Lieutenant, you're the life of the party," she said nastily.

"In case you've forgotten, sweetheart, this is part of my job. I'm not here to party. And these good-time Charlies aren't my idea of a good time anyway."

What inverted snobbery! Sara was glad she'd worn her highest heels tonight so he couldn't look down on *her*. Indeed, if she wasn't mistaken, she probably had the edge on him by at least a quarter of an inch. "I thought policemen were required by law to be six feet tall, Lieutenant Connelly," she inquired haughtily.

"Only if they have low I.Q.'s," he answered.

She was racking her brain trying to think of a clever response when Richard Singer-Murray rescued her. "Sara, dear, there you are, I've been looking all over for you. Have you listened to all this talk?"

"'Listened to all this talk'! I'd have to be stone deaf to have missed it. By the way, Richard, have you met Lieutenant Connelly?"

"I'm afraid not. How do you do, Lieutenant," Richard said. He held out his hand, but not, as it turned out, to Michael, rather to Sara whom he led onto the dance floor where, to the strains of "I've Got You Under My Skin," he whispered exultantly, "Look, we've got to run more pieces, Sara. People are just eating Nigel's column up! We're riding on a crest, and I'd like to keep the momentum going as long as possible. How much material do you have lying around?"

Sara thought they danced very well together indeed,

and she was much less interested in Nigel's material than in nuzzling close to Richard Singer-Murray, inhaling the fragrance of his Brut. "Material? I'm not sure," she said. "Nigel taped a lot of stuff and gave me about five cassettes to transcribe, but I haven't gotten around to them yet."

"Fabulous," he said, taking a big dip.

Almost tripped on that one! Sara thought to herself as she caught her balance.

"Anything else?" Richard pursued, spinning her around.

"I've got two reviews and two columns that are just about ready to go. You know Nigel always worked so far in advance." She blew the words into his ear suggestively.

"Incredible," Richard exclaimed, extending his arm and guiding her into a turn.

She did a quick pirouette, bumping into a man in a white suit. "Oh, excuse me," she said to Fenton Farnabee, then whirled back to Richard Singer-Murray.

"And what about Nigel's little black book?" Richard whispered, holding her close now.

"It's missing," Sara said in a hushed tone.

"Missing?" Richard stood still right in the middle of the dance floor. "Missing?" he repeated. "Oh, well, Sara, you come and see me first thing tomorrow morning, and together we'll work something out. Together, you and I will keep Nigel Whitty alive, at least for a little while longer." He kissed her on the cheek, squeezed her hand, and made his excuses.

Sara watched him snake his way through the crowd, offering a hug to the right, a kiss to the left, a back-slap straight ahead, and a wink over his shoulder. What a piranha, she thought. But he smells good.

Michael Connelly stood leaning against the bar, a glass of club soda in his hand, and watched as Sara Nightingale and that foppish little fruit, Fenton Farnabee, mangled each other on the dance floor. They were trying to work out the crazy rhythms of "Lady of Spain," and as Fenton kept shuffling Sara from side to side, and front to back, the two just couldn't avoid stepping on each other's toes. But still Sara wore an ecstatic expression on her face as though she were Ginger Rogers.

Oh, well, she may not have been the greatest dancer in the world or the most humble person, but she really did look terrific in her pale green chiffon dress with her red hair flying as she moved. Michael would have liked to have taken her in his arms himself, but it struck him as an unprofessional move. He was here to look around and size up the situation, and she was his guide to this uncharted territory. Strictly a business relationship, he reminded himself.

And she'd been helpful, pointing out everyone on Lynn Ericson's screening list so that, one by one, he could observe how they operated. She'd also urged Sammy Nachman to introduce him to one or two. And, just as Michael had figured, when he'd read the statements O'Reilly had prepared and looked through the files Friedkin had put together, they were quite a crew. And any one of them could have murdered Nigel Whitty, from Danny Blue to Lynn Ericson. Even that pimply-faced usher could have done it. But which one? They were all so theatrical, these people, so full of baloney, no, popcorn. They'd all seen too many lousy movies, if you asked him. Even the Europeans.

This Polish ham he'd chatted with tonight, for instance. This Gyorgii Gdansk, the great ballet dancer, who had been so overwhelmed by expressions of grief that all through their conversation he kept dabbing at his big blue eyes and wiping his aquiline nose. He didn't fit Michael's image of a dancer: his short stocky build suggested a bantamweight boxer more than it did some guy who ran around the stage in pink tights. But the guy was handsome all right, with that thick wavy blond hair and those even white teeth.

There was something fishy about that other import as well, Enzo Carbonare. He also acted a little too sorry, a little too stricken, Michael felt, even though in Sara Nightingale's eyes he was the biggest star of them all, the greatest living Italian director. A tall, silver-haired, elegant-looking man, he kept wringing his hands, shaking his head, and patting the arm of his companion, Maria Cortese, a striking woman with dark fiery features who wore a spectacular flame-red evening costume and was almost as tall as Enzo himself. Sara had explained that although Carbonare was one of the most talented directors alive, he had been on a streak of bad luck. He was making a comeback now with his new American-financed film, *The Green Sky,* which was a Festival selection. It was going to have an unusual premiere, though, since the Italian-American Anti-Defamation League was underwriting a benefit showing at the recently refurbished Radio City Music Hall.

Sara had filled Michael in on almost everyone this way, telling him the kinds of things his men were unlikely to come up with, such as what relationships the suspects had with each other and with Nigel Whitty. She'd also thrown in other bits of information, tidbits she'd picked up from Nigel during the last few weeks, such as the fact that the Film Festival had recently had trouble attracting big Hollywood movies and needed to create an exciting new image for itself. Or the fact that Lynn Ericson was now in line for a promotion after having flown out to the coast and single-handedly persuaded Alan Savory to show *Allergic to Love* as the Festival's Closing Night entry. And that, until Nigel had intervened, Sammy Nachman, who had organized tonight's gala (and every other movie gala in New York), had planned to donate all his personal profits from the evening's bash to establishing the Sammy Nachman Seat of Cinema Studies at Yeshiva University. Sara had also told Michael about a letter Nigel had written to the Yeshiva's Dean of Students. "What will the students study?" Nigel had asked imperiously. "Menus from great movie parties?"

Michael smiled now as he thought about that line. Maybe Nigel wasn't so off the wall, after all. Christ! Look at this crowd of phonies in their diamonds and $800 suits pushing each other out of the way, tripping over each other's fancy shoes to get to the chow. And look at what they put on their plates! You'd think they hadn't eaten in weeks. This party had sure been set up for gluttons. There was a huge buffet table in every one of the restaurant's string of rooms, even out here in the garden. And each table looked like it was going to collapse under the weight of those tureens of shrimp, mounds of caviar, platters of ham and prime ribs, casseroles of wild rice and ratatouille, huge bowls of salad and boards of cheese. In every room as well there was a pastry table and a bar. Guests were crawling around each of them like ants at a picnic.

And everybody was on the make for something. He'd never seen people kiss and hug so frequently. They never stopped touching one another, never stopped wanting from one another. Some, apparently, just wanted to get laid, others to get ahead. Still others seemed to want to bask in the spotlight, to shove their faces in front of the continually popping flashbulbs—the place was swarming with photographers—or to make small talk with big names. But most amazing of all, wherever they were or whomever they were talking to, these people never seemed to be satisfied. Their eyes were always roaming the room, hungry for a better catch, a bigger contact.

"Ooooohh, Lieutenant Connelly." Fenton Farnabee danced up to him, Sara in tow. "That was exhausting!" Fenton flung his hand across his brow. "I'll certainly get my beauty sleep tonight."

"It was fun, Fenton." Sara smiled. "Thanks."

"Just call me Fenny, honey. All my good friends do."

Funny, Fenny! Michael thought. This guy has got to be kidding!

"Now, Lieutenant Connelly, though I'd love to ask *you* for the next dance, I'm just too too pooped. Let me take you for a drink instead."

"Never drink when I'm on the job, but I'll join you if you like."

Fenton stretched out his arms, wrapping one around Michael, the other around Sara, and led them toward a small table in the corner of the garden. "Sara, honey, why don't you go and powder your sweet little nose for about twenty minutes." Fenton winked.

Michael nodded, and Sara excused herself.

"Now we can talk strictly *entre nous*." Fenton grinned, settling his chin on his hands and batting his wide blue eyes. Michael judged him to be in his mid- or late thirties, although his pretty baby face and curly dark hair made it difficult to be sure.

"Listen, Lieutenant Connelly. Fenny has a little deal for you," Fenton said, leaning in to Michael. "If you happen to throw a bit of hot news to Fenny about Nigel's sad departure, Fenny might be able to throw a little your way for your little investigation."

"What do you have in mind, Fenny?" Michael asked, drawing back just a little.

"Well, what do you think of Elizabeth Salt and the M-A-F-I-A?" He emphasized each letter dramatically.

"Sure, Fenny, that sounds good. S-H-O-O-T."

"Well, suppose I tell you that she taped some very important interviews with Carmine Capolavaro right before the family had his throat slashed at Sing Sing."

"Keep talking."

"You first." Fenton smiled coyly.

"Sorry, Fenny, honey. I don't have anything to give you right now."

"But you'll keep me in mind." Fenton cocked his head. "Especially because the rest of this story is fascinating. You know, those tapes disappeared. And some say they weren't stolen."

"What was on the tapes?"

"You know—" Fenton smiled widely—"I just can't remember. . . . It must have been all that dancing."

"I know how it is," Michael said calmly. "But I'm being straight with you, Fenny. I don't have any info to buy with right now. Will you take cash instead?"

Fenton shook his head no. "We're all whores—me, Nigel, Liz Salt, the whole kit and caboodle, every critic, every columnist. But cash isn't my style, honey." He paused and signaled the waiter, who delivered a glass of champagne. "But maybe," Fenton began again, fishing around now, "it was Nigel's style. I could never figure out how he lived so well."

"How far back do the two of you go?" Michael asked.

"Back to Noah's Ark," Fenton chortled, "weathering the storms together, if you know what I mean."

"Not exactly," Michael said, "but while you were sailing around, he didn't happen to mention anyone ever threatening him, anyone who carried a heavy grudge?"

"Anyone? My stars, sweetie, everyone!"

"What about an 'everyone' named Rio?"

"Rio? You mean as in 'The Man from' or 'The Road to' or 'Grande,' 'Bravo,' or 'Lobo'?"

Michael shook his head. "Who knows?"

"Well, sweetie, not I."

Suddenly there was a high-pitched shriek from the other end of the garden. The orchestra stopped abruptly. Michael got up and ran in the direction of the shriek, Fenton following in hot pursuit. Maria Cortese, the visiting star, was screaming at the top of her lungs. As she yelled, her hands were gesticulating wildly. *"Putana! Putana! . . . Che bastarda!* How dare you insult Maria! . . . You can't keep your own man . . . go *fock* yourself."

The barrage was directed at a short, chubby blonde half Maria's size and a good deal older, in a pastel embroidered caftan. It was Elizabeth Salt, who was very drunk and very angry.

"You goddamn thief . . . keep your hands off my man!"

"Not your man, a *free* man. . . . He belong to nobody. Did I put pistol to your head, *caro* Danielo?"

She turned to the cause of the battle. It was Danny Blue. He stood slightly separate from the crowd which had gathered, watching these two women with evident amusement. There was a semblance of a smile on his lean, sensual face. He appeared strangely relaxed, his shirt open at the collar, one hand in the pocket of his brown suede pants, the other holding a glass of wine. His posture seemed somehow surly, considering the situation.

"That's right, Danny, just come to her defense," Elizabeth screamed. "I dare you, you bastard."

"Go ahead, bribe him, Mommy, Mommy." Maria shrieked with laugher. "Buy him with money. Buy a man. Buy a *fock,* Mommy."

This was too much for Elizabeth Salt. She literally hurled herself, caftan and all, onto Maria. Maria's lustrous dark hair came tumbling down her shoulders, and the red chiffon scarf that was clasped over her strapless gown tore as, with amazing strength, she pushed her opponent away. She really was a big one, Michael thought, edging his way over to break up the fight. But he was just a little too late to stop Elizabeth Salt from grabbing a plateful of ratatouille and throwing it in Maria's direction. Maria ducked, and the plate went flying into the air, splattering its gooey sauce of peppers, tomatoes, and onions all over a young woman standing behind her.

Maria retaliated now. Plucking the champagne from Danny's hand, she splashed it into Elizabeth Salt's face. "You are all wet, signora," she said, slapping Elizabeth's cheek so hard that the noise resounded throughout the garden.

Elizabeth was stunned but recovered quickly. She was frantically looking for something else to hurl when Michael reached her. "Break it up, everybody," he yelled into the crowd as he gently guided her out of the spotlight, depositing her into Sammy Nachman's ready arms.

Out of the corner of his eye, Michael could see the tempestuous and stunning Maria Cortese striding indignantly out of the room. She was followed by a flustered Enzo Carbonare, and also, he noted, by Danny Blue, a cigarette dangling defiantly from the corner of his mouth. "Bravo, Maria," someone—was it Blue himself?—shouted after her.

A huge sob. Michael turned around to see what was the matter this time. It was Becky Luna, crying like a five-year-old who had just dropped her ice cream. She looked like a kid, too, Michael thought, much younger than her twenty-three years. Ratatouille was dripping from her nose onto her décolletage and down onto the pink ruffles of her organdy dress. "My frock is ruined," she sobbed. "Absolutely ruined! My Mary McFadden original, my favorite frock, my very favorite!" Tears streamed down her round cheeks, leaving big tracks of mascara under her puffy eyes. Her nose reddened and began to run. Bits of tomato clung to her short-cropped dark brown hair. She stood rooted to the spot, clearly unable to move.

Suddenly the orchestra began to play again. Strains of "Smile" filled the garden. How corny can you get, Michael thought. But then what he saw next made him realize that you can get a lot cornier still. For at that moment, Gyorgii Gdansk bounded across the dance floor with what almost amounted to a leap, flung off his blue velvet jacket with a flourish, and wrapped first it, and then his arm, around Becky Luna's heaving shoulders. Gently he guided her toward the door.

Then, it seemed to Michael, quite an extraordinary thing happened. As she reached the door, Becky Luna obviously had second thoughts about the whole fracas, and in a desperate effort to reestablish her dignity, she stopped dead in her tracks, slipped out of Gyorgii's jacket, and led him back to the dance floor just in time to lead him into a mad tango. And why not? After all, Gdansk was considered to be the world's most gifted Polish dancer. No grass is going to grow under his feet, Michael chuckled, no opportunity is going to be lost to this one. Boy, tonight was something else. No wonder people paid a C-note apiece for tickets to events like this!

And the climax was yet to come. For now Michael's attention was grabbed by a spoon against a glass, and then the sound of a familiar female voice. Elizabeth Salt again. She was very drunk and very wet. She also looked very foolish as she stood, fat and blowsy and weaving, atop one of the tables, a drink raised high in her hand.

"A toast!" she announced. "To Nigel Whitty. May he hot-flash through all eternity!" She took a sip, then slammed the glass to the slate floor and collapsed in a heap among the empty glasses and dirty forks and knives.

Michael Connelly stood in front of Tavern-on-the-Green waiting for Sara Nightingale. She'd forgotten her purse and had to go back into the restaurant to get it. As he waited for her now, he yawned. It was late, sometime after 3:00 A.M. It had been a long day, an even longer night. The first to arrive at the party that evening, he was also the last to leave. A lot had happened in the interim, but he wasn't quite sure what to make of it. All he knew was that if Nigel Whitty had gotten to every one of these characters in the same way he'd gotten to Elizabeth Salt, then each one of them had more than enough motive to kill him.

But maybe it wasn't that, either. Maybe, as Fenton Farnabee had hinted, Nigel had been on the take, and whoever was slipping it to him had had enough. Like what was that check for ten grand all about that he'd found in Nigel's files? What had Perdue Pictures been paying him for? Michael decided to begin with the only person who'd been in that screening room who might also know something about the Perdue payroll. He'd begin with Alan Savory and see him first thing in the morning.

"Found it!" Sara suddenly appeared at his side, waving a green beaded purse. "What a crazy night!" she chirped. Then, changing her tone, "Poor Nigel! He would have loved every minute of it."

"I thought you said he was a man of taste?" Michael remarked sarcastically.

"He *was*."

"You're something else, Nightingale. You really like hanging out with these fruitcakes, don't you?" He grinned.

"*I* think they're charming."

"Yeah, who can resist a toast on a tabletop?"

"Very funny, I'm sure," Sara retorted, punctuating her remark with a near fall.

"You mean it wasn't the toast? It must've been the flying ratatouille, then?" he said, putting his hand on her elbow to steady her. Her heels, he noticed, were very high; the gravel, quite rough. And as he helped her into his unmarked squad car and watched her close her eyes and lean her head back dizzily, he also saw that she had had a little too much champagne.

"Feel all right?" he asked, sliding behind the wheel.

"Fine," she said. "I was just thinking, Lieutenant Connelly, how little you understand the artistic temperament. What you don't see is that these people are passionate, sensitive, volatile types whose emotions are the very key to their talent."

"Talent? Yeah, it took a lot of talent to make that stinkeroo we saw tonight. For Chrissakes, who in his right mind would make a movie about a subway clerk who gets his kicks touching the hands of young girls as they slip him their change?"

Sara hiccoughed and delicately covered her mouth with her hand. "Did it ever strike you, Lieutenant Connelly, that *Subway* wasn't really about a subway clerk at all? That what you were watching was a symbolic drama . . ."

"You gotta be kidding! An hour and a half in a subway change booth?"

"And why not? It's a perfect metaphor for the human condition—the sense it gives of being trapped, enclosed."

"I'll say."

"You, my dear detective, quite clearly have nothing to say at all. You plainly didn't comprehend a thing you saw tonight."

"Yeah, all that underground stuff went right over my head." He was beginning to lose patience now. "You know, Nightingale, that movie was full of it, and 'quite clearly,' at this moment, so are you."

"Stop the car right now," she commanded abruptly. "I want to get out."

"In the middle of Central Park?" he asked, stepping on the gas.

"I'm not afraid."

"But I am. We've already had one murder this week. Let's not try for another."

"Really, Lieutenant. I've battled bats in Madagascar and survived hurricanes on the high seas. You don't think I can deal with a mugger in Central Park?"

"I know, Miss Nightingale, it's all in your file."

"What do you mean, my file?"

"Your police file."

"How filthy! You spy, you Peeping Tom, you Herbert Hoover," she sputtered.

Michael laughed. "Just doing my job, Miss Nightingale."

"And I suppose that laughing is also part of your job?" she said haughtily. "Hmmpff!" She was clearly fuming now. "I just want you to know, Lieutenant Connelly, that I'd appreciate silence for the rest of the trip. Otherwise," she paused menacingly, "I'll have you charged with harassment."

"And I'll have you charged with excessive snottiness."

"Ha!" she huffed.

She always had to have the last word, Michael thought.

They drove through the sleeping city. And not another word was spoken until Michael pulled up in front of Sara's apartment on West 11th Street.

She opened the car door and turned to Michael as if, he thought, preparing another one of her dramatic exits. She cleared her throat.

"I'm afraid, Lieutenant Connelly, that not only was *Subway* over your head, but so is this entire case."

She slammed the door and with a flourish marched toward the stoop of her brownstone, running into a garbage can along the way.

Michael laughed. This one, as Bridget Connelly might have said, needed a good thump on the rump and a large helping of humble pie.

Saturday

WHAT NIGEL KNOWS

Tinseltown Tidbits and Tattle

by Nigel Whitty

A CURE FOR ATHLETE'S FOOT? Rumor has it that snazzy producer Alan Savory has had enough of starlet/bride Biffy Adams's sporting life—her nocturnal tackles, her morning volleys, her luncheon serves, and her cocktail-hour scoring. Friends say he plans to dump her if *Allergic to Love* is a flop and his quickie marriage to Biffy has proven to be another unlucky patch in his rash of ill luck. Well, Biffy, baby, Nigel suggests you pack up all your cares right now, for *Allergic* is one of those movies audiences will be avoiding Like the Plague. The 1944 original was bad enough, but this time out, as tailored to the talents of Gyorgii Gdansk and Becky Luna, it's impossible. Get this: A college football hero who also happens to be a Polish exchange student has to pass his English Equivalency Exam in order to play in the Big Game. The night before, he comes down with a giant case of hives, but his tutor. who has a giant case on him, saves the day. Disguising herself as our hero, the tutor, played unfortunately by Becky Luna, first takes the test for him, passes, and then runs 50 yards for the winning touchdown—and all to the tune of "The Warsaw Ghetto Polka," as played by a 60-piece marching band. Need Nigel say more? No wonder Savory has been holding court all week long at his NYC townhouse, plying reviewers with goodies, girls, and movies—no, not *Singin' in the Rain*, dearies. . . . **MYSTERY OF THE MOMENT**: Back to our celebrity feminist. Cookie, we have come across the cutest photos we know you're just dying to eyeball. Don't worry, they're safely tucked away with lots of memories, waiting for you in Nigel's little and very black book. . . . ★

5

STREAK OF BAD LUCK?

Well, Alan Savory could always hock his townhouse, Michael thought as he stood in the morning sun sizing up the elegant white stone building on East 67th off Fifth. With its huge French windows, its pillared entryway, and those hand-tooled wrought-iron balconies up on the third floor, it must've been worth a cool million or two or even three. And this was just Alan Savory's New York pad; he'd given his main address as Bel Air Road in Bel Air, California. Michael had to hand it to him; the guy really knew how to live.

But as luxurious as the place looked from the street, Michael wasn't prepared for what he found inside. For beyond the ground-floor foyer where a slim young man in designer jeans greeted him was an indoor swimming pool almost the entire width of the building. "Right this way," the man said, leading Michael through the glass doors into a glass-enclosed and glass-ceilinged patio dotted with palms and bougainvillea. A little bit of L.A. in New York, Michael thought. Who's gonna believe this one?

"C'mon in for a dip, Lieutenant Connelly." Alan Savory smiled up at Michael from his rubber raft which was now floating in the middle of the green-tiled pool. "Sonny, get the Lieutenant a pair of trunks," he ordered Michael's escort.

Michael quickly declined. "Never dip when I'm on the job." He pulled up a redwood lounge and sat stiffly at the edge of it, trying to digest the scene before him. For next to Alan Savory were two young girls, each floating around on her own little rubber mat and wearing the briefest of bikinis. Both were stacked like Playboy bunnies, but that was all Michael could tell about them, since their hair was completely hidden by golden-wiglet bathing caps with braids of daisies across the crown, while their eyes were obscured by identical green plastic goggles, protection from the row of sunlamps above.

As for Alan Savory, he was Mr. Hollywood himself. He wore dark-tinted aviator glasses and white Lastex bathing trunks with a huge monogrammed *A.S.* at the side. His carefully tanned and perfectly shaped body was small, smooth, and hairless, and his thick black hair was as slick as his body. His features were small and even, and his smile sparkled plenty.

"Lieutenant Connelly, let me introduce Cheri and Colette."

Simultaneously, the girls took off their green goggles to reveal four of the longest sets of eyelashes Michael had ever seen. Actually, they looked like spider legs. "Hiya, Lieutenant," they said in unison, revealing that, names notwithstanding, they probably hailed from Jersey City. The salutation done, they replaced the green goggles and concentrated on their suntans.

Alan Savory climbed out of the pool and wrapped himself in a white velour robe that bore the same monogram as his trunks. "Now let me take the old bull by his horns," he said, sitting down. "I suppose you want to talk about Nigel Whitty."

Michael nodded. "I know you've run through this with my men before, but let me just get a few of these basics out of the way. First, just why were you at the screening the morning of Whitty's death?"

"Good question, Lieutenant, which I already answered for your man, O'Reilly. Perdue Pictures was thinking of picking up the American distribution rights to *The Last Gasp*, and I was checking it out for the company."

"Were you sitting alone?"

"No, I was with my stars, Becky Luna and Googie Gdansk."

"Did you get up at all during the screening?"

"No."

"Did you hear anything strange during the screening?"

"Not a thing. I was totally absorbed. I love stories about the disabled; they really touch me where it counts." He tapped his heart to show Michael where it counted.

"Where were you before the screening?"

"I was in my office at eight. Had to okay some publicity stills and send them to the lab by ten."

"Anyone who can confirm what time you got there?"

"Well, I don't punch a time clock." He smiled condescendingly. "And my secretary hadn't come in yet."

Sonny arrived with a tray on which sat two Wedgwood cups and saucers, a silver coffee urn, and a basket of brioches. "Help yourself," Savory offered.

"Thanks." Michael poured himself a cup of coffee. "When did your secretary arrive?" he continued.

"About ten."

"And no one saw you from the time you arrived at eight until ten?"

"I'm afraid not."

That was a suspiciously late start for a secretary, Michael noted to himself as he sipped his coffee. But this was the movie world and God only knew when and if they ever started. Now he took a new tack. "Tell me about your relationship with Nigel Whitty. How long did you know him?"

"Forever. During the best years of our lives."

"How many years was that?"

"Six years, maybe seven."

"Describe your relationship."

"Well, part of it was professional, but we were really good friends. Blood brothers. Like two peas in a pod. Like this." Savory wrapped two fingers around each other and held them up to indicate his closeness with Whitty.

"You knew, then, that he hated your new film?"

"Sadly, yes. But I'm not the kind to hold grudges. Others may have, but to me, Whitty was an incredible guy, the most incredible I've ever known."

"How so?"

"He was a genius, a real, honest-to-God, eighteen-carat genius."

"So I've heard."

"You haven't heard the half of it." Savory sighed with what Michael assumed should be taken for grief. "Someone should make his life story. I'm going to begin negotiating for the rights right now. I want Sean Connery for the part."

"Let's come back to Whitty's life story. We've had a lot of trouble putting it together. He apparently had no family, but one newspaper article about him said he was born and brought up in New Rochelle. . . ."

"New Rochelle?" Alan Savory looked sincerely shocked. "Never. He was born and brought up in India. His father was a colonial magistrate . . ."

"I thought his father was in plumbing supplies?"

"Never!" Alan Savory was insistent. "Nigel was much too classy for that."

"Maybe," Michael said wryly. "Tell me, what else do you know about his past?

"Only that he was a man of great substance and principles. A real prince."

"Did he ever know a princess named Rio?"

Savory shook his head and sniffed a couple of times. Maybe he had a cold, Michael thought. Too much sunbathing, no doubt.

"I'd like to ask you something." Michael suddenly began to feel the heat of the sunlamps. Or maybe it was the bullshit that was beginning to stifle him. In any case, he loosened his collar. "Did Whitty ever work for you?"

"Never." Sniff. Sniff.

"Well, can you explain this?" Michael handed him the $10,000 check record made out from Perdue Pictures to Whitty.

"Oh, that," Alan Savory said without flinching. "Well, I thought you meant, did he work for me *directly*. Yes, indeed, he did do a little work for the company—a little consulting."

"A little ten-grand worth of consulting? Or maybe twenty grand? According to Nigel's bank, there was another ten-thousand dollar payment from Perdue six months ago. And twenty thousand the year before."

"Look, Lieutenant Connelly, I know that sounds like big money to you, but in my business that's chicken feed." Sniff. Sniff. Drip. Drip.

Clearly this was no cold.

"You know, Nigel was one in a million. We'd show him scripts, and he'd be able to tell you in a minute what worked and what didn't. His advice wasn't worth ten grand—it was worth a million. We got him cheap."

"Just exactly what scripts did he advise you on?"

"You want the names?" Savory shrugged. "Hard to say—we see so much stuff." And he sniffed again.

Michael couldn't believe his ears. "You mean you don't remember the name of a single script he advised you on?" Savory, from his symphony of sniffs and snorts, was obviously a snowcone, a coke head; but even with his muddled thinking accounted for, he'd have to do better than this.

"Lemme think about it Lieutenant, and get back to you."

Michael let it drop and handed Savory a Xerox copy of the letter he'd found in Nigel's apartment. "Would this help you to remember, maybe?"

"Oh, this," Alan Savory chuckled, reading aloud: "'*Dear Nigel, It's always best to know which side your bread is buttered on. From one gourmet to another. A.'"* Then he explained. "Nigel had such a palate. Had he moved out to the coast, he would have been the best celebrity chef in Hollywood. He could have written a cookbook: 'What Nigel Knows About Noshing'—it would have been Number One on the bestseller list."

"Come on, Savory, get off it—this is a threat, isn't it?"

"Threat? To a man who fried the best potatoes in the Western Hemisphere? To my best friend? To a buddy whose death has had me crying my eyes out for the last three days!"

"Crying whose eyes out, you goddamn phony?" a voice bellowed.

Michael turned in the direction of the voice. It was Biffy Adams who now stood at the entrance to the pool, flanked by three gargantuan men in sweatsuits.

"Your best friend!" she hissed. "You hated his guts, you liar."

"Biffy, my love," Savory said, his voice calm and syrupy, "I'd like you to meet Lieutenant Connelly from Homicide."

"I don't care if he's Columbo himself. What did you do, Lieutenant, clean up Forty-second Street and bring the dregs over here?" She stared daggers at the bathing beauties. They in turn lifted their green goggles to see what was happening, smiled mindlessly, and then covered their eyes again. "What a joke!" Biffy now threw at her husband. "You can't even do it with one, and you're trying *two*! What do you do, watch them do it to each other?"

Michael took in the newly arrived quartet, wondering what *they* did. Here, in the flesh, was Whitty's baton twirler, and the three bruisers at her side looked like linebacks on the team she twirled for. She was pretty in a hayseed kind of way, blond and big-boned, healthy with a vengeance. Savory's taste was certainly eclectic.

"Miss Adams, if you don't mind, I'd like to talk with you for a few moments in connection with Nigel Whitty's murder," Michael requested.

"Sure, Lieutenant, glad to tell you anything I can about that lousy shit. You know, I literally laughed when I heard about his death. The only person I'd be happier to see go—" and she turned to her husband who was now examining his polished fingernails—"is that piece of slime."

"How charming, my dear. You always did have a silver tongue."

"Shut up!" she screamed. "And let me tell you a thing or two. I saw the papers this morning, and if *you* think *you* are dumping me, you've got another case coming. *I* am dumping you, buster. I'm just home now to pack my bags." She nodded to her team. "Come on, boys."

"Just a minute, Miss Adams." Michael detained her. "I'd just like to know where *you* were the morning of the murder."

"At the beauty parlor. Just check with Kenneth. But, believe me, if I could've strangled that turd myself, I'd have canceled my appointment. And whatever my phony husband tells you, he would've loved to break Nigel's neck, too."

Sara was in heaven. She couldn't believe her good fortune. When she'd been to Richard Singer-Murray's office that morning, he had been ecstatic. "Do you know how many calls I've received this morning alone, asking about Nigel's column?" he exulted. "Sixteen! Imagine, sixteen! Everyone wanted to know how many more pieces there were, how long we'd be publishing "What Nigel Knows," who Nigel's victims would be, and who was putting the columns together. And do you know who's been calling, Sara, dear?" Richard had leaned back in his brown leather executive swivel chair. His pause had been so long that for a moment Sara thought she was supposed to guess. "At least three publishers with offers for posthumous books; ABC News—they want to interview me tomorrow—and such luminaries as Henry Kissinger, George Plimpton, Becky Luna, Liz Salt, Clint Eastwood—maybe he wants the movie right—and even the Italian director, Enzo

Carbonare—he told me what a great fan of Nigel's he was." Richard had swiveled with joy, making a complete 360-degree turn. Then he'd stopped and leaned forward as though he'd had something momentous to announce to Sara.

And indeed, it was momentous, Sara now recalled as she walked briskly up Columbus Avenue on her way to the 20th Precinct. "Sara," Richard Singer-Murray had said, seizing her hand, "this is your moment. Everybody knows that you're the one who's putting together Nigel's column. Now I'm going to give you something of your own, your very own shot. I want you to do a piece for me entitled 'One Hundred Twenty-Two Minutes In the Dark with a Dead Man,' or 'What Nigel Whitty's Death Means to the Film Community.' And I'll tell you how I want you to do it. Get hold of every person who was in the screening room with Nigel, and plumb for their true reactions. In other words, what was it like watching a movie with a corpse? How did they really feel about his death? Did they hate him? Did they love him? Get me a lot of sensational stuff, and get it to me fast. By the end of next week. Ten thousand words. We'll run it as a three-part series, front page of the arts section. Sara, dear—" he smiled patiently—"I know that nobody else has been able to get to these people, but I'm confident that you can. And when you do—" he winked—"I'm going to make you a star."

At first Sara had some trepidation about this assignment. It seemed so cheap, so cruel, like picking at the carcass of a dead animal. What if these people had only awful things to say about Nigel? Could she betray his memory so? Then again, she knew damn well that Nigel wouldn't have had any hesitation had the shroud been on any body other than his own. Moreover, she also knew that in her hands, Nigel's spirit would get as fair a shake as possible, and so she finally consented.

Poor Nigel! she thought once again. There he was, lying on a slab in the morgue, while here she was, happy as a lark, with the sun shining and opportunity beckoning. Her good luck, she felt, was a direct result of Nigel's misfortune; and since she really didn't know how to cope with such pangs of conscience as she was now having, she decided not to cope with them at all. What she concentrated on, instead, was that she was about to take on her first big-time assignment. And the prospect was thrilling.

The trick now was, how to get these people to see her. Fenton Farnabee was no problem; he had already called her three times to find out where Nigel's columns were coming from. Though she'd admitted nothing, he knew, of course. He was just hoping she would give him some item he might use; he could always be talked into a tradeoff.

Sammy Nachman also might come across; he certainly understood the value of publicity. The others, though, would pose a challenge. In fact, they might prove impossible. Which is why she decided to make peace with Lieutenant Michael Connelly. She knew he was going to interview every one of the people who had been in the screening room. If he would only take her along with him and allow her to throw in a question or two of her own, she'd have it made.

She pranced up the steps of the precinct and in her most authoritative manner asked the first uniformed man she saw to show her to Michael Connelly's office. The Lieutenant was just finishing off a sandwich and a container of milk when she arrived.

"Sara Nightingale!" He smiled quizzically. "To what do I owe the honor?"

She fluttered her eyelashes and looked down at her feet. "Lieutenant Connelly, I'm here to apologize for last night. I was such a beast, I don't know what got into me."

"Oh, that's all right, Miss Nightingale. We all have our off moments."

"Please call me Sara."

"Okay, Sara."

"Can I call you Michael?"

"Sure."

"Okay, Michael." She hesitated. "I just wanted to say that I was truly rude. And I'm sorry."

"Well, I wasn't too charming myself."

"Don't be silly, you were wonderful." She started to fiddle with the buttons on her blouse. "And about that movie last night, I just wanted to tell you that I've thought about it a lot. You were right. It *was* pretentious."

"I'm glad you've seen the light. You've probably been sitting in dark rooms too much."

She laughed her favorite light trill. "I hope you don't consider it too forward, Michael, but I'd like to cook you a dinner as a gesture of friendship. I'm a very good cook, if I do say so myself."

"Dinner?" He raised an eyebrow.

Was he hesitating? She'd better act fast. "How about tonight?" she blurted out, aware that her voice was growing thinner, frailer. She took a deep breath. *Easy,* she told herself. She didn't want to blow it.

"Lemme see," he answered. "What time do you want me?"

"What's your schedule?"

"Well, I'm supposed to meet Becky Luna in about ten minutes. And—"

"That sounds like it might be interesting," Sara interrupted sweetly. "Would you mind terribly if I came along?"

He cocked his head, thought for a moment, and threw her a suspicious glance.

"I could take notes for you," she said hurriedly.

"Notes?"

She bit her lip. Had she gone too far?

"What are you up to, Nightingale?" His voice was suddenly stern.

"Nothing. Absolutely nothing."

"Come off it, Sara. I'm not an idiot."

"I really do want you to come to dinner," she said. "Really. But this absolutely fabulous opportunity came my way to write an important piece about Nigel's death, and I've just *got* to see all those people who were in the screening room. I was hoping you might help me."

"Let me give you a piece of advice, Sara Nightingale." He stood up and reached for his corduroy sports jacket. "Next time you want something from me, just ask me straight, and I'll answer you straight. Don't ever use those cheap feminine wiles on me."

"Oh, Michael, I'm sorry. Honestly. But you've just got to take me along to see Becky Luna."

"Forget it, Sara. Just forget it." He started walking out of his office. "You can't come with me to see Becky Luna, and that's that," he said, stopping at the door. "And you know what? I just lost my appetite. See you around the precinct, kid." He waved and strode down the hall.

Sara was stunned. She thought this guy would be a softer touch. But she wasn't going to give up now. She scrambled down the corridor into the precinct lobby, and then out into the street. A squad car was pulling away from the sidewalk, and she could see Michael sitting beside the driver. She called out, but he didn't seem to hear. She just couldn't let him get away.

"Taxi!" she screamed. A yellow cab screeched to a halt.

"Follow that car," she ordered as she leapt in.

"But, lady, that's a police car." The cabbie looked puzzled.

Sara reached into her purse and pulled out a bill, slipping it halfway into the change pocket of the glass partition. "There's ten dollars here," she told the driver in her toughest voice. "Lose the car, and you lose the tip."

"Look, lady. The only thing I'm about to lose is a *loco* like you." He slammed on the brakes and turned to Sara. "You want a cop?" he asked. "Cop a walk, cookie."

"Stamp-hop-step-step . . . Move those tootsies! Turn, turn . . . slide, slide. Use those hands, don't let them hang. . . . Smile, smile, slide and step!"

Michael leaned against the mirrored wall of the rehearsal studio, watching Becky Luna finish up her tap dancing lesson. She was running a little late, she'd told him when he'd arrived, and would he mind just waiting ten minutes while she and her instructor, Bernie, finished running through this routine? And why not? Michael shrugged. It wasn't every day he had a chance to see a big star like Becky Luna working out in a pink tutu together with a little black pansy in yellow tights. Bernie was tapping for all he was worth, working his feet as if he were Ann Miller. Opposite him, Becky Luna was plugging away.

"C'mon, Loony-toony, can't you hear that beat?" Bernie spun around the floor and started to sing along to the music which blared from a tape recorder sitting in a corner.

"Hear the beat
Of dancing fe-et
It's a song I love
The melody of
Forty-second Street . . ."

"Where's the pitter-patter of your little feet?" Bernie called out, snapping his fingers to the music. "All I hear is the clatter of cannon-boxes."

The perspiration was running down Becky's forehead. Better than ratatouille, Michael thought as he watched her struggling to keep up with her instructor.

"Move those heels/Let's not *kvetch* it," Bernie chanted in rhythm now, "we don't wanna look like/Stepin Fetchit."

"Have a heart, Bernie," Becky panted, hopping up and down like a frantic rabbit. "I'm trying my best."

Perhaps she was doing her best, but even Michael's inexperienced eye could tell that her best wasn't good enough. For if Bernie, with his flying feet and flashing smile, was a dead ringer for Ann Miller, Becky was something else altogether. With her stiff arms and bow-legged shuffle-off-to-Buffalo, she was, if not quite the Jiminy

Cricket Nigel had seen in her, at least a lot like little wooden Pinocchio.

"Left foot, Loony! Left, left," Bernie barked like a drill sergeant in the WACs. "I'm gonna tie a little red ribbon around your pinky so you'll finally get it straight. Left is *left,* and right is *right*. Got it, mama?"

"Aagh, I'm exhausted." Becky threw herself down on the floor and tried to catch her breath.

"Sweet-patootie, this will never do!" Bernie reprimanded her. "We're going to have to tune up your tootsies if it kills us."

"It's killing one of us," Becky moaned from the floor. Her face was flushed and her dark hair was wet and matted now, with a little pink bald spot winking out from beneath her cowlick.

"Come, come, we don't want to be a flopsy-mopsy, do we?"

At these words, Becky burst out sobbing. "Oh, Bernie, what am I going to do?" she whined in despair.

"There, there, my yammie-pie." Bernie bent down to comfort her. "You're just a tired little Loony-tune. We're going to call it a day, aren't we, my minuscule melody?" He helped her up and gave her tutu a maternal little pat as she headed across the floor to the small curtained changing room.

"I'll just be a minute, Lieutenant," she said to Michael and heaved one last sob before she drew the curtain.

The minute was closer to fifteen. And the calm, relaxed woman who emerged in sophisticated black silk slacks and halter top bore little resemblance to the sobbing girl who'd entered in a pink tutu. As the pair left the Carnegie Hall Building on Seventh Avenue and walked around the corner to the Russian Tea Room, Michael noticed a peculiar aura surrounding Becky Luna. She seemed to be neither walking nor clomping, but floating.

He suspected something. And when they sat down at a table and he had a chance to check her out more carefully, he was sure. She was on something. Probably 'ludes, he figured. Quaaludes. Her voice was thick, and her eyes were closing.

"Two cups of coffee," he told the red-jacketed waiter who'd recognized Becky Luna immediately and had launched into a lengthy reminiscence.

"I used to serve your dear late mother," he said reverently. His Slavic accent was thick, but no thicker than his eyebrows which grew like great unclipped hedges over his hazel eyes. "Your mother used to sit at this very table, and she'd say to me, 'Igor, you look like a prince,' and I would say, 'I *am* a prince.'" He grinned proudly. "A Romanoff! But your mother was a queen. When Billie Glover cracked a joke, my sides, they would split. She was the greatest comedienne of them all."

Becky Luna sat there nodding assent. Michael had the feeling she'd still be nodding even if Igor hadn't been standing there singing her mother's praises.

"The coffee, Igor, if you don't mind," Michael reminded him. "And throw in a couple of pastries. Whatever Billie Glover used to order."

Igor left, and Michael turned to Becky Luna.

"You still with me, Miss Luna?"

She smiled vaguely, her eyes unfocused. "It's all that tap dancing," she muttered. "You know, *stamp-hop-step-step . . .*"

"Think you could manage to answer a few questions?"

"What?" she said, drifting. Then, "Oh, sure, just give me a minute to powder my nose. Okay?" She got up tentatively and wobbled her way back toward the ladies' room. It was a good ten minutes before she returned. Igor had brought the coffee and pastries which sat waiting for her.

"I feel great now," she smiled. "Bright as a penny."

Actually, she seemed bright as a 250-watt bulb.

"You want to know about Nigel Whitty, of course. Well, I'll tell you. He stunk to high heaven. He was low-down rotten trash. Did you see what he wrote about me this morning? He was the cruelest man who ever lived."

"You used that line once before. Do you remember?"

Becky looked at Michael blankly. He took out the letter he had found in Nigel's files and handed it to her. As she read it over, tears came to her eyes.

"That piece of dirt!" Her voice quivered. "The pain he caused me! Do you know how many hours I spent with my analyst trying to work Nigel Whitty out of my system? Do you know how he paralyzed me? I broke every mirror in my house. I couldn't get out of bed for two weeks. I wore dark glasses and hats with wide brims. I bought a ski mask and prayed for winter."

"Was it just what Whitty wrote that hurt you? Or was it anything else? Did he ever do anything to you?"

Becky dabbed her eyes with her napkin. "Did he? I'll say! You won't believe what that filth did to me. Two years ago I was up for my first big break—the musical version of *Cleopatra* with a score by The Who. I was to play the Elizabeth Taylor role. Whitty didn't like the idea—and he also felt like playing God. In other words, he wanted to show just how much power he had in this shitty industry. So he called the head of the studio and told him that if they were stupid enough to star me in a forty-million-dollar production, they deserved to lose every penny of it."

"Nigel Whitty had that much power?" Michael was incredulous.

"Not really, but he knew who he could push around. And he assured the studio bigwigs—and I have this, Lieutenant Connelly, from the horse's mouth, the head of the studio himself—that every critic on both the East and West Coasts thought I was an absolute zero and would pan the movie mercilessly. He told them that in a survey conducted by some cruddy college magazine, I had won first prize as the most unattractive newcomer ever to blight the silver screen! Well, they dumped me, of course, and for the last two years, I've been doing nothing. Thank God, Alan Savory gave me this chance."

"Nigel really did that to you? Why? What did he have against you?"

"Nothing against me. It was my mother. That flotsam

had a big thing for her, and she wouldn't give him a dance. She never went for guys who swung both ways."

Swung both ways? This was a new one, Michael thought. "You mean Whitty went for guys as well as girls?"

"He probably even went for dogs," Becky muttered. "He'd sleep with anything."

"Did he ever sleep with anything named Rio?"

She shrugged her shoulders.

"Know anything about his past?"

"Not much, but my mother told me his father was a Hungarian count who controlled the country's pork exports with an iron fist. The count had been disowned by his family when he married a commoner—some beautician or something who was a fifth cousin once removed of the Gabors."

"The Gabors?"

"Yeah, you know, Zsa Zsa, Eva, Magda, Jolie."

"Okay, got you. And none of them come from New Rochelle?"

"What?" Becky looked puzzled.

"Nothing." Michael shook his head. "A private joke."

"Are you eating your pastry?" Becky suddenly asked.

"No, help yourself."

She reached over to his plate and took the big puff of cream and crust in her hand.

"I have a couple more questions, if you don't mind," Michael began again. "Why were you at that screening the morning Nigel was killed?"

"A couple of weeks ago the French director Jean-Paul Pauljean sent me a script he thought I'd be right for. And before I spoke to him about it, I wanted to see his work."

"Were you sitting alone?"

"No, right between Googie Gdansk and Alan Savory," she said with a mouth full of cream.

"Anybody get up during the screening?"

"Just Googie. He went to the men's room." She swallowed the last of the pastry.

"How long was he gone?"

"I don't know. Ten minutes. Five minutes."

"Long enough to strangle Whitty?" Michael baited her.

"Never Googie," Becky protested. "He's the gentlest man who ever lived. A real softy. One-hundred percent cashmere!"

"And what about Savory?"

"Pure polyester. But I love him anyway."

"Did he love Whitty, is more to the point."

"Can't say. All I know is, they did a lot of bird-dogging together."

"Bird-dogging?" Michael was surprised. "That's interesting."

"Yeah, they both had weird tastes. God knows what they used to pick up and bring home, but only Satan knows what they did when they got there." Just at that moment Becky seemed strangely prim and childlike.

"One more thing," Michael continued. "Where were you earlier that morning, before the screening?"

"At home in bed."

"Please don't be offended, Miss Luna, but was anyone with you?"

"Yes."

"May I ask who?"

Becky's eyes looked wide and watery. "Sure you can ask, Lieutenant. But I can't help you. I don't know."

"Just his name, Miss Luna. I'll keep it confidential."

Becky's mouth dropped open and remained that way for a long moment.

"You don't understand, Lieutenant. I don't know. I never asked."

She blinked emphatically and a single tear sneaked out of the corner of her eye and ran smack into her nostril.

Michael leaned back in his chair, staring at the institutional green walls of his office. He was going nowhere fast with this one. O'Reilly and Friedkin had come up with nothing. The statements they'd taken told little, the research they'd gathered told less, and they hadn't even begun to answer some of the key questions. First of all, who in hell was this Nigel Whitty anyway? All Friedkin had been able to dig up was that the New Rochelle stuff was crap. He'd found that Whitty carried a Swiss passport, gave his place of birth as Buenos Aires, and had been in the United States for the past twenty years as a permanent resident. O'Reilly, on the other hand, had come upon an ancient *Paris Review* interview in which Whitty himself had talked of a childhood in Upper Volta. Surely, Michael had pointed out to O'Reilly, Whitty had been pulling somebody's leg. Or had he?

All the dossiers, clippings, files, and statements notwithstanding, Michael still had a lot of questions to ask, and no answers whatsoever. Like who was the kid with the pussypoppers? Who was this Rio? And what about the photo missing from Whitty's wall? Who was in the picture? And why would anyone want to steal it? Moreover, was its theft the reason—or one of the reasons—Whitty's apartment had been broken into?

This case was a real puzzle. It could go in any direction. And what about the $64,000 Question: What in God's name were those "Mysteries of the Moment" that kept running in Whitty's columns? In this morning's for instance, those references to photos and old memories . . . photos of whom? Memories of what? Goddamn it, where was that little black book? That book in which Nigel Whitty wrote down everything—names, places, dates, all the trash that ended up in his columns. Columns—that was it. The answer had to be in his columns.

But how to break their code? How to unscramble the message? He needed help. And who was better equipped to give it than the very person who was now putting the columns together? Miss Sara Nightingale.

Okay—he knew he'd been gruff with her earlier that day, too gruff perhaps. But somehow he was continually caught off balance by that roller-coaster personality of hers: that nutty mix of scatter and brains, of little girl and big shot. He'd never met anyone like this fluttering bird before. Bird—that was funny. Bird. Nightingale. Birdie. What a perfect name for her. He liked it. He liked her.

Let's give it another try, he thought as he picked up the phone to dial her number.

"Sara speaking."

"Nightingale, it's Michael Connelly."

She was evidently surprised to hear from him.

"Look, remember that I told you I lost my appetite. Well, I'm ravenous now. What are you doing for dinner?"

"Not a thing. Frankly, I was trying to diet."

"You're thin enough. So let me take you out. But I want to warn you, as much as I'd like this dinner to be pure pleasure, I've got to take care of some business, too."

"Whose business, yours or mine?" she asked coolly.

"Both of ours, I guess. I'm beginning to think that the answer to the murder might lie buried in Nigel's columns, and I want to go over all your material—the columns that are ready to go and the stuff that hasn't been organized yet. And I'll make a deal with you. If you keep my confidence as long as necessary, I'll give you an exclusive on my information."

"It's a deal," she said quickly. Then, "Thank you, Lieutenant."

"Where would you like to eat?" he asked now. "I know a great little Chinese restaurant—"

"Look, it would be easier if you just came here. Besides, I really am a great cook. Why don't I run downstairs to Gristede's and pick up a couple of steaks and a bottle of wine?"

"You can cook, but let me buy," Michael offered.

"You can buy, but let me shop," Sara countered. "I'll run downstairs right now."

"Let's compromise." Michael glanced at his watch. "It's seven thirty-five now. At eight-fifteen promptly, I will meet you on the checkout line at Gristede's. Get it?"

"Got it."

"Good." Michael was ready to hang up when he remembered. "Sara, wait! How will I know which Gristede's?"

"Sixth off Twelfth," she answered. "I'll be at the first checkout counter on the left. The shopper with the gardenia in her hair."

Michael smiled as he replaced the receiver. He had to admit, he just loved gardenias.

She hadn't had a gardenia in her wild red hair, but he had to admit she looked pretty terrific anyway. She was wearing beige corduroy pants and a coffee-colored silk blouse, and all of her seemed to match. The shopping was nice, too, especially since she'd left her attitude at home, and for perhaps the first time Sara Nightingale seemed completely relaxed. Now as they walked down 11th Street carrying their shopping bags full of steaks, artichokes, and Häagen-Dazs rum raisin ice cream, Michael found himself singing.

> *"Hear the beat*
> *Of dancing fe-et*
> *It's a song I love*
> *The melody of*
> *Forty-second Street."*

What was he singing that tune for? Oh, yeah, the tapping twosome at Carnegie Hall!

"Well, here we are." Sara interrupted his thoughts.

They climbed up the three flights to her apartment in the rear of the small red-brick Federal house. The light was out in the hallway. "Watch your step," Sara cautioned as she led the way. "As you can see, the landlord's a real skinflint."

"Bet you can file a complaint," Michael said. "This is dangerous."

At the edge of her landing, Sara put her shopping bag down and began to fumble through her purse for her keys. "I've lost them," she wailed but kept searching. Her hand blindly groped through the contents of the huge, unformed tote, and then suddenly stopped. "Here they are!"

She reached down to pick up her groceries, and an edge of the brown paper ripped, sending an artichoke bouncing down the stairs.

Michael quickly hurried after it. "Gotcha!" he smiled as he snatched it up from the threadbare carpet and bounded back up the stairs.

Sara was opening the door. "Where's the kitchen?" he asked, starting into the dark apartment. He was also about to ask, "Where are the lights?" when he felt a blow to his chin that sent him reeling across the room. . . .

He must have passed out. When he came to Sara was holding an ice pack over his head.

"Michael, Michael? Are you okay?"

He blinked a couple of times. Jesus! What was that all about? "What happened?" he asked, still stunned.

"I don't know. I couldn't see. Whoever it was threw a bath towel over my head, then knocked me down and ran out of the apartment. Look!" She rolled up her slacks to show him a big blue bruise on her calf.

"Take some of that ice for yourself," he advised, trying to stand up. His chin ached. "We must have walked in on a burglar. Anything missing?" he asked her.

The green-and-white wicker furniture was all turned over. Clothes and underwear were strewn about. And papers from the small desk in the corner lay, discarded, on the floor.

"Well, your TV is still here. And so is your stereo," Michael observed, scanning the room.

Sara walked into the small flowered bedroom. "My jewelry hasn't been touched. And my raccoon coat's okay."

"Try the desk," Michael suggested. "Look through all your Whitty material."

It took Sara awhile to put things in order and tell what was missing, and what wasn't. Then she turned to Michael. "All Nigel's columns are here. Nothing seems to be gone."

"This must've been the same person or persons who did Nigel's place."

"I wonder what they wanted."

"Obviously, whatever they didn't find at Nigel's."

"Maybe the little black book?" she asked.

"If they don't have it already."

Michael could see Sara begin to shake. Her face grew pale. "It'll be all right," he said, putting his arm around her. "Whoever it was, he won't come back."

"How do you know, for sure?"

"Trust me. I know."

Sara didn't move. She was still upset. "But how did they get in?"

"The same way they got into Whitty's apartment," Michael said as he examined the front-door lock. "The old credit-card routine. You and Whitty had one thing in common: The most primitive locks in New York. A five-year-old could slip this."

No five-year-old, however, could pack that wallop, he thought, rubbing his chin. More likely, a candidate for the Golden Gloves. What a jab!

The phone rang. Sara jumped, then stared at it.

"Answer it," Michael commanded softely.

"It's for you," she said after a moment.

It was the precinct with a message. Michael took out a pad and jotted down a couple of things. Then he reported the break-in at Sara's and asked for a man to be sent over to her apartment to check it out thoroughly, and another to stand guard for her. "Thanks, Friedkin," he ended the conversation. "You take care of this for me, and I'll head down there right now."

As he hung up the receiver, he looked at Sara with concern. "You gonna be all right?"

"Why? What's happening? Where are you going?"

"Down to the *Trib*. Richard Singer-Murray called. Someone broke into his office tonight."

"Oh, my God," she said. She looked panicked all over again.

"Don't worry, Sara. No one was hurt, and nothing was taken. Someone was apparently looking for something he couldn't find."

And whatever that something was, Michael thought, somebody wanted it real bad. Bad enough to kill for it.

Sunday

WHAT NIGEL KNOWS

Tinseltown Tidbits and Tattle

by Nigel Whitty

DANCE, BALLERINA, DANCE: Can it really be—as we've heard tell—that Googie Gdansk's fabled Polish feet are the least of his fabulous appendages? And that if his partners seem a little weak-kneed when they flutter onstage, it's because of the *pas de deux* they've just finished in the privacy of Googie's dressing room, a room which the *corps de ballet* has dubbed "Seventh Heavenski." But, alas, we hear that in the boudoir the great Gdansk's muscular feats have everyone coming (and going) except himself. . . . Speaking of INSATIABLE APPETITES (our favorite kind), our spies tell us that Mrs. Enzo Carbonare, the once-luscious film sensation, Sophia Pisani, has really developed one. As a result, she has ballooned out to such grotesque proportions she won't be seen in public. Is that why hubby Enzo has been escorting shooting star and stargazer, Maria Cortese, around town instead? Or, has the elegant Enzo other appetites to sate? MYSTERY OF THE MOMENT: Which famous "caterer to the stars" is having son troubles? Junior, it seems has done some catering of his own, as all the zonked-out kids in his very exclusive Long Island "high" school can tell you. And so, too, can Nigel who has it all—every pill, every popper, every one of Sonny-boy's connections—down in his little black book. . . .★

6

MICHAEL CONNELLY spooned a heap of Ovaltine into his glass of milk and watched the powdered specks swirl around and then disappear. He really needed a shot of energy, he thought, as he took a gulp of the sweet, thick drink and leaned back on his chair, balancing himself precariously between his desk and the wall. The early morning light was breaking through the slats of the Venetian blinds, and he'd been sitting at his desk since a little after twelve.

What a night! First the fracas at Sara's and then the mess at the *Trib* where, once again, files had been emptied, papers had been rifled and strewn about, with nothing apparently taken. The scattered clippings, with their byline, "Nigel Whitty," inspired him further and on a hunch he'd returned to his office with a carton full of back issues which he had spent the rest of the night reading. Now he was up to his ears in Nigel Whitty. No, better yet, up to his nose—since examining ten years of that bastard's writing was like sniffing through ten years of the world's dirtiest underwear. Michael resisted the impulse to wash his hands and took another swig of Ovaltine instead.

And where the hell was he after all those hours, anyway? So now he knew what Nigel knew. The question was: What the hell did Michael know? Too much and too little. Motives? Suspects? He'd never been on a case where there'd been so many of both. From what he'd read last night, there must have been a thousand people who wanted to tie that typewriter ribbon around Whitty's neck for some slur, some smear, some filthy revelation. It made things a little easier that only eleven of those thousand had been in the screening room the morning of the murder. But only a little bit easier. That pimply-faced usher, Dwayne Jones, could have been lying. And Lynn Ericson's goddamn list could have been phony. And even if it wasn't and both were telling the truth, which of the goddamn eleven? Every one of them had been raked over in Whitty's column at one time or another and so had some sort of motive, while none had an absolutely airtight alibi for his or her whereabouts during the hours right before the screening—that is when Whitty's apartment had been rifled. Quite simply, Michael had never come across so many people who had been nowhere so consistently.

What a case! Even each clue pointed in a different direction. The typewriter ribbon suggested to Michael that Whitty had been killed as a vendetta for something he'd written. The check from Perdue Pictures, however—whatever cock-and-bull story Alan Savory might have handed him—hinted at something more like blackmail. Besides, Savory looked like the type who would pay anything to keep his public image pretty and his black soul lily-white. As for the break-ins, Michael couldn't quite figure out just where they were leading him. All he knew for sure was that whoever had broken into Sara's and probably Whitty's and the *Trib* as well threw a pretty good punch. Unfortunately, that glove didn't seem to fit anyone. Fenton Farnabee? Alan Savory? Come off it. Neither of them could have punched his way out of a paper bag. What about someone like Maria Cortese? She was big all right, but somehow not big enough to have swung that punch. Certainly, then, it couldn't have been a chubbette like Elizabeth Salt, who might have the weight, but not the strength. And surely not Becky Luna—not unless she'd taken enough angel dust to turn her into the Incredible Hulk. But then who knew? Perhaps, beneath her tears and spaced-out smiles throbbed a murderous heart. In a way, if that were true, Michael couldn't blame her. Whitty had stabbed Becky repeatedly in print when he was alive, and even now, in death, he was still twisting the knife.

Under other circumstances, Michael might have asked Richard Singer-Murray to cancel the Whitty columns, but he'd made up his mind that the Beckys of the world would have to grin and bear the last few gasps of "What Nigel Knows." For even if Michael was wrong and those blind items led down a blind alley, perhaps somewhere among the bitchery and tattle still to run lay something which would serve as bait for the killer. He didn't have any idea what this bait might be or how the killer would reveal himself, but the continued publication of "What Nigel Knows," was probably the best shot yet.

In the meantime, Michael did what he could and found out what he could. For instance, in going through those backdated reviews and those endless numbers of "What Nigel Knows," he had come across a couple of interesting items. For one, there had been a mean and insulting Whitty review of Enzo Carbonare's last movie, *I Scaloppini.* "The work of a butcher or a meathead," Whitty had written. "Whichever, *I Scaloppini* isn't fit for human consumption." The review was dated six years ago and came together with a barrage of reader correspondence which continued for weeks, accusing Whitty of systematically destroying the great director's career, or at least his audience in America.

For another, Michael had discovered that for the past five years Whitty had been doing continual battle with Vernon and Beatrix Leakey. Though their celebrity certainly was slighter than that of many of the others Whitty attacked, the two repeatedly showed up in his columns. The onslaught had begun on the occasion of the Leakeys' silver anniversary party. Nigel had written: "When a second-rate critic has gotten together with a third-rate poetess, you can be sure that they'll have spent their lives making fifth-rate music together." Whitty had also suggested that the Leakeys' marriage had simply been an ode to a couple of vegetables: "The grape as it applies to wine, the potato as it applies to the vodka martini. And the whole mess finally leakeying all over their prose and poetry."

The item Michael found most interesting and most surprising of all, however, was one suggesting that "flack publicist" Sammy Nachman and his "flaky flack assistant" Lynn Ericson were having a hot romance. "Public relations has never been so involved with private parts," the eight-year-old blurb began. Nachman and Lynn Ericson! What a weird couple! Coincidentally, Nachman was also an item in today's installment of "What Nigel Knows." Surely, Whitty's not-so-mysterious "Mystery of the Moment" referred to the son of Sammy. And so, Michael felt, today should be Nachman's day. There was something about that guy that bothered him. He was just a little too sweet, a little too gushy. His praise for Whitty still echoed in Michael's ears: "The most intelligent critic alive! A brilliant genius! His mind was deeply profound and so was his heart." What crap! As soon as it was a reasonable hour, Michael would give the "caterer to the stars" a ring and set up a meeting for that very afternoon.

The Broadway Life Potency Spa smelled like the inside of a box of dusting powder, the kind kids bought at the dime store for Mother's Day. The perfumed odor made Michael feel just a little bit sick.

"Can I help you?" asked a perky little blonde in a black leotard. Her breasts were so huge that Michael guessed they'd been shot up with silicone.

"I'm supposed to meet someone here." Michael smiled pleasantly. "Has Sammy Nachman arrived yet?"

"Oh, yes, he's inside."

"Inside where?"

"Oh, you've never been here before?" Her voice registered genuine shock.

With false rue, Michael admitted that no, he hadn't.

"Well, aren't you lucky!" Her silicone breasts seemed to dance in celebration. "We're having a special on membership at this very moment." She reached below the desk and took out a pink sheet of paper which she waved at him as if it were a semaphore flag. "This week only it's two hundred dollars off, plus free disco lessons every Monday night. Co-ed."

"Gee whiz, I'll have to give it some thought," Michael said. "Meanwhile, where can I find Nachman?"

"Down the stairs and to the left." She flashed him a dazzling smile. "I'm sure once you see the facilities, you won't be able to resist."

Michael squinted at the Day-glo-orange shag carpet which traced its charged nylon path down a flimsy-looking metal-rimmed spiral staircase. So this was where Sammy Nachman came "to take a breather," as he'd put it that morning when Michael had phoned him at home in Great Neck.

"Sure, I'd be happy to see you, Lieutenant," he'd said over a background chorus of barking dogs and screaming kids. "But I'm up to my neck today. Yes, today, even on Sunday." Nachman had then gone through the list of things he had to do in preparation for a party to be given that night at the old celebrity haunt, Studio 54, in honor of Gyorgii Gdansk. He certainly hoped the Lieutenant would come as his personal guest. Not only was the great *danseur* making his movie debut in *Allergic to Love*, but it was Googie's thirtieth birthday, and here he was, away from his poor mother in Bialystok. Nachman's voice had broken in commiseration. But since on such hectic days, Sammy always took an hour out to relax his nerves at the Broadway Life Potency Spa, he invited Michael to join him for a brief workout. Michael had declined the exercises but had taken Nachman up on the invitation for Studio 54 as well as on the one to meet him at the spa. They'd agreed on noon, which was fine with Michael. It gave him a couple of hours to go back to his apartment, shower, and shave.

"Over here, Lieutenant, over here." Sammy Nachman, in a yellow sweatsuit, waved from atop his electric Exercycle.

Michael strode over, leaned against the orange wall, and looked about the room which was filled with gleaming chrome machines of various sizes and shapes. Except for Nachman's cycle, none of them was presently in use. Indeed, the room was empty except for a single young man whose oiled biceps, now straining under the weight of a massive-looking barbell, suggested that he might be a contender for the Mr. World contest.

Nachman followed Michael's gaze. "Don't worry, we can talk in front of that one." He winked. "He's got muscles between his ears. Shoot, Lieutenant." The cycle spun around in circles so fast that Nachman's strikingly undersized feet seemed to have trouble gripping the pedals. "Good for the heart," he panted. "Good aerobics." He reached into a pocket and pulled out a bag of peanuts. "They're good when you lose salt," he said, grabbing a mouthful, then placing his hands on the bicycle bars. His upper torso began pumping back and forth in time with the machine.

"You sure you want to talk while you're on that thing?" Michael asked.

"Why not? It doesn't bother my concentration at all. Here, try this one—" Sammy gestured toward the empty machine next to him. "You'll see what I mean."

"No, thanks," Michael said, pulling a piece of paper out of his pocket. "What do you make of this?" He thrust a Xerox copy of Nigel's eight-year-old item about Sammy and Lynn Ericson in front of Nachman.

Sammy glanced at the paper and started.

"Nothing, nothing. I don't make anything out of it."

"You mean it's all a lie?"

Sammy was silent.

Michael pressed on. "Or is it the truth, after all?"

Sammy still said nothing.

"Come on, Mr. Nachman, it's either one or the other, and I'm afraid you're going to have to tell me."

Suddenly, Sammy stopped pumping, and as the machine raced on without him, he was thrown off his balance, tumbling in a yellow heap onto the orange padding surrounding the Exercycle. A multitude of jujubes scattered all over the floor. This guy was a walking candy store. No wonder he was so sweet.

"Oh, my liver," Sammy wailed, rubbing his ample midsection.

"You all right?" Michael asked.

"No, I'm not. I'm terrible. Oh, Lieutenant, you've wrenched me back to the saddest part of my life," he said, wiping his nose on the sleeve of his yellow sweatshirt. "I loved her so."

It had all started almost a dozen years ago, just a little while after Sammy had set up his own highly successful firm, Sammy Nachman Associates: Public Relations for Primary People. Lynn Ericson, a young divorcée from Kansas City, Kansas, had come to work for him as a Gal Friday. "She was gorgeous, real refined, in that white-bread kind of way, if you know what I mean." Nachman had nudged Michael. "And such efficiency. She worked her fingers to the bone for me."

At the time, Nachman had been—in fact, still was—a happily married man. He had three kids, a dog, two cats, three gerbils, a doting wife, wall-to-wall carpeting, and a house with a built-in vacuum cleaner system in the best section of Great Neck. He had a lot to lose and nothing to gain. But he'd fallen for Lynn all the same. There was nothing he wouldn't do for her. He taught her everything he knew about the business, gave her her own clients—

"big names, too, the biggest"—and an office with a view—"a great view, the greatest." They even had a couple of great nights together before . . .

"What do you mean, a couple of great nights?" Michael interrupted.

"You know, extramarital. Nooky nooky," Sammy explained.

"I know, extramarital," Michael persisted. "But what do you mean, *a couple*?"

"Not that I was counting, but it was three. Three beautiful, perfect nights. It was all milk and honey." Sammy Nachman's face turned a deep scarlet. "I guess I was counting, Lieutenant. I remember every minute, every second, as though it were yesterday."

But then, Nachman went on, everything turned sour and began to go wrong. First, out of the clear blue sky, he lost his biggest account, E.G.O. Pictures. A 70-millimeter print got lost right before the Opening Night Invitational Gala, and five hundred guests who'd paid $100 per person to come out in the zero-degree temperature had to be shown a 16-millimeter print of Walt Disney's *The Three Caballeros*, dubbed in Serbo-Croatian, the only movie lying around in the projection booth at the time. "Actually, the gala got pretty good reviews in the *Village Shriek*," Nachman inserted. "But what a mess! What a stew!"

Then came the item in Whitty's column. "But I swear to you, by then nothing was going on," Nachman said. "Still, Shirley threatened to walk out on me. Boy, what it took to win her over! Two weekends at Grossinger's, a blond mink stole, a dinner at Mamma Leone's, and a guest appearance by Jack Benny, may he rest in peace, at the Great Neck Hadassah Chapter."

But the business with Mrs. Nachman wasn't the worst of it. Without any warning, Lynn left his company one day, taking with her six of his largest accounts: the New York Film Festival, Danny Blue, Perdue Pictures, Television Tinsel Incorporated (in which Elizabeth Salt had major holdings), Kiss My Ass, the great glitter-rock group, and Quondam Quality Books, the biggest religious publishers in the world. Lynn had also, mystifyingly, ended up with his lost account, E.G.O. Pictures. "But I'm not the type to hold grudges. I always wished her bread and chocolate, wine and roses. Always wanted her to be happy. No matter who she was with."

"And who was that?" Michael asked.

Once again, Sammy Nachman blushed. Out of a pocket somewhere, he picked a box of Raisinettes.

"Would you like one, Lieutenant?"

Michael shook his head, no. Sammy Nachman stuffed the entire contents of the box into his mouth and began to chew vehemently. This guy's dentist, Michael thought, had to be a millionaire.

Now Nachman got up and walked over to a punching bag hanging from the low mirrored ceiling. "Well, it hurts me to tell you this," he said, hunching his narrow shoulders forward and letting go with a left jab that managed to just miss the bag. "But it was Whitty." He jabbed again, missed again. "Nigel Whitty." This time his hand connected to the bag. "Ouch," he said, "I think I'm hurt."

Nigel Whitty! What the hell was that story? "You mean Lynn Ericson and Whitty had an affair?"

Sammy looked glum. "I almost keeled over when I found out," he moaned dramatically. "It really got to me, almost gave me an ulcer. But," Nachman sighed, "what could I say, really? Look, there was one important difference between Nigel and me. Mainly, he was free and I wasn't. He could take her to fancy-schmancy places and show her a good time. What could I do for her? Hide with her in closets? It wasn't a good life. And I think that maybe Lynn wanted to get married again herself, have kids and a home. Anyway, she knew I'd never get a divorce." He paused dramatically. "I feel guilty. Like I pushed her into Nigel Whitty's arms, if you know what I mean."

Michael didn't know at all but he nodded encouragingly,

hoping that Sammy would continue his talking jag. Privately, he thought that any woman who would fly first into Sammy Nachman's arms and then into Nigel Whitty's had to be a real sickie—a sadist, a masochist, or both. Though he was no Cupid and rarely took notice of these things, Michael figured that such matches as Lynn had made were definitely not arranged in heaven.

"This divorce business," Sammy was saying now, "it goes against my grain. Frankly, Lieutenant, it makes me sick. No matter how much heartache, no matter how much trouble, you make a promise and you keep it. I mean, the little woman—Mrs. N., that is—is not like an old car you trade in when something better or newer comes along. Sammy Nachman's rule of thumb, the rule I live by, businesswise and personalwise, is: 'A promise is like a diamond. It's made and it's forever.' You know what I mean. Lieutenant?" His eyes shining with sincerity, Sammy looked at Michael, clearly searching for a sign of agreement.

"I agree," Michael said gently. "But let's get back to Whitty and Lynn for a moment. What do you know about their relationship?"

"Not much." Sammy shook his head. "Why should Lynn have told me anything? She knew I was eating my heart out, as it was. And Whitty? He'd never give me the time of day. Believe me, Lieutenant, not that I want to say anything bad about him, he should rest in peace, but the guy caused me a lot of grief—love grief, work grief, just plain grief."

"How do you mean?" Michael asked.

"You know, Lieutenant Connelly, we PR people are a strange breed. We live to push gossip around, to place an item here or a story there. It's a round-the-clock job, but it's what makes you look good to your clients. You tell them: 'I can get you a mention in Suzy's column, a line in Liz Smith, a paragraph in "What Nigel Knows." ' But Whitty was a peculiar fella—he wouldn't take a thing from me. Or give me anything either. Like when I'd handle a movie, all I'd want was a little something, a little phrase for an ad. Nigel could kill the movie in his review, who cared so long as he'd give me a little something to quote. Like 'Farrah Fawcett's most profound performance to date,' or 'Henry Mancini's most triumphant musical score.' Not Whitty. I couldn't get a thing from him. Ever."

Nachman sat down at one of the Universal exercise machines and started to use the leg press, pushing his spindly feet up against the weighted chrome plate. "Wanna give it a try?" he puffed, motioning to Michael. "It tones the calves."

It struck Michael that Sammy Nachman was probably the first man he'd ever met who worried about toning his calves. But all he said was, "I'd rather hear more about you and Whitty. Why do you think that Whitty wouldn't work with you?"

Nachman was panting now as his muscles tensed to defy the heavy chrome bars. His face was turning red from the exertion and the veins on his neck were pulsating wildly. All, Michael thought, for a pair of lousy toned calves! "It's a little hard to explain, Lieutenant," Nachman finally said, as his calves proudly held the machine's weight steady. "But who knows, maybe he did have a reason, if I wanna be very honest with you. I mean, Sammy Nachman may be an honorable man, but Nigel Whitty had principles up to here—" he gestured way over his head. "And he was a perfectionist to boot, a real one. Anyway, once I made a little boo-boo. I took a little something out of context. You see, Whitty wrote, 'a terrific bore,' and I quoted, 'terrific!' So sue me. It was a mistake. With the others, the other critics, you can always do that. And they don't give a hoot. Actually, they love it, love, love, love seeing their names advertising a movie. Like Farnabee. He and I have a good relationship. Look, Lieutenant, I'll tell you a little professional secret, if you promise to keep it under your hat."

Michael wore no hat, but he touched his lips with his fingers to assure Nachman that mum was the word.

"You have to make a few deals to survive in this business. You have to make a few trades. You shmooz them, they shmooz you. Get me?"

Michael nodded.

"So I give Fenton a little something, oh, maybe a tip on who's screwing who, who's got money troubles, who's got job troubles. And Fenton, in return he drops a nice line onto one of my clients. Like he writes in his column: 'The beautiful so-and-so, happily ensconced in her Nantucket beachhouse with her loving hubby and four kids, has been offered four scripts, blah-blah-blah . . .' You get the system?"

Michael nodded.

"Well, I tried to get the same thing going with Whitty, but he wasn't taking. Maybe my gossip wasn't hot enough for him or my clients not big enough. He was good, you know, and pretty classy, too. So who knows why he wouldn't touch me with a ten-foot pole?"

"Maybe," Michael suggested, curious as to how Nachman would react, "just maybe, you weren't mean enough?"

Sammy giggled and dug into his pocket which was obviously deeper than it looked. This time he came up with a small bag of golden candy corn which he promptly began to nibble.

"Aww, Lieutenant, you've got him all wrong, really! But between you and me, I always figured that tradeoffs were what he really wanted from Lynn. She had a way with people, still does. She can get anything out of anyone. Her talent is, she makes them feel relaxed, real relaxed." Nachman pause, then sat quietly, almost as if he'd just run out of steam.

"Go on," Michael prodded. "Please."

"Well," Nachman hesitated. "I don't like to say anything bad about anyone, but sometimes . . ."

"Go on," Michael encouraged.

"Sometimes I think Whitty used Lynn, really used her. You know, got her to give him very secret stuff. Real dirt.

You know why I say that? Lynn changed when she got involved with him." Nachman wiped a bead of perspiration running down his forehead. He shook his head sadly. "She really did change. The Lynn Ericson you see today just isn't my sweet little Waspy True-heart Susie anymore. She's not the same little girl I used to know. Today she's a real tough cookie."

"Tough enough to murder Whitty? If she were disappointed enough, hurt enough?"

"Are you out of your mind?" Sammy was now at the barbells, adjusting the weights, taking off all but the ten-pound discs. "Lynn's not that kind of person. She wouldn't hurt a gerbil, let alone a living human being."

Maybe not, Michael thought, but she was sure as hell going to be his next stop today. He knew he'd find her at the press office at Lincoln Center.

"Then how about you, Mr. Nachman? Could you have murdered Nigel Whitty?"

One of the discs slipped off the barbells and rolled across the orange carpet. "You crazy or something?" Sammy's eyes popped so far out of their little sockets that for a moment Michael was afraid they would follow the disc across the floor. "I loved him like a brother, like a brother, I tell you."

"You mean, Whitty was like an uncle to your son?" Michael pushed another piece of paper—this morning's column—under Sammy's nose.

"Look, he didn't mention any names, did he? That's what I call a gentleman. And a real pal, may he rest in peace."

This guy was either a good liar or too good to be true. But unlike the other suspects. Nachman at least had some sort of alibi for the time of the first break-in. He had visited his chiropodist in Great Neck at 8:00 A.M., or so Nachman claimed and Dr. Hayden Foote, D.P.M., A.A.F.S., confirmed. If both were telling the truth, in order for Nachman to have gotten from Dr. Foote's to

Nigel Whitty's in time to rifle the apartment and get up to Lincoln Center for the screening, he would have had to take a helicopter or sprout a pair of wings. And that was pretty unlikely, Michael thought, even for would-be angels like Sammy.

Not again! Sara pulled the pillow over her head. The phone had been ringing all morning, it seemed, and she'd hardly had any sleep at all. The police hadn't left until almost eleven last night, after which she had spent the next three hours alternately quaking with fear and straightening up the mess. Even then, she had slept fitfully, her rest constantly troubled by some shadowy figure she imagined looming behind her peacock chair or waiting for her behind her bathroom door. "Buckle up, Nightingale, you've traveled the globe, seen the Abos and Incas and the bats and wombats, you're a strong independent woman with a blackjack in your night-table drawer," she kept telling herself, trying not to wish so hard that Detective Michael Connelly were there to take care of her, to watch out for her. He wasn't really such a bad guy after all, kind of warm and sweet and sensible, she thought, as she wrapped herself in her silky pink comforter. Then she'd hear a noise that would jar her out of her reverie. Again the shadowy figure would seem to skulk in the darkness, waiting to pull a typewriter ribbon around *her* neck. It wasn't until the dawn's comforting light that she was able to truly fall asleep.

At precisely nine o'clock, however, her parents made their weekly Sunday morning call, the one that always came right before her mother went to church and her father went off to his golf game. Actually, it was the second time this week that they'd called; the first had been on Thursday night, after hearing about Nigel Whitty's murder on the six o'clock news. They had been very concerned and her father had suggested politely, but in his most imperious tone, that the intelligent thing to do would be to pack up immediately and catch the next flight back to Grosse Pointe. Sara had assured them that going home wasn't necessary, that she would be all right, that *her* life certainly wasn't in danger. Now, she wondered. Still, it was their fears which kept her from telling them about her own, and so she had said nothing to them about the break-in. Had her father known, he would have personally dragged her home or, even worse, moved her into the Barbizon or some other hotel for women.

Another phone call had come in the interim, but she hadn't picked it up until it had rung a half-dozen times, and by then, whoever had been on the other end had already hung up. Now, once again, that damned insistent ring. Slowly she grappled for it, bringing the receiver under the covers with her.

"Hi there, sugar plum, it's Fenny."

She grunted a giveaway yawn into the phone.

"Rise and shine, rise and shine. Come now, it's eleven o'clock, slug-a-bed."

"Hi, Fenton, how are you?" She tried to sit up and force her voice to sound alert.

"Good girl, that's better." She could almost hear Fenton smile. "Any news? Any news for your friend Fenny who is sitting chained to his typewriter without a single sensational item to write up."

"Fenny, I don't know a thing," Sara said wearily.

"Oh, come now, Sara, no new developments as to who nipped Nigel in the bud?"

"Well, nothing about Nigel, but I do have some news to tell you, after all."

"Oh?"

"Guess who's going to be writing her own series for the *Trib*? A piece called 'One Hundred Twenty-Two Minutes in the Dark with a Dead Man' or 'What Nigel Whitty's Death Means to the Film Community'?"

"That's absolutely lovely, sugar plum, but how in heaven's name are you ever going to get a series out of that topic? I can give you your answer in a word, or rather two. What does Nigel's death mean to the film community? Orgasmic relief, sweetest, orgasmic relief."

"Can I quote you on that, Fenny?"

"As long as you spell my name right."

"Very funny. But seriously, I'm really going to need some material. And a little help. Look, I hate to ask you, but do you have any time to see me in the next few days? After all, you were Nigel's arch-rival and your comments would be invaluable."

"How flattering, sugar plum. And to show you that flattery will get you everywhere, how would you like to come over for lunch today? I prepare a mean tuna on rye."

"I'd love to, but I'm meeting Lynn Ericson for lunch."

"Hmmm. Very, very interesting. About Nigel?"

"Yes. I thought that was an easy place to begin; that is, with Nigel's relationship with PR people."

"And she agreed to see you? Frankly, my dear, I'm a bit surprised."

"What's so surprising about it? Lynn has done business with Nigel for years."

"More than business, sugar plum, and that's the point."

"What do you mean, Fenton?"

"Just ask her about Nigel's birthmark."

Nigel's birthmark? Whatever it meant, it sure sounded as if it would be great for openers, Sara thought—that is, if she wanted Lynn Ericson to end the interview then and there.

"Thanks, Fenny," she said sarcastically. "Talk to you tomorrow."

"Not tomorrow. See you tonight at the big party at the old Studio 54. Also, sugar plum, I want to give you a raincheck on that lunch. Tuesday night, Fenny has a real treat for you—better than tuna on rye. I'm screening a great movie classic for a group of my closest friends, and I' d love you to come."

"Great," Sara replied, wondering just who Fenton regarded as his closest friends. But instead she asked, "Which classic is it?"

"It's Fenny's surprise," Fenton said coyly, "but I'll give you a few clues: It starred Baby Jane in her younger days; she played a Jezebel but that wasn't her name; she *didn't* say, 'Petah, Petah, give me the lettah'; and in case you haven't guessed it yet, it was also on Nigel Whitty's all-time Ten Best list. Got it, sugar plum?"

No, Sara didn't. Moreover, it was hardly the most pressing riddle on her mind at the moment. Still, unlike all the other mysteries surrounding Nigel Whitty, she took some small comfort in the fact that this one, at least, would have an easy and happy solution.

When Sara arrived at the Lincoln Center press office, Lynn Ericson was on the phone. She waved Sara to a seat, her salutory smile contrasting strongly with the sharpness of her words. "Thanks, Nachman, thanks for nothing," she said into the phone before slamming down the receiver.

Immediately, the phone rang again. This time the caller was Michael Connelly, Sara gathered. She felt as if her ears were swelling but tried to look nonchalant, completely inattentive. "Yes, three o'clock will be fine," Lynn was saying. "Meet me right here at the press office. Yes. See you then." She hung up and turned to Sara.

"You don't happen to have a Valium on you, do you?" Lynn asked, slipping on her tan suede jacket and picking up her purse.

"No, sorry," Sara returned.

"An aspirin then?"

"No."

"Well, then, I guess a drink will have to do it," Lynn sighed, beginning to shut off the lights in the press office. "Where do you want to go?" she asked Sara. "The Ginger Man? O'Neal's?

"No," she answered her own question. "They'll be

packed at this hour. Look, why don't we try that French restaurant down the block. *Les Frites*? The food's lousy, but it's quiet. And right now, I don't think I can face much noise."

Obediently, Sara followed Lynn out of the press office and waited while she locked the door. Then the two women made their way across Broadway to the small restaurant where, apparently, the food was so bad that not a single patron was present. In fact, it was even hard to find a waiter. At long last, a stocky woman of about forty-five, adorned in a starched lacy apron and a crisp Breton cap under which her flaming red Madame Pompadour wig sat equally stiff, set menus and glasses of water on their table.

"*Voulez-vous* order your *repas,* madame et mademoiselle? You are mother and zee daughter, non?"

Lynn Ericson blanched. Sara wanted to crawl under the table with embarrassment. This, she knew, was no way to begin an interview.

"A double martini, straight up, with a twist," Lynn ordered decisively.

"Isn't that a leetle, how you say, too strong for zee *déjeuner*?" the waitress remarked in an accent growing ever stronger and more blatantly artificial.

"Where did zey get you from, Central Casting?" Lynn asked, her depression turning to annoyance now.

"I beg zee, how you say, pardon?" The waitress huffily sashayed off, shaking the prissy bow of her apron behind her.

"Who does she think she is," Lynn muttered out of the side of her mouth, then sharply called the woman back to the table to take Sara's order.

"A white wine," Sara requested meekly. "And a Salade Niçoise."

"Make that two," Lynn Ericson commanded with the same kind of authority which in a mere eight years had turned her small public relations firm into a thriving and immensely profitable enterprise.

But as soon as the waitress had left with their orders, Lynn burst into tears. "Forgive me, Sara, I'm just a wreck," she sobbed, taking a lace monogrammed hanky out of her pocketbook. "Everything's a mess."

Sara didn't quite know how to respond. She stretched a hand tentatively across the table. "If you'd like," she offered, "we can do this interview another day. After all, 'What Nigel Whitty's Death Means to the Film Community' can wait."

"That's just it, it can't. Nigel's death is closing in on me. The chickens are coming home to roost."

Sara began to fidget in her seat. She wasn't sure what Lynn was leading up to, but she felt peculiarly ill-equipped to handle it. What was she supposed to say when a stranger, someone she had spoken to maybe a dozen times in her life, and someone who was also old enough to be her mother, broke down in front of her like this? Was she supposed to use this for her article? God, no, she thought. She wasn't Nigel Whitty. Not now. Not yet. But she did intend to be a crack reporter, and so she figured she'd better begin this interview while Lynn was still in one piece.

She turned on her tape recorder. "During the screening of *The Last Gasp*," she began, "did you have any premonition that things were going wrong, that something had or would soon be going amiss in the screening room?"

"Of course not," Lynn answered testily.

"Can you recall, Miss Ericson, what went through your head when you first heard that Nigel Whitty was sitting in the screening room, dead?"

At that Lynn Ericson spilled her glass of water. The liquid ran all over the table and the glass rolled off the table and smashed into tiny pieces on the concrete floor. Lynn Ericson began to shake. Sara knew that this time she had stepped on a mine.

"Sara, can I talk to you off the record?" The tears began falling from Lynn's eyes again. "I have to talk with someone, and I know, I can just feel it, that I can trust you. But could you please turn off that tape?"

"Of course," Sara muttered. Lynn was ruining her interview, but what else could she say?

"Well, I'm sure," Lynn continued, "there's a lot you know already. After a month with Nigel, I bet you know everything."

Sara shook her head. "He told me very little, Miss Ericson."

"Call me Lynn," she said, giving Sara a skeptical glance.

"Honestly, Lynn," Sara repeated. "I hardly even got to know him."

"Come on, Sara. What kind of a fool do you think I am? You mean to tell me that after a month with Nigel Whitty, you still didn't know him, that you two never were the least bit intimate, that you never went to bed with him?"

"Are you kidding?" Sara exclaimed. "He was my employer. You think I'd sleep with my bread and butter? Besides, if you really want to know the truth, he scared me."

"Yes," Lynn said, more softly now. "He was terrifying. I suppose that's what attracted me to him." Her eyes grew distant, and Sara wasn't sure for a moment whether this reminiscence was giving Lynn pain or pleasure.

The drinks arrived. Lynn belted hers down and ordered another. The waitress looked extremely disapproving. "Tsk, tsk, tsk," she chastised through clenched teeth, then removed Lynn's empty glass from the table.

As soon as the waitress was out of earshot, Lynn leaned toward Sara. "Did you know about us?" she asked.

"No," Sara answered, thinking at that moment of what Fenton had told her to ask Lynn. "Birthmark." The word slipped out.

"What?" Lynn Ericson sat erect.

"Birthmark. Fenton said Nigel had a birthmark."

"That shit. I knew all along that he and Fenton must have had something going. What a pig Nigel was. He had something going with everyone."

The waitress arrived with the salads and Lynn's second double martini, all of which she slapped down in front of them. "*Bon appétit!*" she piped.

Lynn drank the martini in a gulp and handed the waitress her empty glass. "Fill 'er up." The waitress shook her head in despair.

"I could kill that Sammy Nachman," Lynn said, as she started forking tuna into her mouth. "He had to open his goddamned trap to that Lieutenant and then call me to warn me. That poor, silly slob. He never could control himself." And she began relating to Sara the sad, tortured story of her difficult road to success. And of the terrible price she had paid.

First there had been her brief marriage to her high school sweetheart, Bill Ericson, a prosperous businessman who owned a grain elevator outside Kansas City, where both of them had grown up. The marriage started off all right but foundered after a movie company came to town and Lynn had snared a part in *The Invasion of the Atomic Locusts,* playing one of several victims of a horde of insects bred to mammoth size by atomic fallout. It was her job to lie in a wheatfield under a 101-degree sun for seven hours with fake blood pouring out of every orifice. She'd never had such a wonderful time, she told Sara, she'd never felt more alive.

And so came the end of Bill Ericson and the wheatfields of Kansas. For, a week after the movie company left town, so too did Lynn. She'd originally planned to go west, but the first train that came into the station was heading east, and that was the one she'd taken.

How to break into the movie business in New York puzzled her at first. She hit every employment agency in town, the offices of every movie studio, and finally, she got to Potemkin Pictures. It wasn't much of a job, only a receptionist's, but, as Mrs. Lillian Potemkin would smilingly remind Lynn over and over again while she sat in the filthy windowless suite on West 44th Street that was crowded with huge packing boxes full of order forms for Potemkin Pictures' catalogs of 8-millimeter wild-life documentaries, it was still show biz. And better than Kansas City.

Lynn was fast beginning to doubt this and was just about ready to pack her bags when Sammy Nachman came into her life. He was Lillian Potemkin's brother-in-law, a publicist working in the *real* show biz world. He was just setting up his own public relations firm and asked her to be his Gal Friday. She was thrilled to death! The people who'd walk in and out of *his* office! Not just the grimy postman. Not just the retarded delivery boy. But real stars! Real celebrities! She'd be talking to them on the phone every day, bringing them coffee with one sugar or two. She may not have known it beforehand, but this job was exactly what she wanted.

The only trouble was that Nachman had begun to fall in love with her, something Lynn could sense long before he himself probably knew about it. Those strange little self-conscious gestures—fixing the knot in his tie, holding in his stomach every time she walked into his office. Those inexpensive but thoughtful presents which always turned up on her desk: a little bouquet of daisies, a fresh danish, a warm muffler, a little sweater with an imitation fox collar to wear in the office on chilly days. Well, finally, more out of pity for his bumbling emotions and out of gratitude for instructing her so well in his business than out of any real feeling for Sammy himself, she gave herself to him. And what a mistake that turned out to be! One or two revolting nights together—she really couldn't remember how many—and she was stuck with his oppressive passion forever. She felt she was being stifled. She really had to get away from Sammy Nachman, well meaning though he was. And as soon as possible.

Sara began to cough.

"Am I shocking you, my dear?" Lynn asked, suddenly embarrassed.

"No, not at all," Sara reassured her. "It was just an anchovy sneaking down the wrong pipe." She sipped at her wine to relieve the irritation. She was annoyed at herself. Somehow, she didn't want to interrupt the flow. But she knew she was losing the interview. She had to get the conversation back to her article. "What about Nigel Whitty?" she asked and deliberately switched her recorder back on.

Lynn didn't notice. "Whitty was my way out, as it happened. Naturally, working for Sammy, I came in contact with Nigel. Sammy was always trying to get an item into his column, to prime and soften Nigel for a picture he was promoting. Sammy knew he always rubbed Nigel the wrong way, and so I became the liaison." She paused. "Well, I became more than that." Lynn's voice suddenly became very thick.

"I seenk you are *fini* wees entrée, non?" the waitress interrupted.

"No!" Lynn waved her aside and went on with her story. She had been crazy about Nigel at the outset. She would have done anything for him, or so she thought, until she heard what he wanted her to do. And that was to spy on all of Sammy's clients and feed Nigel the worst, the dirtiest, the most disgusting bits of information about their private lives. He went so far as to encourage her to become the intimate of the stars, to accept their hospitality and their friendship, to get into their homes and tape telephone conversations. Nigel even suggested that she crawl into bed with them so that she could discover their sexual predilections. "And the joke of it was that none of them could have been sicker than his," Lynn added with a bitter laugh.

"Why didn't you just tell him to get lost?" Sara asked. She was truly bewildered by Nigel's Svengali effect—by any man's, in fact. She herself had never been under such a spell and never, she swore to herself, intended to be.

"Tell him to get lost? But I was crazy about him—even though he never gave a damn about me or about anyone or anything, for that matter. The only thing Nigel ever gave a hoot about was going to Rio. He used to moan, 'Rio,

Rio,' in his sleep. And once when I asked him what the hell was in Rio besides the Copacabana, he slapped my face."

Rio? Wasn't that the name on the leather box: *To Nigel from Rio*? Didn't cities give keys, not music boxes? But before Sara had any more time to think about it, Lynn went on:

"But even if I hadn't been nuts about him, what could I do? I was in so deep, he could have ruined me. And he still can."

Tears welled in her eyes. "Sara, let me give you a piece of advice. Always be above-board and clean as a whistle. What I did was so stupid, I can't believe it. And I've regretted it every day for the past eight years."

What Lynn regretted most, as it turned out, had to do with a lost film, a lost 70-millimeter print. It all happened while Lynn was still Sammy's assistant. On the afternoon of a huge gala at which the film was to be shown, Sammy had asked Lynn to pick up the print at the airport. It was being flown in from California for the evening's premiere and was to be hand-delivered at Kennedy. The only print in existence other than the original negative, this work print of W. D. Capillari's nine-year effort, *Epiphany Soon,* was a five-hour feminist tract loosely adapted from George Eliot's *Middlemarch.* The movie, according to those who had seen it at sneak previews in Westwood and Van Nuys, was a masterpiece, a work unlike anything ever before created on film. But the opinion of those few viewers was never to be confirmed or contested, for *Epiphany Soon* went astray somewhere between California and New York.

"Sara, you must never repeat this," Lynn said, her eyes glazed over with drink, "but it was I who lost *Epiphany Soon.*" Recalling her running tape recorder, Sara felt a twinge of guilt, but she was now a reporter, and the image of a *Trib* headline reading "The Truth Behind Who Lost *Epiphany Soon*" flashed through her mind.

"Oh, Sara," Lynn sobbed, heedless of the recorder, "it was such a terrible coincidence—the lab containing the original negative burnt down that very day. And so it was I who was the cause of Capillari's subsequent suicide when he found his nine-year, nineteen-million-dollar effort had disappeared without a trace. Nigel knew it. He was with me when I picked up the print. He was with me at the little bar off the Van Wyck Expressway where we stopped for a couple of drinks on the way back from Kennedy. And he was the one who realized, after we returned to Manhattan, that we'd come back without the film."

It was also Whitty, she went on, who testified that the Perdue courier had never met them at the airport. In this way, he had saved Lynn her job and reputation but only, she added, at the expense of first the courier and then Sammy Nachman. "Everyone assumed it was Sammy's negligence that caused the whole incident, and Sammy never wanted to put me on the spot. So Perdue Pictures canceled their contract with him." As Lynn spoke, the tears started flowing again, but dried quickly enough. "Ironically," she went on, "when Nigel encouraged me to go out on my own, Perdue Pictures became my biggest account. If they ever knew about this, I'd be dead."

That was the hold Nigel had over her, Lynn explained. And all those years that was what he used to force her to be his main source of gossip, to be his main line to the sewers of the stars. Starfucking? She became the biggest starfucker of them all, fooling around with everyone—from Gyorgii Gdansk to Danny Blue and worse. What just deserts! When she'd been back in Kansas, that's what she had dreamed about—screwing the stars. How appealing, how sexy all that glamor had seemed! What a laugh! No, that was wrong, it wasn't a laugh at all. "In fact," she whispered to Sara, "fucking around with all those perverted pricks—and that's what they are, perverted—has been hell. Absolute, horrible hell."

Worse, now she was forty-five, alone, and with Whitty's murder and this goddamned investigation, she was also absolutely terrified. What if her whole past surfaced like some bloated corpse in a murky river? Nachman had already blabbed too much to Lieutenant Connelly, and now with the Lieutenant coming over to question her in just a little while, she felt as if she were sitting on a time bomb—a time bomb of her very own making. Nigel had always warned her that he had every detail, every fact, written down in his little black book. If she could only get her hands on it, she'd be able to protect herself. But now, it was probably too late anyway. The chances were that the police had found it. Did Sara know? Lynn squeezed Sara's hand. "Sara, please tell me. Between us. From one woman to another?"

Sara shook her head. "I don't think so, but I don't know. All I can tell you, Lynn, is that you can trust Lieutenant Connelly. I'm sure of that. He's a really straight guy."

"And zere are not enough of zem een zees city, I tell you," the waitress said emphatically. Abruptly, two *tartes tatins* appeared on the table. "Compliments of *moi*," the waitress said, smiling sympathetically at Lynn as she poured out two cups of coffee. "In Bretagne, we have an old saying, eet goes *comme ça:* 'A *tarte tatin* a day keeps zee troubles away.'"

"Oh, thank you," Lynn said, evidently truly touched. "It's very kind of you."

Sara nodded in agreement.

The waitress winked and tilted her Breton cap. "By zee way, I could not help but overhear a leetle of what you were zaying. And zat you are a friend of Danny Blue. My daughter, she ees just crazy for Danny Blue. I hate to trouble you, but could you get me hees autograph? For my daughter, of course." She blushed. "You zeenk maybe he could write, 'Wees love, to Sadie'?"

7

MIDNIGHT. And still too early to show up at Gyorgii Gdansk's birthday party. Sara yawned and poured herself another cup of black coffee. She lay down on her bed and pulled on the white stretch satin jeans she had bought precisely for the occasion. Dammit, the zipper wouldn't close. She got up and went to the kitchen to get a fork. Now, lying on her back on the living room rug, her knees bent to relax the pull of the elastic cloth, she inserted the fork into the utility zipper and tugged. Whew! That did it. She stood up and breathed easy, then bent down to pick up the fork.

Suddenly, she felt the air hit her belly and heard the ripping sound of the zipper tearing away from the cloth. She sighed. Sixty dollars down the drain. She'd have to wear a pair of everyday jeans instead. Oh, well, she could apply a bit of dash somehow, she thought, pulling on her blue tank top and splashing some gold glitter dust on her shoulders and hair. Then, she added jewelry: long feather earrings and a necklace to match. And finally she slipped into a pair of gold wedgies. Was it all too much, she wondered, examining herself in the mirror. Hell, no. After all, she was going to the renowned old Studio 54, which was being restored tonight, thanks to Sammy Nachman, to what it had been during its days of glory. And she was going there for a purpose as well: to get material for her article. She threw another handful of glitter dust over her shoulder just for good luck, then checked to see that her shoulder pouch held everything she needed: pad, pencil, pen, and her small tape recorder, just in case.

She looked at the clock. Twelve-twenty. What the hell! So she'd be the first one there. It might not have been too chic for a regular person, but she was a reporter. She checked her reflection once more. She kind of liked the burnished look the glitter dust gave her hair. Brenda Starr? She smiled and danced out the door.

The scene at Studio 54 was indeed precisely as it had been in its heyday—that is, precisely as described in the hundreds of articles and items that had been written about the notorious discothèque. Sammy Nachman had obviously done a terrific publicity job tonight, and masses of people, having heard about the festivities, were milling around at the barricaded entryway to get a look at celebrities or possibly to be among the chosen few to gain entry themselves. Some of them were teenagers; others suburban types and tourists in elegant gowns and tuxedos; still others painted and costumed freaks—one, for example, with a bright red face and a feather boa. But mostly, the crowd, as it always had, consisted of thirtyish male hairdresser types in leather jackets and leather vests, their key rings and hankies hanging out of the back pockets of their designer jeans. All, it seemed, wore neatly clipped beards, sparkling earrings in one ear, dozens of chains around their necks, and bracelets on each wrist. With all that hardware, Sara thought, the only thing that seemed to be missing was their barber shears.

She slipped through the crowd and gave her name to the huge bouncer standing at the door. He nodded and made way for her to enter.

"Who's she?" somebody in the crowd called out. "Andy Warhol's sister?"

"What's she got that I ain't, sweetie?" A bald-headed young man of ample girth threw out his hip defiantly.

"Sugar plum, wait for me." It was Fenton running up

behind her. He was accompanied by a spectacularly beautiful young boy who couldn't have been more than seventeen. "Sara, I'd like you to meet Bruce. Bruce is from South Dakota. He's a real cowboy."

The cowboy held out a manicured hand. "Pleasure to meet you, ma'am."

Fenton threw a quick hello to the bouncer who was obviously an old acquaintance and slipped his arms around both Sara and Bruce, leading them past the cloakroom, into the shadowy lobby. Here, the scene seemed very much like the one outside: figures of every conceivable size and shape and in every conceivable variety of costume, just standing about trying to catch a glimpse of whomever was to be seen. Behind them, music blared and lights glittered. Sara followed Fenton and Bruce toward the center of the action. Her first impression was one of overwhelming disorder. This was how she imagined Mardi Gras except that here the beat was disco. The dance floor was huge and filled with gyrating figures over whose tossing heads and shaking shoulders colored lights danced in constantly changing hues and patterns. As many people seemed to be off the dance floor as on, some of them standing around a large circular bar to the rear of the room, others lounging on the rows of cushioned banquettes that ran along the side, some standing on the moving bridge over the dance floor, and most simply watching the dancers from the edge of the raised floor. The smell of grass perfumed the air.

"What a fabulous party," Fenton said. "Everyone's here. There's Brooke!"—he pointed Bruce's eyes somewhere in the middle of the dance floor. "I must introduce you, Brucie, you'll adore her."

A figure in a white tennis shirt brushed against them. "Vitas, Vitas, great match this afternoon." Vitas gave him a big grin and moved on.

Fenton winked at Bruce and started snapping his fingers to the beat. "Sara, would you forgive us if we tripped the light fantastic for a moment or two?"

"Of course." Sara smiled, but she felt a twinge of panic as Fenton and Bruce disappeared into the crowd. What was she supposed to do? Where was she supposed to go? She positioned herself between the bar and the dance floor and plastered a congenial smile on her face, as her eyes skimmed the room for someone she might know. Curiously, she'd really felt like dancing before she'd arrived, but as she watched the people on the floor, she found herself becoming more and more self-conscious, more and more distant. She couldn't quite understand why. Finding no one, she moved back to the bar and asked for a glass of white wine. Everything was on the house tonight, the bartender explained. The party.

A medium-sized man in a business suit and button-down shirt came over to her. "You look very unhappy."

She smiled politely.

"Don't know anyone here? Neither do I. I'm the accountant for the movie company, for Perdue Pictures, that is. Scruffs, Wolfson, and Sons, Certified."

"How nice," Sara murmured. "How's the company doing? Should I buy stock?"

"Don't quote me, but after this bomb, I strongly advise against it."

"You mean, even with stars like Googie Gdansk and Becky Luna, you don't think *Allergic to Love* will make money?"

"Not a red cent, not a wooden nickel, wanna dance?"

"No, my doctor advised against it. Inner ear trouble. My balance is shot to hell."

Scruffs, Wolfson, and Sons, Certified, looked at her askance. "You pulling something on me?"

"Yeah, wool over your eyes."

"Sara, darling!" It was Richard Singer-Murray, wearing sunglasses now, as if to give his brown corduroy jacket and khaki pants a little dash. "Have you seen Maria?"

"Maria? What are you talking about?"

"Maria Cortese, of course. Haven't you heard, we're an item. What kind of a columnist are you going to be?"

Sara's heart skipped a beat. Could she have missed out on the biggest news of the day? And could she have missed out on something else as well? She was jealous of Maria and at the same time annoyed at herself for the sensation.

"What kind of columnist? A really terrific one if everyone kisses and tells the way you do."

"Sara, you've got me wrong." Richard put his arm around her and nuzzled his cheek against her hair. A little glitter dust rubbed off on his lip. "I wasn't kissing and telling. I was sharing my happiness. It isn't every day a brilliant small-town boy from Youngwood, Pennsylvania, and a gorgeous movie queen from sunny Napoli find love and mutual satisfaction at the Hotel Carlyle."

Sara's jealousy vanished on the spot. What a boob, she thought.

"No, really, Richard. I'm absolutely delighted for you. And for me. Think you could use your influence to get Maria to talk to me for our article?"

"No problem, sweetheart. Actually, I told her all about you and what you were doing and she was really impressed. As soon as she comes in, I'll arrange a little powwow."

"Richard, glad you could make it." It was Lynn Ericson. "And hello, Sara," she said warmly.

"Hi, Lynn. You look terrific." Sara meant it sincerely. Lynn's eyes were bright, her smile open, she looked rested and relaxed, and had clearly pulled herself together since this afternoon. Michael Connelly must have put her very much at her ease.

After exchanging a few meaningless words with Lynn, Richard excused himself. Now Lynn put her arm around Sara.

"Thanks a million for today. I really hope I didn't impose myself on you."

"Not at all. If you ever need me . . ."

"And if I can ever be of any help to you," Lynn offered.

"Well, in fact, you can," Sara said quietly. "If you could just introduce me to a few of these people here tonight, maybe I could really get started on my article."

"What about Googie for starters?" Lynn suggested. "I think I just caught a glimpse of him."

Sara thought Gyorgii Gdansk would be perfect. She followed Lynn through the crowd around the rim of the dance floor until they were at the very rear of the massive room. In front of the cinderblock walls, a row of bleachers had been set up. Behind them, Gyorgii, wearing jeans and an Edwardian blue silk shirt, was leaning against the wall. He had found the only private spot in the room. Two beautiful young girls, each with a swan neck that seemed about a foot long, and a dark braid falling down her back, were flanking him. Gyorgii was alternately kissing one and then the other.

"Perhaps another time would be more appropriate?" Sara tried to stop Lynn.

"Don't be silly." Lynn laughed. "You don't know Googie. He just adores publicity."

Lynn took Sara over to Gyorgii and made the introduction, explaining Sara's article to him. Would he mind answering a few questions for her? Not at all, he smiled.

"Vat you vant to know? Vatever, I tell you." He patted his two girls on their rumps, a gesture that sent them on their way. Then he turned his cool eyes toward Sara and began scrutinizing her so carefully that she found herself blushing.

She nervously fumbled for her pencil and paper. "You knew Nigel Whitty personally, didn't you? What did you think of him?"

"He vas beautiful. Arrogant. And sensitive like a Polski."

"In other words, like you?" Sara smiled.

"Naturally." Gyorgii smiled back, lowering his lids suggestively.

Sara coughed. With Gdansk, she decided, the less friendly the better. "In your opinion, Mr. Gdansk," she persisted in her most businesslike voice, "what was Nigel's influence within the film community?"

"Nigel! Nigel! Ve talk of Nigel, but not here, not now, somewhere else, later. Ven it quiet." He pulled her toward him. "Now, it time to stop moving vith your head and start moving vith your heart, your feet. Ve dance, you, Miss Sara from America, and Mr. Googie from Bialystok, yes?"

The whole idea terrified her. She, Sara Nightingale, who couldn't help stepping on her own feet, dancing with the great Gyorgii Gdansk! And with everybody looking? What if she stepped on his toe? What if she broke his toe? What if she broke her own?

"I'm sorry," she said primly. "I'd love to dance with you, but I'm working." She began to scribble furiously on her little yellow pad.

"Vat? You refuse Googie Gdansk, the world's greatest Polish dancer? I von't take no for an answer." He swept her up in his arms. Her pencil jabbed straight through his blue silk shirt. He jumped. The shirt ripped.

"Ven you say no, you mean no. No?" He stopped short for a moment and looked at her with admiration. "But I like girl who mean vat she say." He leaned toward her. Instinctively, she pulled away, but he grasped her firmly around the waist and swept her around the floor.

"Happy birthday to you,
Happy birthday to you,
Happy birthday, dear Googie,
Happy birthday to you."

It was Becky Luna, wearing a pink paper birthday hat and leading a contingent of well-wishers. "Googie, Googie, I've been looking for you all evening, my darling." She threw her arms about him and kissed him passionately on the mouth.

"Ah, my Becky," he said with dismay. "I can't get too far away from you, can I?"

She giggled and pulled Gyorgii around the dance floor. "Never, never, you Polish wolfhound, you," she said, snuggling up to him and grinding first one hip, then the other, into his pelvis. Sara could hear her voice doing battle with the music, singing gaily:

"Won't Gdansk, don't ask me,
Won't Gdansk, my Polski,
Won't Gdansk, except with you . . ."

Once again, Sara was left alone. The music pulsated in her ears as she moved along the edge of the crowd toward the opposite end of the room, running smack into Richard Singer-Murray on the way. He was still waiting for Maria and puffing on a joint. "Here," he said, handing it to her, "I've had enough."

Five minutes later, Sara's head was floating. The colors of the room were softening: everything was taking on a pretty pink haze. Somebody led her onto the dance floor, and she found herself moving with unexpected abandon. It felt good. Someone else grabbed her. Whoever it was, together they seemed to move perfectly in time to the music. Her partner broke something under her nose—amyl nitrite, he said it was. She felt an incredible rush. Everything melted together, like water colors . . . the music, the lights and shadows, the people. . . .

And how famous they all seemed! Somewhere out of the corner of her eye, Sara thought she saw Dustin Hoffman and Deborah Harry standing together chatting, but then she shook her head. Impossible. A pretty unlikely couple. Still, the place seemed to be crawling with celebs, and despite her hazy vision, Sara found herself playing a game: Seek out the Stars. Wasn't that Steve Martin over there? And Princess Caroline dancing with some young man who sure looked like a Kennedy? Sara also thought she saw

Peter Allen pounding away to the disco beat with his ex-wife, Liza Minnelli.

Sara seemed to be somewhere in the clouds when Richard Singer-Murray found her standing near a wall, how many minutes since he had handed her the joint, she couldn't quite tell.

"Sara, I've been looking all over for you. Here's Maria."

A very tall woman in a very bright dress—fuchsia? shocking pink?—held out her hand. "So this little Sara! Ricardo tell me all about you. Nigel Whitty, he tell you all about me?"

Of course not, Sara thought, but she was learning fast. She smiled widely. "Nigel thought you were a very gifted actress. And that you would become a big international star." Actually, if she remembered correctly, Nigel had thought exactly the opposite, or had written some such in his review of *The Green Sky* which would run later in the week. But Sara didn't want to think about that now; she'd deal with it some other time. Tonight, after all, she was making Maria happy.

Or was she? Maria, at this moment, looked skeptical. "That what Nigel Whitty say? He say I become big star? You are *certo*?"

"*Certo*. Quite sure." The only way to get out of this bind was to lie. But just a white one, surely.

Maria gave Sara a Mona Lisa smile. "You will go far, Signorina Nightingale, like shooting star. Bang, bang!" She laughed hysterically. "Ricardo say to me you write all Signor Whitty's columns now. He say you have your own column soon. You are young woman on way up. What your sign?"

"Capricorn," said Sara, fumbling for her tape recorder.

"Good, I do your chart."

"Would you mind if I asked you a question or two first, Miss Cortese?"

"What question? About how I learn movement of planets? And how I—"

"No. This is about Nigel Whitty . . ."

"No comment," said Maria, and abruptly turned away.

Damn! Sara thought. She was left holding the tape recorder as if it were an empty bag. One of these people she'd needed to talk to had wanted to dance with her, the other had wanted to chart her course in life. Meanwhile, she could see her big opportunity to break into print as a journalist fading away.

"Sugar plum!" Fenny again. "I've been looking for you all evening. I have the most super stuff I want you to try. Brucie is waiting for us up in the balcony. I left him sitting with Vitas and Barbra. I hope they don't abscond with him. A good cowboy is hard to find."

Fenton led Sara across the dance floor and up the steps to the balcony. Once upstairs, he led her down a few steps to one of the cushioned seats. How strange this place was, Sara thought, sinking back. From this vantage point, she could see that Studio 54 was unmistakably a converted old theater. Not only that, it seemed that the crowd of dancers below, and the throng of observers on the bridge, had become part of a giant stage show, a crazy, confused performance invented by a spaced-out choreographer. Fenton now took a joint from his pocket and lit it with a gold Dunhill lighter.

"Here, sugar plum," he said, passing it to her. "This is something special. It will send you to heaven and back."

Sara took a couple of puffs and had to admit that, if this wasn't heaven, it was, at any rate, fantastic. The lights from up here on the balcony began to make stupendous patterns on the dancers below. Sara slowly got up and fought her way down to the first row, all the better to glimpse the show. Snow was fluttering down from the ceiling now, coming down in a gorgeous white cascade on the celebrants downstairs. Sara leaned over to watch the patterns.

There were so many people standing here near the railing, too many. And it was dark. She felt claustrophobic, uncomfortable, and she was beginning to identify another feeling as well—guilt, nagging, niggling prickles of guilt which were seeping into her awareness. Her interviews, her work! What was she, Sara Nightingale, doing, stoned out of her mind, looking down from this balcony onto all these blurry antlike creatures hopping this way and that? She had to pull herself together and begin her interviews. She was acting so unprofessionally, she thought; she ought to be out there hustling her career along with the others. That three-part series in the *Trib* was, Sara knew, her stairway to stardom. Yet, she was too distracted even to begin the climb.

Her head was swimming now. In just a minute, she'd make her way down to the ladies' room to freshen up. In just a minute, she'd snap out of this haze. She breathed deeply and tried to get hold of herself. What was it she'd smoked? Grass had never done such strange things to her before. She took a step and felt herself weaving. Slowly, slowly now, another step. She grabbed somebody's elbow to steady herself and leaned over the edge of the balcony, watching the movement below from beneath her heavy, half-shut lids. Her head was reeling.

Suddenly, she felt herself losing her balance. Where was the railing? My God, what was happening? "Watch it!" she screamed. She could feel a hand on her back. It was pressing, insistent. My God! Somebody was pushing her off the edge of the balcony. She wanted to call out for help, but her voice seemed lost in the noise and movement. All she could do then was push back, kick, try to resist, and this she did with all her might. Everything was blurry, vague, but now, suddenly, she was steady again, safe, free.

"Who was that?" she shouted to a man standing beside her. He didn't seem to know what she was talking about. Incredible terror gripped her. She was shaking now and began to shiver, cold chills running through her body. She had to get off this balcony. Where was Fenton? Who could help her? She began to push her way through the crowd, to run. She stumbled down the steps now, taking them two at a time, beads of perspiration rolling down her forehead. Move, Nightingale, move, she told herself just before she tripped and fell right into the arms of Lieutenant Michael Connelly.

"Sara Nightingale." He smiled. "Always crashing through life. Never out of character."

"Oh, Michael, don't joke," she sobbed. "Somebody just tried to kill me. You've got to get me out of here. Right now."

She was shaking as he put his arm around her and led her out into the lobby, past the jeering crowd waiting outside in the cool September night.

"Okay, buddy," somebody shrieked to the bouncer. "Two of us can go in now."

"Right," Sara heard the bouncer answer. "But it ain't gonna be you."

All the way home from Studio 54, Michael kept reassuring Sara. Everything was going to be all right. Nobody was trying to push her off balconies or throw her down staircases. Nobody was trying to harm her. In fact, she had most likely imagined the whole incident. Besides, wasn't she lucky that he'd finally decided to take Sammy Nachman up on his invitation to the party on a hunch that something might happen? It was kismet.

At first, she had been angry. He was unsympathetic, she told him, huddling into her corner of the front seat of the car, as far away from him as she could get. He was also, she pointed out, a perfectly lousy policeman. Here she was being attacked right under his nose and what had he done about it? Had he combed the disco for her assailant? No. Had he sealed off the dance floor, locked the doors, fingerprinted the dancers? No. Had he been interested in a detailed account of the incident from the victim? Not on her life.

He pleaded guilty. No, he hadn't combed the disco. What was he supposed to do? Check every hand in the place for evidence of Sara's glitter dust? Or blindfold her and ask everyone on the balcony to give a sample push, just to see which hand fit the small of her back? And if he was doing all of these things, who was going to take her home? Had Sara forgotten that she had been the one who insisted that they leave Studio 54 immediately? She probably had. After all, she was high as a kite, too stoned to remember anything. Who the hell knew what was in those joints she'd so evidently smoked?

"Only God and Fenton Farnabee," she returned, no longer high at all, just a little bit woozy. "But I have to tell you, Michael, it was the strongest dope I've ever smoked."

"Probably, because it was laced with something."

"Like what, for instance? Speed?"

"Maybe, but I don't think so. I'd bet on PCP. Angel dust."

"Oh." Sara thought for a long moment. "You know, that occurred to me myself when I was high."

"Did it?" There was a sarcastic ring to his voice. "Do you really know what angel dust is, Sara?" Obviously, he didn't believe her.

"Of course I do."

"You know then that it's an elephant tranquilizer?"

Now she didn't believe him. "A likely story. Do I look like an elephant to you?"

"Only around the ears."

In spite of herself, Sara laughed.

"More seriously," Michael went on, "that's very dangerous stuff. It can really freak you out. People do crazy things on it. They steal, they kill, they leap out of windows, they . . ."

". . . throw themselves off balconies, thinking that they're being pushed."

"Who knows?"

Who knew indeed? Angel dust! Maybe, she *had* imagined the whole thing. She felt like an idiot for having created such a fuss. Had her mind simply played tricks on her? She couldn't believe it and she couldn't get rid of that vague sense of terror. The idea of going up to her apartment alone really unnerved her. But on the other hand she didn't want Michael to think her hysterical, or worse, cowardly. The trick was, when his car pulled up in front of her brownstone, to get him upstairs without letting him know just how needy she was.

"Can I offer you a cup of coffee, a glass of wine, some ginseng tea, a hot chocolate?" she asked.

He smiled. "What is this, Miss Nightingale's Tea Room and Corner Coffee Shop?" Michael leaned over to open the car door for her. "Thanks, Sara, I'd love to, but I really should get some sleep. I was up all last night, and I've got a lot to do tomorrow."

She felt a twinge of panic. She just *had* to get him to come upstairs with her! She fiddled around in her purse. "Oh, no, I forgot my keys," she said, pushing them deeper into a corner of the leather bag. "Didn't you say you could slip my lock with a credit card? Would you mind?"

Michael sighed. "Nightingale, you'd forget your head if it wasn't screwed on." He parked the car, then followed her into the building and up the narrow staircase.

At the door, she handed him her Bloomingdale's card. In moments, the lock slid open and they were inside her apartment.

"Okay, Nightingale, sleep tight," he said, turning around to leave.

"Don't go, please don't go." The words slipped out unguarded. She was terrified, her pulse suddenly racing.

Michael looked at her.

"What's wrong, Sara?"

She hated herself for having to say this. "Michael, I know you'll think this is crazy, but I'm scared witless. Really scared." Her shoulders started to heave and a small sob escaped her lips. The tears began gushing down her cheeks in a veritable downpour. "I'm so embarrassed, so embarrassed," she cried in distress as she ran toward the privacy of the bathroom. But she was torn, and halfway there she returned to the foyer where Michael was standing. What if he went home while she was in her bathroom, crying her heart out? Which was worse, that, or that he could see her now, so fearful and so emotionally naked? She was out of control and felt completely humiliated.

Michael put his arms around her. "Sara, Sara," he said with obvious concern, pulling a handkerchief from his breast pocket and dabbing the wet spots on her cheeks. "Calm down, Sara, everything will be okay. You're safe. I'm here and you're safe, I promise you."

"I'm so scared. And so embarrassed," she muttered, snuggling up to him. She could feel the nub of his tweed sports jacket brushing against her chin, and she could smell the clean, male scent of his body. She raised her head and saw that he was looking at her tenderly. With their faces so close, she could feel his warm breath against her cheek. Right now, more than anything else in the world, Sara wanted to kiss him. Obviously, he felt the same way, for, like two magnets, their lips began pulling toward each other. Tentatively, his grazed hers, then more determinedly they searched each other out for more. This time, their kiss was long and lingering.

Unexpectedly, Michael broke away. "Nightingale," he said softly, "you're wonderful, but this is all wrong. All wrong."

She lowered her eyes and focused on a spot beyond his left shoulder. She knew Michael was right, but at the same time, she wanted him terribly. "Oh, Michael," she managed to say. It was ambiguous enough. So were her feelings.

"Sara, this isn't going to work," he said quietly. "I know this sounds corny, but we live in two different worlds. And you, more than anyone, understand that."

She was almost at a loss for words. "Why? Just because I go to films and you go to the movies?"

"Yes, sure, that's part of it."

"You're probably right." She backed away. If he didn't want her, then she certainly wasn't going to force herself on him. "Well, thank you very much for stopping by."

"Come on, Sara. Look, if you like, I'll stay here tonight. Just to ease your fears."

"You must have been a Boy Scout," she said. Then she paused dramatically. "But, for your information, I'm not the least bit afraid."

"You mean, all your carrying on was just a ruse to get me into your bed? Sara, I'm flattered," he chuckled.

Maybe it was all that dope, but Sara was speechless, and her emotions were running like a roller coaster. This guy had been coming on to her all week, she thought, and finally, now, when she was showing a little interest—no, when she was practically flinging herself at his feet—he had the nerve to reject her. And with utter coolness. The bastard! She wanted to tear his eyes out. Before she knew it, she was lunging at him. On trying to.

Just before she would have fallen, he caught her by her waist. "Sara," he said, pulling her close to him, "do you think this is easy for me? Do you think I don't want you?" And he began to kiss her like crazy, her eyes, her nose, her forehead, her chin, her neck.

"Oh, Michael, Michael," she murmured as they sank down onto the Greek Flokati rug.

"Ouch!" Michael bolted up to a sitting position. "Something just attacked my back." He reached behind him and pulled up one of the gold disco wedgies Sara had been wearing. "You know," he smiled. "I think the bedroom might be a little more comfortable." He got up and gave Sara his hand. His arms around her, he led her into the bedroom and pulled her down on the plump, pink comforter. They were not alone, Sara realized to her horror.

"Ouch!" Michael cried out again, pulling a hardback copy of Eisenstein's *Film Form* and *Film Sense* out from under his back. He turned to the left. "Damn!" he muttered, removing an open felt-tipped pen from under his jacket, which now was dotted with green. He rolled over to his right. "Jesus!" he exclaimed as a motor began to whir beneath him.

"Oh, get off my hair blower. You'll break it." Sara laughed.

Michael sat up now. "You're a dangerous woman in more ways than one. This goddamned apartment is one big booby trap. How about doing a quick clean-up before we make another move?"

They stood up and began collecting objects that lay scattered about the bed. In addition to the hair blower, the book, the pen, Michael found two wire hangers, a lipstick, a hairbrush and comb, three subway tokens, two lace-fringed pairs of underpants, a T-shirt saying, "Film Is a Four-Letter Word," and an unopened pack of Carefree chewing gum. "This bed is a mine field. Or is it a gold mine?" he said, picking up a handful of loose coins.

Sara blushed. She made a mental note not to be such a pig anymore. Tomorrow she'd clean the place without fail!

"Listen, birdie, I think we'd better shake this comforter out, just to be on the safe side," Michael suggested. "I mean, I value my life just a little." He picked up two ends of the quilt; Sara took the other two. Together, they began to shake.

In a moment a golden cloud of glitter dust formed and burst, sending a shower of tiny, shimmering particles over everything. Michael looked as if he'd been laminated. He glistened, his hair, his eyelashes, his tweed jacket. Sara couldn't control herself and began to convulse with laughter.

"My bottle of glitter dust. Oh, God, I shouldn't have bought the giant size. Michael, I'm sorry, I'm so sorry."

Insofar as she could make out his expression underneath the golden coating, he seemed to be smoldering. "You bitch! You loon! You goddamn monkey! Take off those clothes!"

For a moment, his tone confused her. But then she saw him taking his own clothes off, and she followed suit.

In seconds, they were standing opposite each other, naked except for a few flakes of glitter dust which were floating up from their clothes and freckling their skin.

"God, you're gorgeous," they exclaimed in unison.

They reached out for each other and, bodies entwined, fell back onto the bed. One of the cinderblocks supporting the shaky leg must have slipped, for just at that moment the bed lurched. Then, with a resounding crash, it collapsed beneath them.

"Kismet," said Michael.

Monday

WHAT NIGEL KNOWS

Tinseltown Tidbits and Tattle

by Nigel Whitty

BILLING AND COOING DEPARTMENT: Scoop! The most fabulous twosome of the week, our spies have it, are dashing young editor-about-town, Richard Singer-Murray, and the exquisite sex symbol of three continents, Maria Cortese, soon to be seen in *The Green Sky*. Debonair Singer-Murray has won her over and away from the band of suitors lining up outside her Hotel Carlyle door each morning. What's your secret, dashing Dickie? . . . **QUESTION**: Has "esteemed" critic Vernon Leakey been forgetting to pay his bills lately? Not only do we hear that Con Ed might be turning off his lights, but someone else whose electricity is still working might start playing his old records. And we don't mean on the phonograph, dearies. Now for wifey, Beatrix, that Wonder Woman from Wolverhampton, Wallasey, or is it Wimbledon? In any case, she can smash balls with the best of them. And if she doesn't start serving reminders to Vernon, Nigel will have to take another look-see in his little black book. Do you hear me, Leakeys? . . . **MYSTERY OF THE MOMENT:** This one, dear reader, has to do with a certain screen heartthrob who, currently racked with ambition to turn himself into a director with a "personal vision," thinks that the purchase of a pair of glasses will do the trick. You've seen all those cover shots of him lately, haven't you? And if you haven't and if you're having trouble guessing who, here's another little clue: He's been getting mobbed for years, and we don't mean by his fans. Got it? If you don't, Nigel does—down pat in his little black book. . . .★

8

THAT SCHMUCK! That boob! That jerk!" Sara sat up in bed reading the morning *Trib*. Michael nuzzled close to her, glancing at the paper over her shoulder. He rubbed his cheek into her hair, luxuriating in its silkiness.

"What's the problem?" He kissed her on the shoulder. God, her skin was gorgeous—so fine and delicate, it was almost translucent.

"That Singer-Murray! Did you see what he did? He put that goddamned item about his romance with Maria Cortese into the column himself."

"Who cares?" Michael slid down in the bed and with his finger traced the line from her clavicle to her navel.

"You know, birdie, you have freckles in the most spectacular places."

"Can you believe what an egotistical creep he is!" Sara exclaimed.

"Yeah, I believe it, I swear on a Bible. Now—"

The telephone rang. Sara reached over for it. "Hi, Fenny, honey," she said after a moment.

"Oh, no!" Michael rolled his eyes heavenward. "Make it quick." He burrowed his nose under Sara's smooth armpit. She began to laugh and squirm, but Michael couldn't tell whether it was because of what Fenton was saying to her or what he himself was doing.

"Michael, please, this is important," she whispered. "Honestly, it's urgent. Michael!"

Michael ceased and desisted. As he listened to Sara's

"Really's!" and "No kidding's!" and "Oh, Fenny's!" he wrapped himself into a spoon position around her, his lips softly grazing her thick tangle of red curls, his legs gently twining around hers. He pulled her to him and folded his arms around her breasts, stroking them absentmindedly until he could soon feel the nipples getting hard and tight under his fingers. Suddenly, Sara slapped his hand and wriggled away from his grasp.

"Look, Fenny, I don't know how to thank you. That's great. I'll be there at noon on the dot." She leaned over and returned the receiver to its cradle.

Once again Michael pulled her to him, this time more urgently.

"Michael, please. Fenny just came up with something important."

"Only one thing's important now." He nibbled her ear, almost swallowing it.

"Oh, stop it." She pulled away. "Listen, Fenny just set up an appointment with Danny Blue for me. Don't you have a meeting with him today, too? Isn't that a terrific coincidence?"

"Terrific," Michael murmured. 'Mmmm, kiss me, birdie."

"Someone should lock you up. You're practically a sex maniac."

"Only—" he could tell she was having trouble resisting him now—"when I run into luscious redheads with freckles in unmentionable places."

"Oh, stop it," she moaned.

But he wasn't about to stop. He pressed his lips against her belly and began working his way down. And she didn't say another word.

It was close to ten o'clock when Michael got to the precinct, and he knew he'd have to hurry. He had an appointment with the Leakeys, who had asked him to meet them at the studios of WFOX. They were to be guests on the "Fenton Farnabee Hour" which was broadcast live in the mornings and then on tape at night. The show was devoted, as was Fenton himself, to movies, gossip, and miscellaneous frivolous folderol. This morning's discussion, though, was to be a bit heftier than usual, Vernon had explained. After all, unlike most in this frequently crass cinema world, he and Beatrix definitely were not interested in trivia but instead in matters of the mind and cinematic metaphor. Indeed, Lieutenant Connelly really should come early and listen, Vernon had added expansively—he was sure to find it an education. In what in particular, Michael wasn't quite sure, but he promised to try and make it.

He was just opening his office door when Friedkin came running up to him, waving a piece of paper. "This just came in from Washington," Friedkin said breathlessly. As usual, his shirt hung out of his trousers and his face was shadowed with a two-day dark growth of beard.

"Friedkin, haven't you heard the news?" Michael said, slapping the young man on the back. "If you want to get ahead in life, you've got to shave."

But Friedkin was unconcerned. "Aren't you gonna read the stuff? It's hot, real hot."

Michael scanned the memo. "Wow, this is something. You absolutely sure?"

"Yeah."

"How'd they find this?"

"The FBI was in contact with the CIA, who received a transatlantic cable from Interpol. They ran a channel check through the BBC, who SOS'ed Scotland Yard. And so here we are."

"Good work, Watson."

"Thanks, Holmes."

"This may break the case," Michael said, looking at the paper again. "And perfect timing, Friedkin. Couldn't have been better in fact. I'm just going over to see the Leakeys now. Anything else before I take off?"

"Just a few messages—they can wait."

"Keep trucking, Friedkin," Michael patted him on the shoulder, "and you'll be a sergeant in no time."

Michael didn't even bother to enter his office. He closed the door and started back down the hallway toward the exit. He was feeling good. Sara had brought him luck. For though he may or may not have found the person who'd killed Nigel Whitty, at least now he had a murderer.

The program was more than halfway finished by the time Michael arrived at WFOX, or so a gray-haired guard informed him in hushed whispers before directing him to the control room. Here, he took a seat next to the "Fenton Farnabee Hour's" producer and two technicians, all of whom sat badgering one another in similarly hushed voices.

The studio was barren and colorless. A large rectangular table stood in the center of the room, accompanied only by half a dozen folding chairs and decorated with two microphones. On one of the chairs sat a tall, big-boned woman in her mid-fifties. Her long gray hair was tied around her head in a braid that gave her the peculiar aura of having just come down off a mountaintop with her flock of sheep. Her ruddy complexion and watery blue eyes enforced the impression. She was wearing an ankle-length paisley skirt and a gray cowl-neck blouse. Next to her sat a man who seemed just about half her size. Fleshy, round, with pepper-and-salt tufts on both sides of his shiny pate, and thick-lensed horn-rimmed glasses, he had the sallowest complexion Michael had ever seen. It was as if no ray of sunshine had ever touched his jaundiced skin. Fenton Farnabee, in one of his little white creations, sat facing the two. All were in the middle of a heated discussion revolving around the topic, "The Significance of Fruit Imagery in Hollywood Movies."

"Consider Carmen Miranda," Beatrix was saying in her BBC contralto. She had obviously had a drink or two, despite the early hour, and kept slurring her words. "Those hats," she was saying, "it's really as if she were wearing her genitals right on her head."

"Oh, now, Beatrix, you don't mean that," Fenton shrieked. "Carmen? Little Carmen? Carmencita?"

"Yes, Fenton," Beatrix replied with a burp. "Fruits in movies are always sexual symbols. And it's indicative of Hollywood's prudery that they continually opted for the custard pie rather than the apple or peach. I mean, a cherry pie in the face? It would have been cunnilingus on the screen!"

"Oh, *cunning linguists*! Yes, of course, the language of film. Yes, Beatrix, my dear, remember, my dear, we are on the radio!" Fenton exclaimed.

"How bloody bourgeois!" she humphed.

"Not to interrupt," said Vernon, "but I do think this is an appropriate moment to mention my seminal essay, 'Notes on Non-Bourgeois Cinematic Imagery.' I, too, mention fruits in my discussion of banana republics and their socialist-realist films."

"Really," Fenton yawned, "how interesting. But now back to Hollywood. And back to you, Beatrix, and your original point. Isn't it a bit sweeping to say that all fruit imagery in films is sexual in nature?"

"Not at all, Fenton. And though I hate to return to bananas, since Vernon has just mentioned them in the most banal and predictable of contexts, I can't help but offer the film *Bananas* as proof of the banana pudding. You're not going to deny, are you, that Woody Allen's film reveals an obsession with matters phallic? Or that—to cite another telling example—Kubrick's *A Clockwork Orange* isn't concerned with things testicular?"

At that, Fenton coughed and sputtered and sneezed, the better, Michael thought, to muffle Beatrix's words.

"In my highly controversial analysis of the descriptive syntagma in the milk bar sequence in that film," Vernon added excitedly, "I point out that the *mise-en-scène* carried a hidden revolutionary code addressed to the hungry and starving citizens of Third World nations."

"How fascinating," Fenton sighed. "But let's get back to Hollywood. What about a movie like the Marx brothers' *Coconuts*, Beatrix? Surely . . ."

"I'll tell you about *Coconuts*," interrupted Vernon. "A perfect instance of the way in which Hollywood encoded its political messages. As I wrote in my internationally acclaimed essay, 'The Marx Brothers' Maniacal Marxism,' the coconut is a secret symbol for the impenetrable womb of capitalism and . . ."

"Good God, Vernon!" Beatrix exclaimed, coming very close to falling off her chair in her annoyance and stupor. "That's a paltry piece of projection, if I ever heard one. Coconuts, as anyone worth his Ph.D. in Cinema Studies knows, are obviously hairy balls."

"*Harry calls,* yes, of course!" Fenton frantically glossed over her words for his listeners. "And then Dick calls and then Tom, with Ginger Rogers as a telephone operator, keeping them all on the line. *Tom, Dick, and Harry's* the flick, a B masterpiece, if you ask me."

"Oh, the party line, you mean," Vernon inserted. "In my historical essay about the symbolic connections . . ."

Beatrix hiccoughed. And at that very moment, Fenton began to wrap it all up by announcing that their time, sadly enough for all passionate moviegoers and greengrocers too, was up. "I want to thank you both. Ladies and gentlemen, I've been talking with America's foremost film critic and founder of the school of Filmophobic Esthetics, the incomparable Vernon Leakey. We've also had the pleasure of chatting with his wife, the fabulous poetess, Beatrix Leakey, whose latest book of verse, *I Don't Give a Fig*, is a runaway best-seller. So until next time, all you sweetpeas in the garden and petunias in the patch, perk up! And Fenton will see you in his dreams." The music faded in, and a chorus of "I Gave My Love a Cherry" provided the program's finale.

"Beatrix, thanks a million." Fenton kissed her, once they were off the air. "You really gave the show a charge."

"Don't talk to me about charges, or anything else electrical," Beatrix sneered. "Did you happen to read today's revolting column by your colleague Nigel Whitty, who is fortunately no longer putrefying the air I breathe?"

"Oh, I know it was shocking, Bea." Fenton shook his head in exaggerated disapproval.

"Hic!" Beatrix added her private little exclamation point.

Michael had listened long enough. "Mr. and Mrs. Leakey," he said, walking into the studio, "I'm Lieutenant Connelly."

"But of course. We have an appointment with you right now, don't we?" Beatrix extended a strong right hand.

Aha! thought Michael. Despite all the booze, she was his first contender for the sock-on-the-jaw sweepstakes.

Fenton offered effusive greetings, after which, on Michael's request, he whisked himself away.

"Can we talk here?" Michael asked, glancing over to the control room and noting that the two technicians and the producer had left.

"Why not," said Vernon.

"Would you like us one at a time or together, Lieutenant?" Beatrix asked. "Perhaps you'd like to talk to me first."

"Let's try together for starters," Michael said.

Beatrix reached into her Greek tapestry bag and pulled out an aluminum thermos. "I hope you don't mind. After all that blather, I'm really parched. You don't want any, do you?" she asked Michael in peremptory fashion.

He shook his head. He sure wouldn't want to be sharing a lifeboat with this one. "The first thing I want to know," he began, "is why Nigel Whitty had it in for the two of you? I mean, he never stopped hitting on you in all these years."

"Jealousy," Vernon said, "pure jealousy. Beatrix, do you have another cup?"

"I certainly don't. And don't answer for me," she snapped. "What Professor Leakey should have said, Detective"—Beatrix turned to Michael—"is that Nigel sold out and we didn't. He was brilliant, you know, and I'm always the first to give credit where credit is due. But he was also a louse and a swine."

"Could you spell that out for me?" Michael asked. "I mean the business about selling out."

"Of course," Vernon said. "When Whitty started out in this business, he was a first-rate critic. A really serious student of the motion picture arts. His film esthetics ranked with the best, that is, if I say so myself, with my own. *Cinema Clarified* is a classic—required reading for anyone involved in film. But then money turned Nigel's head."

"Only partly," Beatrix interrupted, after taking a belt from her cup. "You never see the whole picture, Vernon—and I mean that literally and figuratively. It was also that Whitty was a twisted person and bloody cruel as well."

"Not at heart, Bea," Vernon corrected her gently. "It was money and power, power and money that got him. When he was given the chance to write that absurd twitter, that gossip column for morons and misfits, his mind went to rack and ruin." He paused. "Can't I just have a little sip?"

"No. Now you'll remember to bring your own cup next time," she said sharply and turned to Michael. "What he's telling you is hogwash, Detective. Whitty was a sadist, a true de Sade, and money and power be damned." She opened her thermos and freshened her cup.

"But what did all that have to do with you two?" Michael asked. "You haven't been very specific."

"We didn't give in, we didn't sell out," Beatrix repeated.

"But you drank, and he never let you forget it. Right?"

"Right. He never let us forget it," Beatrix said. "Not ever."

"But there were other things he never let you forget, too."

"What do you mean, Detective?" Beatrix's voice grew sharp. "What are you alluding to?"

Michael took a piece of paper out of his pocket. "My man just handed me some rather interesting information, including a *very* lengthy cable from Scotland Yard . . ."

Beatrix fell off the chair. "Pardon me," she apologized to Michael, as she picked herself up and brushed off her paisley skirt. "Now whatever could you be referring to?" she asked in a suddenly sugary tone.

"The Wolverhampton School. Why don't you tell me about it?"

Beatrix was obviously cornered. She and Vernon looked at each other despairingly. "Go ahead, Bea." He nodded. "It's all right." And he took her hand in his.

"Don't touch me!" she hissed. She weaved forward one more time, then, by dint of sheer will, sat straight up. "Lieutenant, what you're after seems to be eluding me," she said in the most proper manner she could muster.

"Mrs. Leakey, I know about the Priscilla Pettigrew affair. Why don't you tell me about it in your own words."

Beatrix Leakey said nothing, looking away from him.

"Priscilla Pettigrew," he prodded. "Tell me about Priscilla Pettigrew."

"Priss?" she sighed, after a moment. "Ah, Priss, Priss. The dream of my youth, the girl of my dreams!"

And then Beatrix launched into her tale of ill-fated love. She had been a poor girl, she told Michael, the daughter of a Wimbledon groundskeeper, but she'd always been clever, so much so, in fact, that she'd won a work-scholarship to the Wolverhampton School when she was a mere seven. Her job, which made her a bit of a Cinderella, she now smiled coyly, was to help out in the kitchen. Its work cruelly isolated her from her wealthy schoolmates, but the fact that she'd grown almost to her full height of six feet by the age of ten made her even more of an outcast. But then one day Priscilla Pettigrew came to Wolverhampton.

"Oh, yes, a blessed day." Beatrix smiled radiantly. "Or so I thought at the time." Priscilla, the new audiovisual aide, arrived at school carrying her slide projector in one hand and her 8-millimeter film projector in the other. She was even taller than Beatrix and strong from moving all that equipment about; and as if that wasn't enough, she was fleet of foot and swift of mind, to boot. They soon fell madly in love. "We were like twin flowering cherry trees smiling proudly down on the saplings." Beatrix recalled softly. "Like two tender vines, like two stalks of corn protecting the fresh-plowed field, we towered over the world." Beatrix was now uttering each phrase in a singsongy voice, with appropriate flourishes and pauses, as though she were on stage.

This one is reciting her goddamn poetry to me, line by line, Michael suddenly realized. "Mrs. Leakey," he reminded her firmly, "let's get to the point—and I mean, murder."

"Murder! What murder? It was no murder, it was an accident, Lieutenant. Do you hear me, an accident!" Suddenly Beatrix Leakey was trembling.

"Yes, Lieutenant." Vernon quickly stepped in. "An accident. Do you think this woman of letters, this *artiste* with so much to contribute to the world, would throw it—"

"Keep out of this, Vernon," Beatrix ordered and shakily poured herself another hefty cupful of liquor. Then she looked Michael squarely in the eyes. "It was no murder, Lieutenant, it was a home movie."

"A home movie?" Michael asked. He'd lost her completely.

"Yes, Lieutenant." Beatrix looked down into her cup now, almost shyly. "Priss and I wanted a record of our togetherness, so we took our camera into the woods to film one of our perfect afternoons. Oh, I remember how the sun dappled the mossy ground. Ah, I remember how we took turns shooting. Priss swam as I shot . . . I danced as she shot . . . Priss climbed . . . I ran . . . she napped . . . I jumped. And then we placed our lovely camera on a stump while I ate berries and she ate mushrooms."

As fate would have it, the two girls in their joy and haste had confused the harmless white *Agaricus* with the deadly poisonous white *Amanita*, or death angel. By the time they'd started their return to Wolverhampton at dusk, Priss was already drifting into unconsciousness. She was never to recover.

Immediately the authorities jumped to conclusions and charged Beatrix with murder. Unfortunately, there was a packet of love letters—incriminating love letters, according to the police inspector—recently written by the deceased to a newly arrived six-foot, three-and-a-half-inch physical training major, Samantha Fitzgibbon, whom Priss had affectionately dubbed "Sam." "No matter what I did, they refused to believe my story," Beatrix said bitterly. "They chose to see me instead as the jilted woman."

"What happened to the proof of your innocence; that is, to the home movies?" Michael asked.

"Priss's last—I mean, only—error!" Beatrix closed her eyes, as though the memory were too painful. "In our youthful exuberance, we had forgotten to put film in the camera."

And so, despite her fierce protests, Beatrix was found guilty and sent to the Wallasey Institute for Wayward Women. And here it was that she first began to pursue her lifelong preoccupation. Vegetables were clearly a mixed metaphor for her, yet as penance for Priss's death, she asked to be assigned to work in the Wallasey garden in the warm months and the library in the winter ones. There she was able to bring her interest to perfect fruition—if the Lieutenant would excuse the pun—and after teaching herself the rudiments of poesy made it her task to produce at least one ode to vegetables a day.

"How did Vernon happen into your life?" Michael interrupted her, afraid that this long-winded giantess was, after finishing on her childhood, warming up to a long discourse on "poesy."

"Isn't that in my docket? Didn't Scotland Yard fill you in on that part of my tarnished past?"

"Yes." Michael nodded. "But, again, I'd like to hear about it in your own words."

Her words were, for a change, short and to the point. It

seemed that Vernon, having gone to see the film *A Yank in the RAF*, had decided to become one himself. Stationed in Wallasey for four years—he unfortunately was too blind to pass his flight exam and was permanently assigned to ground work—he used to frequent the local RAF canteen. It was here that during the blitz Beatrix had been assigned to work as the final phase in her rehabilitation. The two met and discovered immediately that they had in common their esthetic pursuits—she poetry, he film, together the poetry of film, just as it had been with Priss, the audiovisual instructor.

Moreover, Beatrix wanted to leave England—and her past—behind her. Coming into the States as Mrs. Leakey solved any immigration problems a woman with a criminal record might have.

So much for Vernon. What about Whitty, Michael asked. How did he find out about her past?

Beatrix shrugged. Whitty claimed that it had come from Samantha—the very same Sam of the love letters—who on graduation from Wolverhampton had decided to become a stuntwoman. Nigel had met her, he said, while she was working as Peter O'Toole's stand-in during the filming of *Lawrence of Arabia*. But Beatrix never really believed him—she was positive the true culprit was Vernon.

As she said this, she threw her husband a venomous look.

"Why would I have told Nigel?" Vernon whined. "You're paranoid."

"Why? So that he wouldn't put you into print and tell the world about your heinous deeds, your weak-spined morality."

Michael had had enough, and besides, it was time to make a move.

"Mrs. Leakey, I've read your statement, and you have no alibi for your whereabouts during the hour before Nigel Whitty's death . . ."

"I told your man What's-his-name that I was at the supermarket."

"Not according to any of the checkers or the manager . . ."

"Ask the fruit man—I was examining the avocados."

"Let's cut it here," Michael said sharply. "Why did you do it?"

"Adjust your tone." Beatrix stood up and drew herself to her full six feet. "I didn't do it—as you so crudely put it. And I think we've said enough. Let's go, Vernon."

"Just a minute, Mrs. Leakey," Michael told her firmly. "I think you'd better sit down again. I'm not finished. May I remind you that a man has been murdered and the two of you are my number one suspects."

"Me?" shrieked Vernon. "A professor of world standing, of high academic repute! A fabled film critic! This is like the witch-hunts of the fifties."

"I'm glad you brought that up, Professor Leakey. Because I'd like you to tell me something about the fifties and about your politics."

Vernon opened his mouth, but no sound came forth. He looked as if he were blowing smoke rings.

"Oh, God, you know about that too," Beatrix sighed and took a swig directly from the bottle.

"Who told you?" Vernon's voice was just a cut above a whisper.

"It doesn't matter. Just tell me your side of the story."

"You got it from Whitty, didn't you?"

"Maybe."

"I can't, I can't," Vernon began to sob.

"Oh, stop slobbering and tell him what he wants to know," Beatrix commanded. "What's the difference now?" And she took another swig.

Vernon blew his nose and began his story: "Bea and I were just back from the blitz and I was a young critic teaching film esthetics at the New School. In those days, it was a very avant-garde thing to be doing. My mentor was Ivan Vasilevetch, the Eisenstein protégé who had made that great revolutionary film, *Boy with a Pickled Herring*, you know, the one with the great shot of the herrings squirming on the cobblestones after the Cossacks viciously knocked over their barrels . . ."

"Who cares?" Beatrix interrupted. "Whoever cared about the bloody herrings. It was the onions that gave that shot significance . . ."

"Please, Mrs. Leakey, I'd like to hear your husband's story."

"Well, Vasilevetch, as you can guess, brought me in contact with the Marxist inner circle. Those people were obsessed with film and its powers. The great mass educator, they called it. But that's beside the point. You have to understand that Communism was an eye-opener for me. I came from a very wealthy family, you know. Very wealthy. It's what has enabled me to pursue my interests all these years. Criticism doesn't pay much, you know . . ."

"More than your platitudinous pieces are worth, however," Beatrix interjected. "Now poetry . . ."

"Please, Mrs. Leakey." Michael turned to Vernon. "Go on. About the fifties."

"Yes, that was when the crunch came and," Vernon let go a small sob, "I didn't have the courage of my convictions."

"You mean before HUAC?" Michael prodded.

"Yes, the witch-hunts." Vernon lowered his head. "I named names. I informed. And I'm so ashamed." Vernon looked at Michael pleadingly, desperately. "If this came out, I'd lose all my respect in the film community, all my friends, my status, my life. My publisher would allow my books to go out of print. The *New Utopian* would never run my criticism. People would refuse to sit next to me at dinner parties. I'd be washed-up, a has-been." His voice trembled and his sallow face darkened.

"How does Whitty fit in?" Michael asked.

"He found out. Ten years ago, he found out. I don't know how. The only other person who knew," and he stared daggers at Beatrix, "was my wife."

"Are we going to go through that again? *Your* paranoia this time? Your insane suspicion that I told Nigel Whitty?"

"Well, didn't you?" Vernon's tone was matter-of-fact, his voice drained of energy. "Didn't you whisper it to him while the two of you were curled up in bed, playing with your ridiculous fruits and odious vegetables?"

"Let's not return to that distasteful subject," Beatrix announced haughtily. She turned the thermos over and began to shake it, but apparently it was dry."

"You were saying, Mr. Leakey?" Michael urged him on.

"Yes, I paid Nigel Whitty all my life to keep his mouth shut—about both of us. On the first of every month I sent him one thousand dollars, plus a seven percent cost-of-living increase yearly."

"Why all the mentions in his column, then, if you sent him money regularly?"

"It was Nigel Whitty's way of reminding me that there was always worse to come if I didn't comply."

"You had a pretty strong motive for killing him then, Leakey. And so did you." He turned to Beatrix. "Besides, unlike any of the other suspects, you had experience in this line of work. You know," Michael paused, "I'd say that the two of you together had more reason to kill Whitty and more idea of how to go about it than any other suspect on this list."

Michael wasn't sure that this was true at all—but he wasn't sure it wasn't true either.

Danny Blue was shooting his new movie at the Cloisters. *Brother, Can You Spare a Dance?* told the tender story of a lonely young monk who inadvertently dons an enchanted cassock to find himself driven into a wild and exhausting "Dance of Death." Or so Fenton Farnabee had reported in his Sunday feature. "A musical fairy tale with a real message," he had written. "*Brother, Can You Spare a Dance?*, which stars Gyorgii Gdansk as Mortimus the Dancing Monk, promises to be the most controversial film of the future. We hear that the Pope himself has asked to see the script." But whatever doubts the Church may have had, Fenton suggested, New York City, delighted with

Blue's extravaganza, *Subway*, was giving its full cooperation. It had offered Blue the Cloisters for the film's chief set and had even arranged with the Metropolitan Museum of Art to keep the medieval structures and their gardens closed to the public for a two-week period.

As Sara walked along the flowered paths of Fort Tryon Park that led to the dramatically situated museum, she couldn't help but recall with amusement and exhilaration the crazy times she'd had on various movie locations with Claude, her Turkish cameraman. But she knew she was intoxicated now for other reasons as well. Not only was the day sunny and crisp, not only was she filled with heady feelings about Michael, but she was also high on the prospects of her article. She thought she could put together a terrific piece and one that would truly be her own. Moreover, it would be work that left her with integrity and pride—unlike her efforts on behalf of Nigel Whitty's mean and caustic columns, which really had begun to trouble her. Oh, well, as she'd told herself for the last couple of days—she'd think about it tomorrow.

Right now it was beautiful, and she was at the Cloisters on her way to see Danny Blue. A few yards away, in an adjacent parking lot, stood several campers, vans, and equipment trucks, all of various sizes and all containing the complicated machinery of moviemaking. The words *Erie Transfer* were stenciled across their sides. As Sara approached, five men who had opened a bridge table onto the black tar pavement were sitting on small wooden camp chairs playing what seemed like a hot game of poker.

"Excuse me, I'm looking for Danny Blue," she interrupted.

"You and every other chick in town," one of the men sneered, then turned back to the game. "Raise you five, Tony."

"Where is he? Where's Blue?" Sara persisted.

"Over there." Tony nodded to a camper behind him.

Just then the door to the camper opened, and Danny

Blue himself emerged into the sunlight, zipping up the fly of his Ralph Lauren jeans. He was evidently having a bit of trouble with the corner of his red plaid work shirt, which was jamming the zipper's path. Danny seemed preoccupied. A moment later, Maria Cortese stepped proudly out of the trailer, tossing her long dark mane and exclaiming. *"Che dolce vita, carissimo Danielo!"*

Wait till Richard Singer-Murray hears about this, Sara smiled to herself. It would take a little air out of his inflated balloon.

Danny walked slowly toward Sara while Maria remained poised on the step of the camper, buttoning her blouse. Although her audience was small—the five poker players, a few onlookers who had wandered by from the park, a sanitation man spearing stray papers from the lawns, and Sara—she didn't stint on her performance. She seemed to want to be sure that no one missed a thing.

"Mr. Blue? I'm Sara Nightingale of the *Trib*."

"Hi, Sara Nightingale." Blue extended his hand and smiled beguilingly.

And was that a wink, Sara wondered, or just a tic? Whatever—here he was, the great Danny Blue! She'd seen him at Tavern-on-the-Green the other night, but only at a distance. Now she saw him clearly and distinctly, looking just the way he did on screen. Maybe even better. He really was a knockout, with those marvelously sensual lips, huge and even white teeth, and veiled blue eyes that in his films always seemed to be focused not at the camera but beyond it, not on his leading lady but beyond her.

"I'm not so sure how much time I can give you, babe," Blue began, "we ran into a few snags this morning."

Sara found herself smirking, her eyes unwillingly drawn to Danny Blue's not-quite-closed zipper.

"*Ciao, ciao,* Sara Nightingale," Maria called from her perch and waved.

Danny Blue ignored Maria and turned to Sara. "Why don't you join me on the set, babe, and as soon as I give instructions to my cameraman and they begin to set up for the next shot, we'll go off into a quiet cloister and talk. What d'ya say, babe?"

Sara nodded yes. Danny Blue clasped her hand and she thought she could feel his middle finger tickling her palm. He must be kidding!

At that moment, a bright red custom-designed Maserati convertible drove into the parking lot, causing the poker players to put down their cards and whistle ferociously. It was as if Miss Nude World or some other similar distraction had arrived.

"Oh, Enzo, Enzo!" cried Maria, waving wildly at the slim, silver-haired man in the driver's seat. "I've been waiting for you. So interesting on the set, better even than Cinecittà," she screamed to him as he untangled his tall body and alighted from the tiny car. "And this place, these old stones"—she gestured to the ancient buildings surrounding her—"just like home. A bit of Napoli in New York!"

Enzo said hello to Danny and to Sara, whom he remembered meeting at Tavern-on-the-Green. Then, together with Maria, all four of them walked into the dark entryway of the Cloisters, then through the chapels and hallways until they emerged into the sunlight again. Now they were in an extraordinary cloistered garden, its patches of golden autumn flowers laid out in a sunburst pattern emanating from the weathered sides of a well at its center. The design would have suggested harmony and order, had the garden not been interrupted by yards and yards of thick black cables; by huge lights on heavy iron stands; by a sound boom on a pole; by massive light reflectors and cameras accompanied by dolly tracks and a crane. There must have been forty technicians jammed into the small plaza, most wearing T-shirts and jeans, and a number carrying walkie-talkies. Five blond surfer types dressed as monks in brown cassocks stood smoking in one of the walkways surrounding the garden. Above, a parapet had been constructed which ran the entire length of one of the garden's sides. From it hung four enormous lights.

"So many lights?" Enzo surveyed the set. "In Italy, we don't work with so much equipment, with such a large crew."

"It's the way to get things perfect, Enzo, baby," Danny Blue said knowingly. "And you know, man, my cameraman is a genius. He has all the tricks of the trade down pat."

"Interesting, very interesting." Enzo nodded. "Very good of you to have me here, Danny. I think I can learn a lot, if you don't mind my just wandering around and looking."

"My pleasure, man. Just make yourself at home." Danny threw one of those dazzling grins again.

Enzo bowed ever so slightly and, taking Maria by the arm, began walking with her around the set.

Danny looked at Sara. "Just one more minute." Then he called out to no one in particular, "Hey, where's my stunt coordinator? I want to talk to him."

A stocky young man barked into a megaphone: "Rick Johnson, Rick Johnson."

In moments, Rick Johnson appeared. He looked, Sara thought, exactly like one of the Marlboro men.

"Have you got everything under control, man?" Danny asked.

Rick nodded. "We're almost ready for the big leap. Another half-hour should do it. One thing, though. Get Gdansk off my back. He wants to do the goddamn jump himself. He thinks because he can twirl his toes, he can also jump off a twenty-foot roof and live to tell the tale."

"I'll talk to Googie myself," Danny said. "You just get everything ready, man. I don't want any broken bones, so take your time. Be cool."

Danny Blue now turned to Sara. "Jesus, these superstars! They give me a pain in the ass. I didn't use any stars on my last flick, *Subway,* and let me tell you, babe, it was terrific. Ter-rif-fic!"

Now there was no mistake about it—he did wink.

Danny led Sara out of the cloister, through the building, and into yet another cloister which was indeed serene and lovely. Canvas director's chairs had been set up by the crew for Danny Blue's comfort, and now they both eased into them.

"Okay, shoot, Sara Nightingale, baby."

Sara took out her tape recorder and held it on her lap.

"As you know," she began, "I'm doing a piece for the *Trib* on Nigel Whitty's death. I know this is awkward, but could you tell me how you felt about it personally?"

"Personally?" Danny laughed. "Personally, it meant relief—great relief. That cocksucker was having too good a time dancing on my back."

"What do you mean?"

"That I don't like any prick but my own making a living off my comings and goings."

Sara swallowed hard and decided to take another tack. This clearly was not going to be easy. "Well, Mr. Blue, what was it like sitting in the screening room with a dead man? Did you have any premonitions, any . . ."

"Listen, babe—" Danny Blue moved his chair closer to Sara's and put his hand on her arm—"let's cut all the crap. Why don't you just come back to my trailer with me?"

This interview was obviously not proceeding as Sara had planned. But she steeled herself and gave it another try. "Why? Can you answer questions better inside than outside?"

"Inside, outside, horizontal I'm at my best," Danny Blue smiled, rubbing his legs together as he spoke. "You see, Sara, baby, I love to fuck. So what d'ya say, let's give it a try."

"You're putting me on," Sara said, but she really wasn't

sure. "Listen, I love looking at you, but I don't think we're meant for each other. For one thing, I'm a monogamist."

"So what? I'm a terrific liar, babe. You'd never know when I fucked somebody else. Not in a million years." Now he ran his hand up and down her arm.

"Not in a million years," Sara echoed him, pulling away and returning to her interview. "Look, Mr. Blue," she said in an effort to put some distance between them, "Nigel wrote some pretty awful stuff about you. Did it ever cross your mind—did you ever think about—well, murdering him yourself?"

"Of course, I did. Who hasn't? He was the meanest bastard in . . ."

Danny's voice trailed off. He'd been taken by surprise. There, standing in the vaulted archway of the cloister, listening to every word they had been saying, was Lieutenant Michael Connelly.

"Mind if I join in?" Michael asked. "This is my favorite subject these days. And I have a few questions of my own as well."

"Naw, go ahead and shoot."

Danny Blue didn't look the least bit flustered. He was, Sara decided, the coolest cat she had ever met.

"Well, obviously, what I want to know about is your history with Whitty, Blue," Michael began, pulling up a chair. "I heard the message you left on his answering machine the morning he died. You were pretty angry."

"Of course, I was angry. Look, man, that goddamn fuck had no right to jump my opening and attack my picture like that. I put a couple of years of my life into that movie. And I didn't do it just so Nigel Witless could throw out some stupid puns about it."

"I understand," Michael said. "But what do you think was behind it all? I mean, how well did you know him?"

"Not well. Hardly at all. Sure, I'd seen him around. You

know, I've been a Hollywood star since I was practically a kid, man. Twenty-two. He was just one of those parasites who enjoyed sucking everyone's blood. A lot of people like him in this business."

"But you were especially angry at him."

"Why not? It was just before the opening night of my movie. I was charged, overcharged. But that's okay, man. It passed. It's over." Danny Blue shrugged and stretched out his long legs as if to prove how relaxed he was. Sara could see his bare feet peeking through his Gucci loafers.

"He'd attacked you before, though—when you were an actor. Didn't that add to your feelings?"

"Sure it did. But let me tell you something, man. In order to hang on in this business, you choose right from the start either not to read your reviews or not to give a flying fart about them. Otherwise, babe, you're dead."

"In other words, you're claiming that Whitty didn't really faze you?"

"Right on, baby, that's it. Let me put it this way. Whitty could attack me with all the goddamn ammunition he had—his hifalutin' language, his millions of readers, his clout with the money boys. But what the hell could he really do to me? Man, I still get a million bucks to star in a picture, and the ladies still die for an hour in my bed." He licked his lips and gazed at Sara. She wondered how Michael was registering this one-sided flirtation, but his face, she noticed, seemed impassive as he kept throwing questions at Danny Blue.

"Before he died, Whitty wrote some pretty suggestive stuff about your relationship with Elizabeth Salt."

Danny shrugged.

"Was it true?" Michael pressed.

"Sure, babe. The stuff about Lizzie and me being a hot number, anyway."

"You mean, you admit you were using her?" Michael's tone revealed his distaste.

"Using? Who's using who, babe? Does the chicken use

the egg or does the egg use the chicken? Elizabeth Salt and I had a perfect arrangement. She got her kicks in the sack, and I got my movie, *Subway.* What's wrong with that?"

Michael frowned. "And what about the secret Whitty mentioned?"

"Secret? Bull. I don't know what he was talking about. Liz and I were fucking. Period."

"But what about her and her connections?"

"Can't help you there. I know she has some powerful friends, a rich daddy, and a list of husbands. What do you want from me? Whether one of those husbands was the Godfather or one of his sons, I don't know. Go ask her."

"Just a couple more questions, Mr. Blue. Where were you right before the screening. About eight-thirty or nine A.M.?"

"Getting laid. What else do you do at that hour?"

"Do you mind telling me who was queen for the day?"

"No problem. Liz. But not for the day, babe, just for the morning."

Sara shook her head. This guy belonged under glass in some laboratory somewhere.

"And where did you go right after the screening?" Michael asked.

"I had a date."

"With whom?"

"Sorry, babe, that one I can't tell you. It might bust up a marriage and leave a very lovely lady absolutely penniless."

One of the young men with the walkie-talkies suddenly appeared. "Sorry to interrupt, Danny, but we're ready."

Danny rose. "Would you like to watch us do this shot?" His question seemed to be directed to Sara.

Sara looked at Michael. He nodded. "Sure. Why not? Besides, I'd like a few minutes with Gdansk."

Danny Blue ushered Michael and Sara across the quiet cloistered garden and back into the dark passageways leading to the movie set. As they walked, she suddenly felt a finger working its way insistently between her buttocks. She stopped short.

"What's the matter?" Michael asked.

Sara glared at Danny Blue. "Nothing," she said between clenched teeth.

Danny Blue lowered his lids seductively, and the three walked on. "Later, babe," he whispered to her when Michael was out of earshot. "I knew you'd change your mind. I can tell you're hot, that you're gonna be something special."

"Not to you," Sara hissed, turning on her heels.

The set was a madhouse, somehow even more crowded than it had been earlier. In the center of the garden, Enso and Maria were deep in conversation with a man in a beret standing by the big 70-millimeter Panavision camera. His T-shirt read: "Watch the birdie."

"How about one of those for you?" Michael smiled at Sara.

Rick, the stunt coordinator, was shouting instructions to a group of men who were laying down stacks of corrugated cardboard to protect and cushion the stuntman about to leap from the roof.

The stuntman himself was standing in a corner with the star, Gyorgii Gdansk. In their brown cassocks the two men could indeed have been monks deep in a heated theological argument. But no one would have mistaken them for men of the cloth when, quite suddenly and simultaneously, they removed their cassocks, threw them down to the stone floor and, wearing only their bikini underwear—one in a black set, the other in blue—began flexing their muscles for each other.

"Okay, Twinkle-toes," the stuntman challenged Gyorgii in a voice so loud that the technicians halted their tasks and turned around to see what was happening. "Can you do this with your dorsal fins?"

The stuntman then turned so that his back faced Gyorgii. He wiggled first the muscle under his left wing, then the one under his right. Each muscle jumped up and down a couple of times before the stuntman turned his face toward Gyorgii again. Now he began rotating his pectorals simultaneously in complete circles. The act was just like a stripper's. All he needed, Sara thought, was a pair of tassels.

Gyorgii now performed the very same motions—only faster and smoother. "Easy! Vot's so hard, vot?" he said airily. Then he drew himself up to his full height, extended his right leg in front of him so that it made a 45-degree angle with his body and wiggled a thigh muscle. "Try this, Amerikanski," he invited.

The stuntman followed suit but couldn't raise his leg to the sufficient height. Gyorgii looked at him with disdain. "See, Amerikanski, you're soft, like putty. Sissy!" he said disgustedly. He gathered up his cassock and stalked off.

"Googie! Googie!" It was Maria. "*Ciao, bellissimo, ciao*. We see you soon. It in the stars. You be big hit." She blew him a series of farewell kisses. Then, as she and Enzo tramped across the garden, she blew first Danny, then Sara, then Michael their kisses in turn. "*Ciao*, Lieutenant, we see you tomorrow, no?" she called out to Michael at the last minute. "At ten, yes? At Hotel Carlyle, no?"

"Yes," Michael called back.

"Quiet on the set," an assistant director announced into the megaphone. "Morrison, get up to the roof. You can flex your muscles later," he sneered.

It took at least ten more minutes to get Morrison ready for his jump and to obtain the necessary silence. Danny Blue whispered something into his assistant director's ear. Then he whispered something into the ear of the man in the beret. Then he walked off to the side where Gyorgii was sulking and whispered into his ear. Finally, just as Michael left her to make his way to Gyorgii, Danny stopped to whisper to Sara, "Change your mind, babe? My camper in twenty minutes?" His mouth brushed against her cheek.

"Is that the message you've been sending around?" she asked wryly. "If so, it's going to be quite a party."

"No, special for you, babe." He winked, then continued on to his place beside the Panavision camera.

"Okay, everyone, quiet, please," the assistant director ordered through the megaphone. "Places."

Finally, there was quiet. As Sara waited for the camera to grind, she was struck by the complexity of the American moviemaking process and also by the fact that, on the American set, the real stars seemed to be the technicians and the machinery and not the actors at all. In Europe, whenever Claude, the mad Turk, had taken her on location with him, everything had seemed so communal and informal and *intime*. The technology, the equipment had been simple and the actors—even the biggest of stars—had been friends to everyone, not gods and goddesses who held themselves at a distance. Here, in this country, the machinery of the production seemed to overpower everything else, at least, here on this set, at this moment. In fact, Sara thought, the performers seemed to be the most expendable commodity around. For instance, there was Gyorgii Gdansk, the world's greatest Polish dancer and the star of this movie, standing about so bored that he'd had to strip down to his blue bikini underpants just to give himself something to do. Here they were shooting a scene in which he was supposed to be featured but in which a stuntman was playing him instead, making him so unnecessary that he could stand about, as he was now, being interrogated by Michael.

The director didn't seem particularly essential to the process either. When Blue wasn't whispering into Sara's ear, he was just sitting in his chair, at most directing traffic. But when it was all up there on the screen, who would know? Gyorgii Gdansk would get the credit and so, too, would Danny Blue. And though their names would appear briefly on the screen, no one would remember Morrison, Rick Johnson, or the man in the T-shirt that read "Watch the birdie."

"Okay, Morrison, you ready?" the assistant director called up to the stuntman who now hung by his hands from the roof of one of the chapels like a giant bat.

"Yavo!" Morrison called.

"Camera ready," cried the assistant director.

"Scene Ninety-one, Take one," called the clapper, a boy of about twenty who ran in front of the camera, clapping together the wooden hinges of the black-and-white slateboard which indicated the names of the film, director, scene number, and the number of takes as well. In the editing room, Sara knew, this slate would serve to clarify the particular takes. And that precise moment when the clapboard was slammed together would also be used to synch up the sound.

There was total silence. Sara watched intently. She was utterly fascinated. Morrison dove from the roof, his cassock billowing in the air as he sailed into the stack of corrugated cardboard which collapsed under his weight.

There was a hush until Morrison picked himself up, safe and sound. Then everybody began to applaud.

"Not bad!" Danny Blue commended Morrison. "But let's try it again, and this time, Morrison, baby, smile, for Christ's sake." He got up and walked off the set, obviously headed for his camper. Who, Sara wondered, was the lucky lady in waiting?

The hubbub began again. The stunt crew went to work setting up the corrugated cardboard. A cable ripped and had to be replaced. A new roll of film had to be loaded into the camera. "Move that boom a little to the left," an A.D. called to the boom operator.

"Sara! Sara!" she heard Michael shout. "Watch it!"

Then, before she knew it, somebody tackled her and pushed her into a bed of yellow chrysanthemums. It was at that exact moment Sara saw the huge light crash to the grass, just inches from where she lay. *Oh, my God!* Sara thought. *Oh, my God!* She watched the glass shatter into tiny pieces at the very spot where she had been standing.

And then she fainted dead away. . . .

"How do you feel now, birdie?" Michael asked, handing Sara a cup of tea.

"Better." She smiled as she sank back into the cushions of his worn brown corduroy couch. She pulled a plaid wool blanket around her and sipped the warm drink, tasting the brandy he'd added.

Michael's apartment, Sara thought, could have used a woman's touch. The walls were beige and stark, and the tweedy furniture comfortable but uninspired. The only suggestion of taste in the whole place was a splendid Navajo rug on the floor, and the only indication of personality the bookcase at the other end of the room which was crowded with dog-eared paperbacks. A kitchen that looked as if it might have been used twice in three years was off to the left, while off to the right was a small bedroom with a window looking out on an airshaft.

Michael sat down on the couch beside Sara and took her hand.

"And you thought I was imagining things!" she said, shivering at the recollection of her close call.

"Well, it did cross my mind that you might have seen one too many movies."

"I can't believe you!" Sara exploded. "What do you think? You think I'm crazy? Lieutenant Connelly, there is no history of insanity in my family. And never before in my life have I ever thought that anyone was trying to kill me. As further evidence, let me submit the fact that my employer just happened to have been strangled less than a week ago. Coincidence, you say? You're the one who's out of his bloody mind!"

"Take it easy, birdie." Michael patted her hand.

"And stop being so goddamned patronizing," she practically shrieked.

"Calm down. Calm down. I was only teasing. I do believe you. But still . . ."

"One more 'but still,' and I'm going to leave." She could have bitten her tongue. Why did she say such a jerky thing? The thought of going was even worse than the thought of staying.

"I'm sorry," he said. "I stand corrected."

"I accept." She cuddled up to him. "Put your arms around me, will you?"

He grabbed her up in a big bear hug and kissed her forehead. "One good thing about Nigel Whitty's death," he teased, "and that's you." He ran his finger inside the waistband of her jeans. "And I won't let anything happen to you, I promise and I swear."

"You're not Superman."

"But maybe I'm Supercop."

"So tell me, Soupy, whodunit? Who tried to light up my life today?"

Michael leaned back and reached for his beer. "First, let's try to find out why. Because what happened today really changes the picture. When someone broke into your apartment the other night, we figured that they were looking for something. Now, it seems that that thing might have been you."

"But why in God's name would anyone want to kill me?"

"Because they think you have something they want. Like maybe the little black book. Or because they think you know something."

"But I don't know anything," Sara moaned. "Nigel never told me anything."

Michael looked at her. "Maybe he did and you just don't remember."

"You think I'm keeping something from you? No," she

said, "definitely not. Nigel Whitty kept to himself. He may have been the biggest gossip in the world on paper, but in conversation, he never said boo."

"I trust you, birdie," he said. "But somebody else doesn't. Somebody's scared of you."

"But who?" she persisted.

"The most obvious person would be someone who was on the set today: Danny Blue, Gyorgii, Gdansk, Enzo Carbonare, Maria Cortese. But what's obvious isn't necessarily what's right."

"I know," she answered. "I wasn't born yesterday."

"Glad to hear it. You'd be pretty boring if you were," Michael said, putting his arm around Sara and pulling her closer to him. "But what I mean is, it's also possible that it wasn't any of the suspects on the set. You know, it's pretty easy to hire someone to do your dirty work for you. And Fenton Farnabee or even Sammy Nachman could have paid someone to do the job. After all, who in his right mind would take the risk of climbing up on that roof and being seen in broad daylight?"

"Is a murderer ever in his right mind?"

"You got me there, birdie."

The phone rang. Michael reached over and picked up the receiver. "Oh, hello, Ma."

Sara smiled. So Lieutenant Michael Connelly had a mother. Good sign, she thought. Good person, too. Still, Sara's father and mother wouldn't have thought so. A policeman? A cop? "But he's a real Dick Tracy," she would tell them.

"Save that for the Sunday funnies," her father would probably reply.

"Yes, Ma, I did meet Danny Blue," Michael was saying, his voice trying to disguise his amusement. Or was it impatience? "Yes, Ma . . . Was he handsome? I dunno, I guess so . . . No, he doesn't look like Cagney, a lot taller . . . No, he's not Irish, definitely not . . . You want his autograph anyway? All right, I'll get you his autograph. . . ."

So, Sara thought, Michael Connelly's mother was a movie nut. An idea struck her. She hurriedly scribbled a note and handed it to Michael: *"Invite 'Ma' and 'Pa'? to the Radio City Music Hall Wednesday night. Star-studded premiere. I can get tickets."*

Michael smiled as he read the note. "Listen, Ma," he said aloud, "you and Father Fitzgerald free Wednesday night? I've a big treat for you. Danny Blue in person. . . ."

When he got off the phone, he gave Sara a big kiss. "You're a good girl, birdie."

"And you're a good boy, Mikey."

"Ma's gonna love you. You know what she's gonna say to you when she meets you? She's gonna say, 'Miss Sara Nightingale, begorra! You're the spittin' image of Maureen O'Hara.'"

"Maureen O'Hara! You've got to be kidding!" she said. But she ran her fingers through her hair and imagined herself a spitfire in a gingham dress, standing at the doorway of a log cabin.

Michael laughed. "I know what you're thinking. *Rio Grande.*"

She shook her head.

"McClintock."

"Nope, but you've got it down pat for someone who hates movies," she said in amazement. "What happened in your deep dark past?"

"Too many Saturday afternoons at the movies with Ma."

"Real child abuse. Didn't you like any of it?"

"I'll show you what I liked, ma'am." He rose to his full five feet nine and tipped his imaginary ten-gallon hat. "May I be of assistance, ma'am?"

Without waiting for a reply, John Wayne swept Maureen O'Hara into his arms, carrying her across the prairie and into the bedroom that looked out over the airshaft.

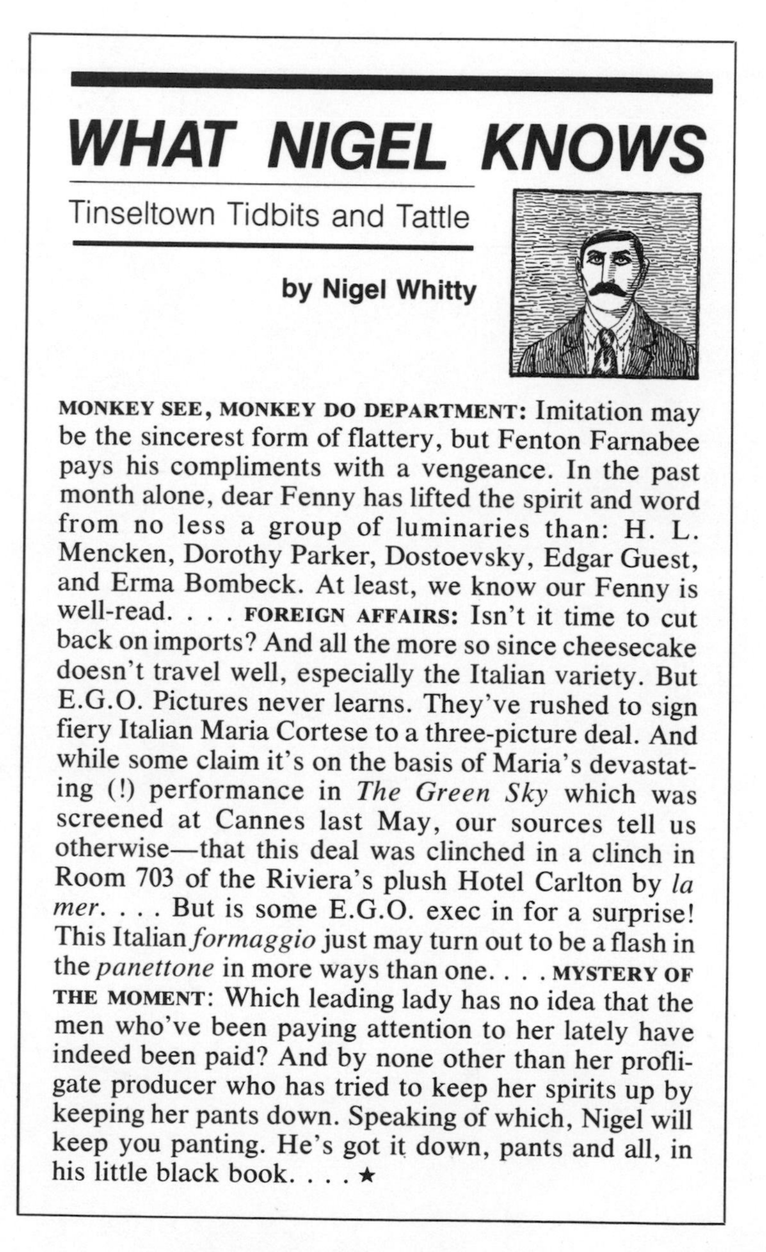

WHAT NIGEL KNOWS

Tinseltown Tidbits and Tattle

by Nigel Whitty

MONKEY SEE, MONKEY DO DEPARTMENT: Imitation may be the sincerest form of flattery, but Fenton Farnabee pays his compliments with a vengeance. In the past month alone, dear Fenny has lifted the spirit and word from no less a group of luminaries than: H. L. Mencken, Dorothy Parker, Dostoevsky, Edgar Guest, and Erma Bombeck. At least, we know our Fenny is well-read. . . . **FOREIGN AFFAIRS:** Isn't it time to cut back on imports? And all the more so since cheesecake doesn't travel well, especially the Italian variety. But E.G.O. Pictures never learns. They've rushed to sign fiery Italian Maria Cortese to a three-picture deal. And while some claim it's on the basis of Maria's devastating (!) performance in *The Green Sky* which was screened at Cannes last May, our sources tell us otherwise—that this deal was clinched in a clinch in Room 703 of the Riviera's plush Hotel Carlton by *la mer*. . . . But is some E.G.O. exec in for a surprise! This Italian *formaggio* just may turn out to be a flash in the *panettone* in more ways than one. . . . **MYSTERY OF THE MOMENT**: Which leading lady has no idea that the men who've been paying attention to her lately have indeed been paid? And by none other than her profligate producer who has tried to keep her spirits up by keeping her pants down. Speaking of which, Nigel will keep you panting. He's got it down, pants and all, in his little black book. . . . ★

9

MICHAEL WAS IN the shower singing "My Wild Irish Rose" and musing on the details of Whitty's latest column when the telephone rang. It was Sara. She'd just gotten home from his apartment only to discover that she'd left her tape recorder behind, and since she was going to interview Alan Savory this morning, she needed it. Could Michael possibly leave the key under the mat so she could pick it up on her way?

"Sure. But if the TV is gone, remember you'll pay."

"It's a deal," she told him.

"Oh, by the by," he said, noticing a red leather case on the couch, "you left your wallet here, too."

"Then I'll pay by credit card, okay?"

"Okay." He paused. "I miss you already."

He really did, he thought, as he readied himself for his meeting with Enzo Carbonare and Maria Cortese. He was really getting involved with Sara Nightingale and a warning bell rang. Get hold of yourself, Connelly. Snotty girls from Grosse Pointe can only give grief to Irish cops from Bay Ridge. Still, when he put the key in an envelope, he couldn't resist drawing a picture of a flower. All he could manage was a daisy, but she'd get the point. He sealed the envelope, slipped it under the doormat, and headed for the Carlyle.

"Pull up a chair, Lieutenant Connelly," Enzo Carbonare advised.

He was sitting at a small breakfast table which had been set up in the elegant Carlyle suite provided for him by E.G.O. Pictures. Maria Cortese, who had a suite of her own across the hall, had joined him to await Michael's arrival. In her Schiaparelli-pink lounging pajamas, she now lay sprawled on the plush gold carpet, thumbing through a copy of *Astrology Today* and munching on a bagel spread with cream cheese.

"Coffee? Tea? Something to eat? Please, Lieutenant, feel free to join us," the director offered graciously.

Michael shook his head and began by asking Enzo Carbonare where he'd learned his perfect English.

"My mother," said Enzo Carbonare, clipping a small bunch of green grapes from the fruit bowl in the center of the table and methodically peeling them one by one, before dropping them into his bowl of corn flakes. "She is British and speaks impeccably. My maternal grandparents were titled, you know. And I spent all my boyhood summers on their estate in Cornwall. Ah," Enzo sighed as he sprinkled some wheat germ on the grape-dotted cereal, "ah, the manor. How I loved hopping and skipping and prancing together with the foxes and pheasants over the hills and dales and moors and marshes of the 1,574.31 acres, including the abbey and the castle and the 8.3 meter moat, that we called home."

Sir Enzo, Michael thought, or was it Lord Carbonare? Was this guy really what he claimed to be? Did they really peel their grapes in England, or wasn't that just a joke in a Mae West movie? And why couldn't Michael take his eyes off this guy's silver hair which looked like two cumulus clouds kissing? Now he got it: it was because those clouds kept moving—just a little to the left, then a little to the right.

"I recall," Enzo went on, "those happy boyhood days. There was a cricket on the hearth, cakes and ale were always in the kitchen. Ah, what great expectations we had, what a paradise we lost!"

Maria, apparently, was untouched by Enzo's reveries.

"Oh, you and your boyhood! You and your cakes! You and your dukes and duchesses," she whined. *"Che annoiato*! How you say in English, how boring!" She tossed aside her copy of *Astrology Today* and joined the two men at the table. "I forget to ask you yesterday, Lieutenant, what is your sign?"

"Maria, please," Enzo said wearily. "Must you?"

"Must I what? Please what?" she huffed. "Who ask your interruption?" She turned to Michael. "Tell me, what is your sign?"

"My sign? My astrological sign?" Michael said, glancing at her magazine.

"*Si*. Sun sign? Moon sign?"

"August. What's that?"

"You mean you never find out your sign? Never chart your course in life?" Maria looked sincerely shocked. "*Impossibile*. You tell Maria your birthday—day and year and minute and place you born—and Maria tell you exactly what life hold in store for you. August what?" She winked.

"August seventh."

"Mmmm." Maria licked her lips. "You Leo. You Lion. Grrr." She growled with delight. "You passion. You sexy hot. What you doing late?"

"Busy, sorry." Michael forced a smile. "But do you mind if we leave the stars just now and get on to Nigel Whitty?"

"*Che annoiato*," Maria sighed.

"How well did you both know Nigel Whitty?"

"Fairly well." "Not at all," both answered simultaneously.

"Can we begin with just you, Signor Carbonare?"

"Actually, it's *Dottore*," Carbonare corrected. "I have a D. Litt. from Oxford and a degree in philosophy from the University at Padua."

"And I have diploma from primary school in Napoli," Maria said, getting up and striding toward the bedroom. "I come back, Lieutenant, when you want talk about me," she said over her shoulder. "Better I leave than fall asleep with yawning."

A moment later, the sound of the television set burst into

the room: "How would you describe your husband making whoopee on your honeymoon night?" asked an unctuous baritone. *"Blazing Saddles? High Anxiety? Midnight Express?"* Gales of laughter answered. "Or would you say, *Magnum Force?"* the voice went on. "Ten seconds, ladies, to write it down on your magic slates . . ."

"Lower the telly, Maria, *per favore,"* Carbonare called out. In response, Maria turned the volume up.

"She's an idiot," Enso announced. "But so are they all. All actors I mean. Pigs, sheep, cattle . . ."

Enzo Carbonare was running through the list of barnyard denizens as Michael got up and closed the door to the bedroom, shutting out the sound. "You were about to tell me something about Nigel Whitty, signor—I mean, *Dottore* Carbonare."

"Yes, of course. How well I knew Nigel Whitty." Enzo Carbonare pushed aside his cereal bowl and reached into the pocket of his blue silk dressing gown which, Michael noticed, bore a crest. He pulled out a small silver box with a similar crest and opened it.

"Would you like some snuff?"

Michael shook his head, no, and watched Carbonare insert some powder into his left nostril. Was it really snuff, or had the noble Carbonare the audacity to be inhaling cocaine right in front of him and offering him to partake as well?

"Well," Carbonare began after a deep whiff, "I first met Whitty, it must have been twenty years ago. At Taormina, at the film festival. I was staying at the palazzo of the Contessa della Zampanude—I was a beautiful young man in those days." As he uttered this last phrase, Carbonare adjusted his floating clouds of hair.

"Anything special happen at Taormina?"

"Nothing, nothing at all," Carbonare said hastily. "It was only a brief encounter." His eyes grew misty. "I only truly got to know Whitty at Cannes, some five years later, at the film festival there. We—that is, my wife and I and my mother—of course weren't staying in Cannes. Rather, we were at my paternal grandparents' villa in Cap d'Antibes, a lovely, quiet *palais*—fifteen marvelous rooms on 2.8 acres with a 4.2 meter wall—that my grandfather won in a game of quoits from the Marquis de Chien-Andalu. The villa is really quite extraordinary, built sometime . . ."

"Can we come back to Whitty?" Michael interrupted.

"Certainly, Lieutenant." Carbonare filled his other nostril.

It had to be snuff, Michael assured himself—if a bit uneasily.

"Where was I?" Carbonare sneezed, then went on. "Oh, yes, when I met Whitty. As I recall, he telephoned for an interview, and I finally agreed to see him—though of course I rarely gave interviews. But he had written an excellent article on my work. In those days, he was a great admirer of mine. Did you know that?"

"Yes. I went over Whitty's old columns and back in the sixties he called you a genius."

"More than a genius. 'A true poet of the cinema,' he wrote. 'One of the finest minds to have embraced and graced this othertimes vulgar technology,'' Carbonare recited proudly. "That was when Whitty had taste and intelligence, when he was a moral force, an intellectual power, an esthetic guide, a true critic, a . . ."

"He changed his mind about you though, didn't he?"

"Changed his mind!" Carbonare exclaimed. "Lost his mind is more the point, Lieutenant. Nigel Whitty became a pure and unadulterated philistine. When my masterpiece, *I Scaloppini*, came out, he was completely unable to understand it. Here was a film that changed the entire face of cinema and Whitty, fixated on cinema's weary old features, simply was unable to recognize it."

"Are you saying then that there was nothing personal between you two? That the whole cause of Whitty's venom was only a movie?"

"Only a movie!" Enzo Carbonare stood up so abruptly

that his box of snuff fell to the floor. "*I Scaloppini* only a movie! I just told you that it changed the entire face of cinema. It was revolutionary, it was brilliant. It had no drama, it had no actors. It was a visionary voyage shot entirely inside a butcher shop—183.5 minutes of raw red shanks, of richly textured tongues, of shining gelatinous hooves, of meter upon meter of gleaming sausage, of row upon row of cavernous ribs, of gluey white intestines, of marbleized rumps, and all these images accompanied by a *musique concrète* score, featuring the magnified sounds of the digestive track at work. And you call it only a movie!" Enzo Carbonare flung his arms in the air.

Michael stared in amazement. Another loony to add to the bin. He sighed wearily. "Can we get back to Whitty?"

"Whitty? Of course, Whitty. Whitty, who I foolishly believed was my intellectual soulmate, who I stupidly allowed to see an early rough-cut of *I Scaloppini*, who then committed the most flagrant violation of professional ethics ever flagrantly violated! Do you know what he did? He informed the world before my film was even in final shape that it was 'stupid, doltish, obtuse, dense, sottish, blockish, and clumpish.' He clearly used his *Roget's Thesaurus* to muster every insult he could unearth! Worse, he bribed and bullied the entire critical establishment into agreeing with him."

"How could he?" Michael was incredulous.

Enzo Carbonare shook his head, over which a cloud suddenly seemed to be hovering. Actually, it was his toupee which in his excitement had moved precariously toward his right ear.

"I have no idea how," Enzo Carbonare said, breathing deeply and lowering his voice which had reached a high and near-hysterical pitch. "But I assure you that was precisely what he did. And since the only people more stupid than the critics are the public, the public too condemned my film. And since the only people more idiotic than the public are the brokers and the bankers, I was unable to find backing for my future work. And since the only people more imbecilic than backers are actors, no one at all would work with me anyway. Quite simply, Lieutenant, thanks to that scorpion Nigel Whitty, *I Scaloppini*, which everyone in my entire family, including my mother, agreed was a work of absolute genius, was slaughtered and went unheeded, while I, its magnificent creator, was forced into silence for six long years."

"After six long years, you must have been worried about the critics' reaction to your new movie," Michael suggested. "And you must have been especially worried about Nigel Whitty. Suppose he attacked *The Green Sky* the way he had attacked *I Scaloppini*? Killing him was one way to make sure he didn't."

"Don't be absurd, Lieutenant. I wouldn't have lowered myself. I wouldn't have dirtied my hands on his typewriter ribbon. Besides, even that deteriorated dunce would have had to have loved *The Green Sky*. It is, after all, an irresistible masterpiece. Everyone who has seen it adores it—my entire family and especially my mother."

Michael couldn't be sure, but it suddenly struck him that he had seen a review of *The Green Sky* somewhere among Sara's collection of Whitty's columns that were yet to run. Sloppy of him not to have checked it out before coming here.

"What if I told you, *Dottore*, that Whitty saw *The Green Sky* before his death and . . ."

"What? Against my expressed wishes? I told the publicists not to let him into the screening room." Enzo Carbonare's eyes widened and his face flushed. He stopped, adjusted his toupee, and sat down at the breakfast table. "I don't care what he thought. I still didn't murder him, Lieutenant."

Maybe, maybe not. But a guy who had made a movie about a butcher shop just might have become a butcher himself. . . . It was time, Michael decided, to change the subject.

"Tell me about Maria Cortese now. How well did she know Whitty?"

"Not at all. She had never met him. She is new to film, you know. She is my discovery."

"She's pretty old for a discovery."

"Pretty old? She's thirty-three. Or thirty-four. Or thirty-five. And even if she were forty, remember, my dear fellow, in Europe our leading ladies are women—not girls as they are over here in your infantile country."

"If you don't mind my asking, what's your relationship with Miss Cortese?"

"I don't mind at all." Enzo Carbonare took a sip of tea. "She is my discovery, as I told you. She may be an idiot, but she is a brilliant actress. And our relationship is completely professional."

"Nothing more?"

"Nothing more."

"You're telling me," Michael prodded, "that you've been traveling around with that bombshell and your relationship is strictly professional?"

Enzo Carbonare laughed. "Really, my dear fellow, you seem to forget I am a dedicated artist, so dedicated, in fact, that I have abstained from sexual relations for twenty-five years, even with my voluptuous wife, the former actress Sophia Pisani who is also the finest gourmet cook south of the Alps. And I have done so for the simple reason that I do not wish to drain off any of my energies from my art."

Just at that moment, Maria opened the bedroom door and stood posing on the threshhold.

"What do you mean, handsome Lieutenant, keeping Maria waiting like this?" she said to Michael dramatically. "My TV program finished and my mind tell me it is time to go to Bergdorf Goodman where I see bright happy colors and where the lucky number of day is 1072—a discount price if fortune laughs on me."

Michael shook his head. What the hell was she saying? All he knew was that he'd better start talking to her now. She was obviously the restless type.

"I hear my name mention too. How old I am? Old as I feel and that is nineteen and seven months. But I have, Lieutenant, the experience of much more years, of *molti* lives."

She pranced over and kissed Enzo passionately on his forehead, right under his floating clouds. Carbonare stood up. Michael could see from the bulge underneath his dressing gown that twenty-five years' abstention hadn't made it any easier for him. What dedication, he marveled.

"I bore you, Enzo? You no want me to have turn, *carissimo?*" Maria walked over to Michael and sat down next to him, putting her hand on his thigh. "These directors are so *explosivo*, so temperamental, so two-sided, especially when they are Gemini. You know what I speak?" She winked and began working her hand upward and inward toward Michael's crotch.

He pulled away, but Maria's hand followed him.

"But where I was?" She smiled and licked her lips. "Oh, yes, my many lives. You want to hear whole story of my stormy weather, Lieutenant? Maybe we have dinner together. You can cook? I come to your place."

"I don't have a kitchen," Michael said hastily.

"We order pizza then?"

"Maybe," he said, putting his hand on hers and pushing it down toward his knee and holding it there firmly.

"You don't know what you missing," Maria said, her voice now at its smokiest. "Oh, well, story of my many lives. You know I was urchin in Napoli. I had to sing song for my dinner. You want to hear song I used to sing?" Maria suddenly burst into a full-bodied rendition of "Arrivederci, Roma," then stopped as abruptly as she had begun. "They used to throw canneloni at me and I was so hungry I scramble for it on cobblestones. Then I was streetwalker, and if you think my feet bloody as urchin . . ."

The telephone rang, and Carbonare walked over to pick up the receiver. Michael grabbed a throw pillow and threw it across his lap.

"If it for me," Maria called out, flapping a long arm in

Enzo's direction, then swirling around and resting her head on the pillow on Michael's lap, "don't forget I here."

Who could ever forget her presence, Michael thought, even if they tried? She was the most overstated human being he had ever met, her gestures were so extreme and emphatic, her voice so loud and her tone so melodramatic. And her Italianness! It seemed as forced, as phony even, as a TV ad for frozen pizza. But he had a weakness for frozen pizza, and for Maria too. What the hell was happening to him? Was he, Michael Connelly, going Hollywood?

"It's for you, Lieutenant Connelly," Enso said.

Maria's head flopped to the couch as Michael got up. It was Sara, calling from Alan Savory's townhouse.

"Come quick," her words tumbled out excitedly. Biffy Adams was beating Alan Savory to a pulp with one of her batons.

By the time Michael arrived at Savory's townhouse, the place was swarming with police. The battle cries had been so blood-curdling that nine concerned neighbors had each called for help.

Sara greeted Michael with relief and began to pour out her story. She had stopped off at Michael's to pick up her tape recorder, then grabbed a cab to Savory's, arriving just at the moment Biffy Adams did—in fact, their two taxis had almost collided.

"Who the hell are you?" Biffy Adams had said when they both tried to push Savory's bell at the same time. "This morning's cocksucker?"

"I beg your pardon?" Sara retorted. "I am a journalist."

"Yeah, everybody's a journalist these days," Biffy sneered. She drew her long narrow Adidas athletic bag over her shoulder, almost knocking Sara over and, at the point that Savory's houseboy opened the door, charging inside like a racehorse breaking from the gate.

Unlike Biffy, the houseboy, Sonny, was cordial, and

even brought Sara coffee while she waited in the study for Savory to appear. Twenty minutes passed and then, clad in blue paisley Lastex bathing trunks, a French-cut navy boat-necked T-shirt, and seven gold chains—including one around his waist—Savory sped into the study, slamming and locking the door behind him without even noticing Sara's presence. A moment later, someone began to pound wildly. It was Biffy, who was also screaming at the top of her lungs. Savory started screaming back and, after a lot of noise, finally unlocked the door. Biffy raced into the room, only to be greeted by Savory's fist which landed somewhere in the vicinity of her right eye. She was clearly taken aback, but not for long, because in a moment she was unzipping her Adidas bag, taking out a baton and lunging at Savory, shrieking like a banshee. Sonny ran into the room, trying to ward off her attack. She whipped around, doubled up her knee, and let loose with a left to the groin that sent Sonny reeling across the floor, writhing in agony.

Sara didn't know what to do. Biffy was blocking her escape through the door, Sonny her route to the telephone. She finally decided to risk a move, but just as she began to edge her way around the room, Savory came running toward her.

"Who the hell are you?" he'd screamed, grabbing her and pushing her between him and Biffy.

Biffy, however, was not to be deterred. She brought her baton down on Sara, who collapsed under the blow and suddenly found herself sprawled next to Sonny. Now Biffy had what she wanted: clear access to Savory's head. The baton went flying as gold chains went clanking. Screams resounded through the house and, almost simultaneously, police sirens through the street outside.

The baton had left a bump on Sara's head.

"Let me feel it," Michael said, as they sat by the pool. He ran his fingers beneath her tangle of red curls. "It's a big one."

"I'll live." She smiled.

"I'm sure, but let's play it safe. How many fingers do you see?" he asked, holding up his index and middle fingers.

"Three and a half."

"C'mon, birdie, how many?"

"Nine. I feel fine. Really, Michael."

"Still, I want you to just sit here and rest. Promise me you won't make a move while I go in and talk to the happy couple."

"Okay." She looked up wearily. "But I wouldn't promise a thing if I hadn't forgotten my armor and breastplate."

"And obviously your baton, too," Michael laughed.

He started toward the door and was surprised to hear himself whistling. Now where had he heard that tune before?

Biffy Adams and Alan Savory faced each other in Savory's large chrome and glass living room like boxers in a ring, flanked on both sides by uniformed policemen. Savory held ice to his head, Biffy held ice to her eye. Her blond hair was matted on her forehead, there was a large bruise on her cheek, and with her swollen eye, little remained of the wholesome, pretty majorette who had won 150 baton-twirling contests with a flick of her large-boned wrist. In fact, at the moment, she looked a lot more like a brawling streetwalker: there was a huge tear across her white dress, exposing the blue flowered pattern of her bra, and one of her stockings was ripped to shreds. As for Savory, his boat neck had been torn into a scoop neck, and his nose was clotted with dried blood. There were welts all over his arms and legs, interrupting their smooth tanned surface.

"Lieutenant, it's good to see you." Savory looked up from under his ice pack, sniffed twice, and gave Michael a cordial smile. It was as if he were greeting the president of the First National Bank.

Biffy Adams squinted from behind her ice pack. "Who

the hell is that?" Her good eye focused on Michael now. "Oh, Lieutenant, glad you're here. I've been telling these jerks in blue to lock this slime up"—she glowered at Savory—"and getting nowhere."

"Lock *me* up? I'm pressing charges for assault and battery, you bitch!"

"You're pressing charges? That's a laugh."

"Okay, gang," Michael said, "let's quiet it down. Let's take it one at a time." He turned to the policemen. "I can handle this now. Why don't you men just wait outside?"

The policemen left and Michael turned to Savory. "How about you first?"

"*Him* first? *Me* first! Ladies first!"

"Lady! You're no lady, you're a slut, a whore."

"Look who's calling who names." Biffy gave him the finger and Savory responded by gesturing with his arm until, Michael thought, they began to look like an X-rated mime troupe.

"Knock it off," Michael commanded. "Look, if we can't do this in an orderly fashion, I'm going to have to separate you. I just thought you each had the right to hear the other one's story."

Under threat of expulsion, Biffy sat on her finger and let Alan Savory talk.

"It's very simple," Savory began, "since I am totally innocent. I was preparing to take my morning swim when suddenly this woman who, I unfortunately must admit, happens to still be my wife, flew into my bedroom, hurling obscenities at me. I had no idea what she wanted."

"You had no idea what I wanted? None? Not after you instructed the goddamn bank not to let me draw on my account—an account holding money that I myself earned through my baton-twirling."

"What? Four dollars and ninety-eight cents? The money you earned in baton-twirling can't even keep you in batons," Savory sneered.

"I don't need much to live on." Biffy's tone suddenly

became self-righteous. She put one hand on a hip and announced, "I'm a very simple person."

"You can say that again, you moron," Savory said, reaching into a drawer in a small table nearby and pulling out a packet of Tums. "Would you care for one, Lieutenant?"

"Thanks," Michael said. He was going to need more than Tums after this.

"Don't try to change the subject." Biffy spoke up sharply. "Look, pipsqueak, I want my money and that's it. And if you don't give it to me, the Lieutenant here will arrest you for bilking me out of my hard-earned personal property."

"Oh, shut up, you cunt," Savory hissed. "For the hundredth time, I don't intend to allow you and your football team to clean me out."

"You deserve to be cleaned out, you pig, after what I've been through." Biffy's voice had begun to climb.

"Been through!" Savory spat through his snow-capped teeth. "Everything's been through you, but what the hell have you been through?"

"He's asking what I've been through." Biffy turned to Michael, adjusting her ice pack. "Six months of this peashooter coming into the sheets, that's all."

"You have the foulest mouth in Christendom, you cunt," Savory exploded.

"Glad to see you can get it up sometimes," she returned. "But if you'll notice, Lieutenant Connelly, it's only when other people, preferably other people of the male sex, are in the room. Right?" She addressed Savory now. "Why don't you tell the Lieutenant about Whitty and your little gangbang?"

Savory stood up, rattled his chains, and sniffed. "You filthy twat! Who are you to talk? You who've allowed the entire Dallas football team to run ninety-yard dashes up your cunt while you lay there twirling your baton."

"Hold it, you two." Things were getting out of control. Michael had been so stunned, he'd almost forgotten that he was more than a mere ringside spectator. As much as he'd seen, as jaded as he sometimes thought he was, it still offended him that a woman who looked as sweet and wholesome as Biffy Adams could sound so foul and ugly. What a pair! They could run each other ragged, and anyone else as well. But he wasn't going to let them run him off the track. "Let's go back a few steps," he instructed sternly. "Back to Whitty. What did Biffy mean, Savory?"

"I don't know what she meant, she's demented."

"I meant one rainy night when you and Whitty brought home those seven dwarfs . . ."

"There were only three, you birdbrain."

"Three, seven, what's the difference? The point is, they were able to suck your cock without getting down on their knees."

Michael didn't know whether to call Bellevue or the Vice Squad.

"Or what about the time," Biffy continued her harangue, "that you brought home that creep with his leather jacket and two great Danes. Whatever Whitty said, I didn't hear *Hamlet* coming from the bedroom."

Savory put down his ice pack, picked a clump of congealed blood from the corner of a nostril, snorted, and sauntered over to his desk. He opened a mother-of-pearl humidor. "Cigar, Lieutenant?"

Biffy popped out of her seat. "Don't change the subject, you prick."

Savory walked across the room and pushed her back into her seat. "Shut your hole." He flashed a smile at Michael. "How about some brandy?"

"Never drink while I'm on duty," Michael said lamely. "Look . . ."

"You don't mind if I help myself, do you?"

"I'm afraid I do."

It was all going too far, Michael thought, and he had better take control. "Now if you two don't sit down and start answering some questions for me, I'm going to take you both down to the precinct and book you for assault, battery, and suspicion of murder. Now, let's begin at the beginning. Miss Adams, just exactly why did you come here today?"

"Because that prick cut off my bank account and had his lawyer send me a letter telling me I wasn't getting one penny from him."

Michael turned to Savory, who had just lit a cigar and was now sitting back on a leather club chair, puffing away. "Is that true, Savory?"

"In a manner of speaking, Lieutenant. Oh, she's getting something, but if this little gold digger thinks I'm going to pay the way for the Miami Dolphins or any other of her favorite jocks, she's mistaken me for an athletic supporter." He smiled, evidently pleased with his little joke. "And do I look like an athletic supporter to you, Lieutenant?"

"You sure do," Biffy interrupted, "a filthy, dirty one, too."

Well, Michael thought, if she was going to keep on talking, it might as well be about the case. He turned to her now. "Last time I met you, Miss Adams, you suggested that your husband strongly disliked, even hated, Nigel Whitty. Now you're suggesting that they were good friends instead. Which is it?"

"Both. Sex or his sick version of it was Alan's way of buttering Whitty up . . ."

"Can you explain what she means by that, Savory?"

"Haven't the vaguest." Alan Savory puffed a smoke ring into the room.

"Well, I have," Biffy interrupted. "This shit"—she threw a disgusted glance in Savory's direction—"would do anything to get a good review, except maybe make a good movie. He'd kiss Whitty's ass, he'd kiss Whitty's birthmark, he'd even suck Whitty's cock, for all I know."

"Ha! All you know, you moron, you could print on the head of a baton." Savory turned to Michael. "Sure you won't have a cordial, Lieutenant?"

"I got something better for you than a cordial," Biffy said, getting up and walking over to one of the several mirrors in the room and beginning to smooth her hair. "Get a load of this, Lieutenant. You know how much a good review was worth to this chump? Not only a case of clap every other month, but twenty grand a year. The same twenty grand he wouldn't even think of giving me."

"Twenty grand." Alan Savory's voice was suddenly laden with syrup. "Oh, my Biffy, you underestimate yourself. I was thinking of a much more generous settlement."

"Don't try to sweet-talk me. I'm not for sale. And neither, you dumb ox, was Whitty." She looked straight at Michael. "Lieutenant," she said, "did you ever hear of anyone so stupid that he spends twenty grand a year on a critic, greases him up in every other way, and still lets that goddamn sadist get away with giving his movies lousy reviews?"

"Maybe you got tired of letting that critic get away with it, Savory," Michael suggested.

Alan Savory took a deep breath. "I didn't kill Nigel Whitty, if that's what you're insinuating, Lieutenant," he said in a perfectly calm voice.

"But you had good reason, didn't you? He was about to dump on your most expensive movie yet—*Allergic to Love*. And after three failures in a row, you really needed a hit, didn't you? He was also about to turn that blind item of his about you and your wife into a full-blown exposé. And that would have been an embarrassment, wouldn't it have? And finally, you were getting just a little bit tired of paying out twenty grand a year, year in, year out, for nothing. And so one morning you decided to do Whitty in. Right?"

"Wrong. You're crazy as she is." Alan Savory took a long puff on his cigar. "Look, Lieutenant, I've been a lot of things in my life. I've been a camp counselor, I've been a waiter in the Catskills, a stock boy in my father's shoe factory, a door-to-door salesman, a stage hand in summer stock, a CPA for Perdue Pictures, and one of its chief executives. But I've never, never, I swear to you, been a murderer."

"But you've been a hell of a liar. Now, you want to give it to me straight about Whitty?"

Savory was silent for a minute. He puffed on his cigar. "What do you mean?"

"I mean, cut out this bullshit about your relationship with Whitty. You were like two peas in a pod, I believe you said. And also that you loved him like a brother . . ."

"Like a brother?" Biffy snapped. "I'd say more like a *sister*."

Her timing was off. Michael turned to her. "Shut up, Miss Adams, just shut up." Now he looked Savory straight in the eye. "You hated Whitty's guts, didn't you?"

Savory emitted on audible sigh. "Yes, I hated him. Year after year, he'd always say to me, 'I'm going to love your next one, I'm going to make you a fortune. Stick with me, Alan, and you'll go down in history as the world's greatest producer. It'll just cost you!' And every year, it cost me a little more. He tortured me, but he never came through. You know, Lieutenant, I've never been so happy in my life to see anyone die. But I didn't kill him. I promise you, I didn't kill him."

"Oh, didn't you?" Biffy Adams reached into her bag and pulled out a little black book. "See, Lieutenant. Here's the proof. It's Whitty's, and I found it in Alan's bedroom." She handed the book to Michael.

He opened it and thumbed through it. On the first page, carefully printed in blue ballpoint ink, were the words, "NIGEL WHITTY—CONFIDENTIAL." There followed a series of printed names, including those of immediately recognizable celebrities, next to whom were entered phone numbers and an occasional note: *"Sardi's, 6/27—with Jackie O." "21 Club, 9/17—with 007."* There was even a line on Savory himself: *"Remember, collect $10,000. Overdue."*

After the list of names were pages and pages filled with dots and dashes, slashes, little triangles, and other cryptic marks.

"A lot of it seems to be in code," Biffy said.

"I see," Michael remarked. "Want to take a quick look at this, Savory?" He handed the book over.

Savory leafed through the pages. "Come off it, Biffy. This isn't even Whitty's handwriting." He began to laugh.

"How do you know, you shithead? With this evidence, you're gonna fry."

Biffy turned to Michael. "Lieutenant," she said, "I'd appreciate some professional advice. Do you think that in the long run I'd benefit financially as a divorcée? Or, would I do better"—she smiled sweetly in the direction of the man she had just beaten black and blue—"as a merry widow?"

10

Before she even saw them that evening, Sara knew that Fenton had cats. Large and airy as his Central Park West penthouse was, with its high-beamed ceilings, its ornate marble fireplaces, and wall of stained-glass windows opening onto a richly planted terrace, it still had that telltale odor. There were two of them—sister white Angoras named Gertrude and Alice, Fenton explained, and in the snow-white Angora sweater he had donned for the occasion, he looked just like their clone. They were clearly part of the family, to be included in all festivities. Each cat found herself a comfortable spot on the mounds of oversized, overstuffed, multihued Oriental pillows that lay scattered on the floor of Fenton's den, and it was evident that they intended to watch the movie Fenton was showing right along with the guests. At the moment these included not only Sara and Michael but also Richard Singer-Murray and Vernon and Beatrix Leakey.

Michael hadn't really wanted to come to Fenton's and had even indicated to Sara that it might look a little peculiar—after all, these people were suspects in a murder case that he happened to be investigating. But Sara was convinced it would be helpful to him. The more he saw of these people on their own ground, she told him, the more he'd understand what made them tick. Moreover, she would be there. And so, finally, he gave in.

It also took a little persuasion to get Fenton to agree to her plan. He was sour enough about the item in Whitty's column that morning—she and Richard were his dear friends, he complained, and they certainly could have edited it out. But Fenny himself had told her, and more than once, she reminded him, that, "It doesn't matter what they say about you, as long as they spell your name right." Yes, well, he supposed so. But as for bringing that Lieutenant along, he just didn't know what to say. "Think of the undercurrent, of the tension. It'll add some excitement to the evening," she had argued. Fenton had thought awhile. "Okay, why not. It'll certainly make the Leakeys squirm," he giggled maliciously.

And indeed it did. For now, as Fenton sat in what he described as his modified lotus position pouring drinks from a Moroccan brass tray in the center of his den, Sara couldn't help overhearing Beatrix and Vernon buzzing furiously about Michael's presence. The Leakeys' complaints didn't command her attention for very long, however; she was much too distracted by the extraordinary amount of equipment in Fenton's den which turned it into, he announced with a broad grin, his little electronic paradise.

All around were media and more media: at one end of the room, a Sony Trinitron television, an Advent screen, a Betamax, and a movie screen; at the other end, a 16-millimeter sound projector and a home video camera; while along both sides were a tape deck, a stereo and speakers, and shelves filled with records, cans of film, tapes of various sizes, and several rows of oversized books with titles like *The MGM Story, The Warner Brothers' Story, Selznick's Hollywood, Lana Turner: Her Greatest Films, Marilyn,* and *The Encyclopedia of Trivia, Volumes One and Two.*

"The necessities of my life—" Fenton gestured extravagantly. "Fenny's day just isn't complete without a dance from Ginger, a song from Judy, a sashay from Mae, or a moment of emotional truth from the divine Tallulah."

The bell rang. As Fenton excused himself, Sara turned to Michael. He was looking through the titles of Fenton's film cans. "Interesting," he whispered. "There must be at least a hundred murder mysteries here: *Murder at the Van-*

ities; Murder on the Orient Express; Murder, My Sweet; Murder, Most Foul; Murder by Death; Murder in Thornton Square; Murder at the Gallop; Murder at St. Trinian's; Murder, She Said; Murder, Ahoy; The Alphabet Murders; There Are Murderers Among Us. A definite obsession."

She nodded and Michael returned to his titles. But she didn't take her eyes off him. He wasn't handsome, she thought, but he had a nice face, a reassuring face, a face she felt comfortable with, a face she liked to kiss. If only he wasn't a detective! Of course, Bogart had been a detective. Still, it wasn't the same—not at all.

Fenny flounced back into the room. "Two girls and a sailor, ta-ta-ta-ta!" On each side of him stood a young man, each perceptibly balding, each with a large mustache and trim beard obscuring what seemed to be nondescript features. So alike were these two that they might have been indistinguishable had it not been for the fact that one wore black leather from head to toe while the other was draped in burgundy velvet. "Meet Marlon and Monty," Fenny announced.

The young man in burgundy velvet went around the room, shaking everyone's hand and glowing, "Hi, I'm Monty." Marlon, the one in the black leather, chains, key rings, and bandana hankies, stood sulking in front of the Advent screen.

"This one has seen one motorcycle movie too many," Richard Singer-Murray, who had somehow managed to make his way through the pillows and over to Sara, whispered in her ear.

"Well, dearie, stop playing the prima donna and take a seat," Fenton invited Marlon.

"Oh, you meanie," Marlon answered in a peculiarly high-pitched voice. "You know I can't sit down in these pants. They make me perspire."

"Well, if you want to stand there like a rubber dolly while on the very screen before you Bette Davis scratches her way to Chicago, suit yourself," Fenny shrugged.

"Why, Fenton, how wonderful! Are we really going to

see *Beyond the Forest*? Wherever did you get a print of that one?" Vernon exclaimed excitedly.

"Isn't that the one that was such a flop it washed Bette Davis up at Warner's?" Richard Singer-Murray looked to Vernon for confirmation.

"That's the one all right. Did you know that it was Nigel Whitty's favorite film, Fenny?" Vernon turned to his host.

"Of course I knew, sweetheart. In fact, you might call tonight 'Fenny's Memorial Tribute to Nigel Whitty.'"

"You turncoat," Beatrix exclaimed. "Had I known, I would never have come."

"Oh, don't be nasty, Bea," Vernon chided. "Besides, this film was the subject of one of my first seminal essays: 'Rosa Moline's Crawl to Chicago: Linear Narrative, Low-Angle Shots, and the Ideological Struggle.'"

"Frankly, Vernon," Beatrix returned, "as much as I hated him and as much as I hate to admit it, I always preferred Nigel's essay on the film to yours. It seemed, well, less forced, more astute."

"Nigel's essay? What was it called?" Sara asked. "I don't think I ever read it."

"You don't know his 'The Magic of the Forest, the Myth of the Smokestack, or Phallic Failure in *Beyond the Forest*,'" Beatrix cried out. "It was positively brilliant. A remarkable piece of work."

"Why must you always gravitate toward the sexual aspect of things?" Vernon complained.

"When are we going to get this show on the road?" Marlon asked from a pillow he had finally eased onto.

Fenton looked at his watch. "Well, we were waiting for Becky."

"And for *mia cara*," Richard called.

"For who?" asked Monty.

"Maria Cortese. Haven't you heard, we're an item?"

Monty shook his head, and Fenton decided to start the film. As they sat in the dark watching the belching smokestacks of a Hollywood version of a mill town, Michael moved closer to Sara.

"You okay?" he whispered. "How's the head?"

"Fine. How's yours?" she whispered back.

"Reeling. But it's a job, isn't it? I could always get caught in a shoot-out."

"Am I part of the job, too?"

"Yeah, you're the real back-breaker," he said right into her ear. "The real heavy work."

"Aaahhh," Monty called out. "Here it comes: 'What a dump,'" he enunciated in perfect unison with Bette Davis.

"Oohh, oohh," Marlon exclaimed, and also chimed in with the movie: "'You're for the birds, Rosa Moline. You're for the birds.'"

"Uughh, she's in drag. Look at the fright wig," Monty squealed.

"Absolutely grotesque—it's a classic," Fenton inserted.

Fenton was right. *Beyond the Forest* was a classic all right, thought Sara, a classic of overstatement. For there on the screen, in ominous *film noir* black-and-whites, Bette Davis played hussy to the hilt. Her Rosa Moline, an American Emma Bovary, was a monument of selfish dissatisfaction. And to watch her push her way out of the banality of her small-town life and toward the heady excitement of Chicago was to witness screen bitchery at its shrillest.

So this was Nigel Whitty's favorite movie! Sara couldn't understand it. It was a joke, wasn't it—both the film itself and Nigel's loving it? Or was she missing something? Was the whole thing over her head? Or under it?

"What do you think of this movie?" she whispered to Michael.

"I hate it," he whispered back. "Nigel Whitty and I don't have the same taste. Except in Gal Fridays."

"Hmmmphf! I wasn't his Gal Friday—I was his administrative assistant." She tried to force a little indignation into her whisper.

"Did you ever see anyone who wanted to get anywhere as much as Rosa Moline wanted to get to Chicago?" asked Fenton. "Heavens to Betsy, you'd think Chicago were Cannes, Tahiti, Singapore, Rio . . ."

My God, thought Sara. She had completely forgotten to tell Michael what Lynn had said about Nigel wanting to go to Rio—and wanting to go almost as much as Rosa Moline wanted to go to Chicago.

Somewhere toward the end of the third reel, the doorbell rang. And just as Bette Davis, racked with fever and pain after her secret and terrible abortion, crawled toward the railroad in a desperate last effort to get to her Midwestern mecca, Becky Luna wobbled into the room. On screen, the train whistled its arrival, while in real life Becky Luna whined hers. On screen, Rosa Moline fell onto the track, while in life Becky Luna fell over the brass Moroccan tray, passing out on the pillows.

"Get some smelling salts, Fenton," Beatrix ordered.

"Oh, leave her alone," Fenton said, turning on the lights and clicking off the projector. "It's her way of getting attention. She simply couldn't stand Bette stealing the spotlight."

Michael stood up and went over to Becky. "You may be right, Fenton, but I think we ought to take care of her anyway." He lifted Becky from the lavender pillow and carried her into Fenton's bedroom, laying her down on the plush beaver bedthrow. Both Sara and Fenton followed him. "Smelling salts?" Michael reminded him.

Fenton went into the bathroom and returned with a small bottle.

"Some black coffee would be a good idea, too," Michael ordered.

Fenton nodded and pranced off in the direction of the kitchen. "Don't go away, Becky, sweets," he called behind him to the still unconscious woman.

Michael unscrewed the top of the smelling salts, raised Becky's head, and waved the bottle under her nose. She shook her head, and her eyes flew open.

"Where am I?" she said theatrically, precisely as if she were reading a line for an audition.

"In Fenton Farnabee's bedroom," Michael told her.

"Oh, no," Becky Luna moaned. "I didn't, did I? Not

Fenton?" She rolled her eyes up at the mirrored ceiling and down again to the walls draped in black velvet, past the electrified sconces shaped like naked human arms. She passed out again.

Again, Michael put the smelling salts under her nose. "Why don't you get a wet washcloth from the bathroom," he asked Sara.

Fenton's bathroom was better than his bedroom. Miniature statues of Michelangelo's David stood in every corner of the room, while the commode—made of white-on-white ceramic tiles each containing in bas-relief a pornographic scene—was set in a wall of mirrors. Sara picked up a monogrammed washcloth, held it under the faucet, wet it, and returned to the bedroom just as Fenton was bringing in a cup of coffee.

Becky Luna's eyes fanned open. "Ooooh, I'm so embarrassed," she wailed. "Oooh, I can never hold my head high again. How could they have done this to me? I wish I were dead! Dead, dead, dead." Tears splashed down her plump pink cheeks, staining them with dark blotches of running mascara. "Why was I ever born? I'm so ashamed, so-o-o—"

Sara handed the washcloth to Michael, who gently dabbed Becky's cheeks, then held up the coffee for her to sip. Fenton sat down on the edge of the bed and took Becky's hand. "Becky, bunny, don't cry, please don't cry," he murmured with surprising tenderness. "Everything will be all right."

"*Nothing* will be all right. Nothing!" she sobbed. "I'm all washed up."

"No, Becky, bunny, you'll be all washed up if you don't stop crying," Fenton teased smilingly. Becky brightened not at all.

"Tonight was a horror. An absolute horror," she bawled. "I hate myself."

"Where were you? What happened?" Michael asked, concern in his voice.

"I was watching Becky Luna make a fool of herself in

Allergic to Love," she cried. "Savory had a small screening. And I've never been so humiliated in my life."

"Oh, come now. It can't be as bad as all that. Surely someone somewhere will like it. Peoria," he giggled. "Or maybe Fairbanks."

"Oh, yeah. *I* happen to know—"

"Oh, really. How? What happened? Who said what? And to whom? And where? Becky, bunny, tell Fenny everything." Was Sara imagining it, or had Fenton just flipped on a tape recorder?

"Well," Becky related between sobs, "there were maybe ten people in the screening room when the movie began and four people when it was over. I was wearing dark glasses and a hat so no one would recognize me, and when I went into the ladies' room afterward, you wouldn't believe what they were saying. One bitch said that with a voice like mine, I would have been better off in silent pictures. The other bitch said, silent pictures, her eye, the only possible thing to do with a face like mine was to put it on the radio. And you know what was worst of all? One of these dykes said that Nigel Whitty was right, and that I was the biggest no-talent ever to be splattered across the screen. I hate myself," she moaned. "I hate the world. And I hate Nigel Whitty. I'd like to tear him limb from limb, then pull out his eyes and boil them for dinner"—her eyes narrowed for emphasis—"and tweeze out every hair on his body one by one."

"Oooh, sounds lovely, Becky," Fenton gurgled. "But you do remember, honey bunny, somebody beat you to the punch."

Punch! Sara thought and cast a sharp glance at Fenton, Could it have been—? No. He wouldn't have dared!

"Damn!" said Becky. "Damn! Of course, someone got to him first. That's the story of my life. Always the bridesmaid, never the bride." And she collapsed back onto the pillow, the tears flowing all over again.

That poor creature, Sara thought. Kill Nigel Whitty? Tie

a ribbon around his neck? Why, she was hardly able to tie her own tap shoelaces!

Sara helped Becky dry her tears, and with Michael taking the right arm and Fenton the left, all three dragged Becky out to join the others at the buffet table in Fenton's Chinese red dining room. After introductions were made, Marlon and Monty swooped down on Becky.

"Ooooh, we adored your mother," oozed Marlon.

"Beautiful Billie Glover kept me in stitches through my entire pathetic childhood," Monty chimed in, biting on a shrimp for emphasis. "I know every one of her routines by heart. Like the one about hunting for the wild bore. Hahahaha." His hands clutched his velvet belly, and he doubled over with hysterical laughter.

"Actually, my favorite was the one about Heidi and the goats." Now Marlon was clutching his sides.

Becky, however, wasn't laughing at all. In fact, she looked as if she were working up to some more tears. Fenton rushed over with a large tumbler of vodka for her and one for himself as well. She gulped it down as if she were a jogger who'd just run a seven-minute mile, then abruptly placed the glass on the table and threw her arms around her host.

"Fenny, honey, the party's great!" she said with enthusiasm and as if she'd been wide awake and enjoying it throughout the evening. "But I'm just so tired, I must go home and get my beauty sleep."

"Oh, no, not yet, Becky, honey," Fenton protested. He, too, was beginning to look as if he'd downed one tumbler too many this evening. "'*The night's so young . . .*'"

"'*. . . and you're so beautiful!*'" Marlon's girlish voice sang melodiously now.

Becky's face perked up. "I am?"

Immediately, she linked arms with Marlon and Monty and whispered something to each. Simultaneously, the boys nodded and, along with Becky, began to wave their adieux.

The moment the door closed behind them, Fenton announced, "I'll lay you a hundred to one that Becky and the boys end up swapping sad stories and crying in their beer at one of your scuzzier gay bars. Tsk, tsk, tsk, isn't our little Becky-Wecchio just like her mother?"

"What do you mean?" Michael asked.

"Well, I wouldn't reveal this if the police weren't pressing me to talk"—he batted his eyelashes at Michael—"but you do know the true story of Billie Glover and the even truer story of her relationship with none other than the incomparable Nigel Whitty."

"We couldn't care less," said Beatrix, grabbing Vernon's hand and pulling him toward the door.

"But I care a lot," shouted Richard Singer-Murray from the telephone in the foyer where he had been standing for the last twenty minutes trying to get someone at the Hotel Carlyle to tell him something about Maria Cortese's whereabouts.

Beatrix brushed past him, dragging Vernon behind her. "Cherry-o!" she shouted as the door slammed shut, just missing Vernon's hand which was waving a fond farewell.

"I just don't know what's happened to *mia cara*," Richard Singer-Murray muttered, glancing at his watch. "Maybe I should call the hospital. Or the police."

"I'm the police, if you recall." Michael smiled at him.

"Oh, well," Richard said, his pale eyes squinting behind his spectacles. "I guess it's nothing serious. I suppose she just got the address wrong or the time wrong. You know these Italians."

"Of course—intimately." Fenton smiled.

"Or maybe she's at dinner. Those Italians eat so late," Richard went on.

"I'll say," Fenton smirked, downing another tumbler of vodka. "She's probably under the table right now feasting on somebody's linguine."

"I don't think that's very funny," Richard glowered.

"You were about to tell us something about Billie Glover," Michael interrupted.

"Ah, yes, Billie Glover." Fenton pulled up a pillow. "Well, you know the story Becky gives out—the one that Billie herself told? That Nigel was nuts for her and she wouldn't give him a tumble? Well, the truth is just the opposite. Billie Glover was so nuts for Nigel Whitty who didn't give a shit about *her* that she finally slit her wrists over him."

"You're kidding," Sara said. "I thought she had a heart attack while rehearsing her Moby Dick routine for a Royal Command Performance."

"Sure," Fenton said, "sure she had a heart attack. When all the blood ran out of her body, her heart attacked. Whose wouldn't have?" He poured himself another drink.

"But if that's true," Richard said, cleaning his glasses with a napkin, "why would Nigel have devastated Billie and then Becky in turn? I mean, the only thing Billie did was fall in love with him. Whitty should have been flattered. Billie was the toast of five continents. Burnt at the edges perhaps, but still the toast." Richard smiled.

"Well, there's a bit more to the story," Fenton resumed with a dramatic flourish.

"Oh, yeah?" Michael said.

"You see—" Fenton cocked his head coyly—"they originally met when Nigel was interviewing Billie for an article in *Fortunate Times*. It was early in his career and a tremendous break for him—the cover story in a big magazine with the hottest star of the day. And Billie took to him. She let it all hang out—quite literally." Fenton laughed. "Well, Nigel accepted the handout and then quickly got bored."

"How do you know all this, Fenton?" Michael asked.

"I never reveal my sources, sweetheart. Right, Richard? Isn't that one of the reasons why I'm such a great reporter?"

"Sure, Fenton." Richard nodded. "And you're not just great—you're the greatest."

"Go ahead," Michael encouraged Fenton.

Sara wondered if Michael were buying this story, and if in fact it were true. Somehow, she trusted it was. Even given the short time she'd been involved in this world of show biz gossip, Sara had begun to discover that almost every rumor had a solid basis in fact. If you heard that Y was a drunk, you could place bets that he'd passed out at at least a party or two. And if you heard that Z and W were splitting, you knew that their domestic battles had become noisy and were going public.

"But while Nigel got bored," Fenton went on, "Billie didn't. She wanted more. And when he wouldn't screw, she decided to put the screws on him. She called *Fortunate Times* and told them that the article, which they'd sent her when it was still in manuscript form, was totally false. She had it pulled and Nigel blackballed."

"You mean, that's all Nigel had against Billie Glover?" Richard muttered, his pale face scrunching up in puzzlement. "That doesn't seem to be worth ten years of jabs and insults."

"Especially," Sara added, "considering that whatever Billie Glover did, it didn't keep Nigel from going on to his great success."

"Perhaps it all doesn't seem worth it to you two," Fenton said. "But our Nigel, let us not forget, was a very proud man. And also a vindictive cunt. Ooh, whoops!" He looked coyly at Sara first and then at Michael. "Sorry for the vulgarity." Then he continued. "In any case, he never stopped hating Billie for what she had done. And when Billie died, he started taking it all out on her legacy, our poor little Becky-Wecchio."

"Does Becky know the whole story?" Michael asked.

"No." Fenton shook his head. "Even gossip columnists have to draw the line somewhere. And it would break poor little Becky's heart to know that her mother, rather than refusing to give big bad Nigel a tumble, tumbled for him head over heels."

"Draw the line somewhere? You'd better not have too many principles when you work for me," Richard Singer-Murray declared.

Sara perked up. "What?"

"Well, Richard has let our little cat out of the bag," Fenton said, "so why don't we share our happiness with sweet Sara and her little man in blue."

"What is he talking about?" Sara turned to Richard.

"Fenton will explain," Richard said, walking into the foyer. "I want to start calling the hospitals. I'm really worried about *cara* Maria."

Fenton smiled broadly. "Guess who's going to take over Nigel Whitty's column and move to where the grass is greener and the circulation's bigger?"

"And when was this decided?" Sara asked.

"Oh, just a few hours ago, when Richard arrived."

Sara's heart thumped. Her hands went cold. What was going on? Why hadn't Richard hinted at this possibility? She bit her lip and took a deep breath as Fenton continued.

"How does this sound to you?" he was saying. "'What Fenton Feels.' Or do you prefer 'A Penny for Fenny's Thoughts'? Or perhaps you like my very favorite—'Fenny's from Heaven'?"

"Frankly," Michael said, "I don't care much for any of them."

"Well, at least you can congratulate me, anyway."

"Congratulations," Michael said, "on the column and also on having provided yourself with a class-A motive for knocking off Nigel Whitty."

"What do you mean? Am I under suspicion?" Fenton asked.

"You've always been under suspicion," Michael said with a surprising sternness to his voice. Had he really come to some conclusion about Fenton, Sara wondered, or was this only the manifestation of his irritation with the whole evening—with its atmosphere, its tone?

"Lieutenant, you do have an amusing way about you!"

"I'm glad you're enjoying this, Farnabee. You may need your sense of humor in the days to come."

"Lieutenant, dear, now just explain what you mean by that!" Fenton was standing in front of Michael now, his arms akimbo and a drunken scowl on his dark, pretty face.

"What I mean is that Nigel Whitty's job looked pretty good to you. And that you certainly wasted no time going after it."

"I beg your pardon. Are you suggesting that in order to have avoided suspicion, I ought to have nipped my career in the bud?"

"Not at all. You'd be under suspicion anyway."

"You mean because of that nonsense that appeared in Nigel's column this morning? Would I kill for that? Because somebody called me a plagiarist? Besides, Richard just promised to print a retraction."

"It doesn't matter. That's not the issue." Michael looked directly into Fenton's eyes.

"What is the issue then?"

"That eight years ago Whitty caught you with your pants down. You wrote a newspaper article called, 'The Inherent Gentility of Joan Crawford,' which was a word-for-word steal from a 1943 profile of Margaret O'Brien that appeared in *Jack and Jill*. And it was Nigel Whitty who found you out. . . . "

". . . that cunt! He read everything."

". . . and he showed your editors the article."

"No, he didn't! They never found out," Fenton blurted out, then stopped himself. He blushed. "How did you find out, Lieutenant?"

"Nigel's papers. Is that what you were looking for, Fenton, when you rifled the apartment?"

"I never rifled anything in my life," Fenton protested.

"So Whitty was blackmailing you?"

Sara could tell that Michael was fishing now.

"Not exactly," said Fenton, drunk enough now to jump

at the bait. "Let's just say that Whitty liked to have power over people, and that was his power over me. Believe me, I'm only one of many." Fenton minced over to the bar and poured himself yet another tumbler of vodka. "But it's all right, Lieutenant. I know why you're zeroing in on poor little Fenny. Shall we say it's my girlish ways?"

"Not true," Michael protested. "I don't care what you do in bed. Or who you do it with. Unless, of course, you did it with Nigel Whitty."

"Oh, really, Lieutenant." Fenton's voice was shrill now and still rising. "You policemen are really pips. You're all alike. You're threatened by people like me. You're terrified. You don't want to confront the woman inside you. You don't want to admit that you're just a little teensy-weensy-eensy bit of a gay blade yourself."

"Goddammit! Goddammit! Goddammit!" Richard Singer-Murray came screaming into the room, tears streaming down his face. "That bitch! That bitch! How could she? How could she? We're not an item anymore." He flung himself down on a mauve velvet pillow. "She's with him. That cocksman, that stud, that Danny Blue. He answered her phone. He's with her. She's with him. *They're* an item now!" He banged his head against the wall once, twice, and then another time until his glasses flew off and sailed through the air, landing in the remains of a custard pie Fenton had bought in Beatrix's honor.

"And here's an item for you, too." Sara walked up and confronted Richard. "A late news flash. Sara Nightingale, lackey *extraordinaire* and general factotum to the biggest, vainest fool in the entire newspaper business, is handing in her resignation—effective as of twelve minutes ago."

"What do you mean, Sara? You're my right-hand girl."

"Then you're going to be a one-armed bandit the rest of your life, you Judas, you traitor. Let me tell you something, Mr. Dashing-Man-About-Town. I don't necessarily want to spend my whole life knee-deep in that garbage you call gossip, but you might at least have had the decency to talk to me before you handed that column over to Fenton."

"But I assigned you that article, Sara, dear. A three-parter. I told you I'd make you a star," said Richard, fumbling on the floor to locate his glasses.

"Why don't we just forget about the article." Sara's voice was icy.

"Forget about it? Don't be silly. When Singer-Murray makes a promise, Singer-Murray follows through on it." Richard was squinting in her direction. "Sara, dear, you know I'll take care of you."

"You don't seem to understand, Richard. I've made plans just now to sell the article elsewhere."

"You can't!"

"I certainly can."

Now, Sara sought out Michael. "Come on, Lieutenant, let's go."

As they stood near the front door, Sara glanced back into the apartment: at Fenton who was lying on a pillow with a tumbler of vodka in his hand; at Richard who was crawling along the carpet, searching for his spectacles; at Gertrude and Alice, who had climbed onto the dining room table and were now busily lapping up the remains of the custard pie.

"What a dump!" she announced and shut the door behind her.

Wednesday

WHAT NIGEL KNOWS

Tinseltown Tidbits and Tattle

by Nigel Whitty

ITALIAN STREETSONG: Remember Carmine Capolavaro, the Mafia bigwig whose throat was slashed at Sing Sing? The story is that he sang sang first and trilled on about Danielo Azzurro a.k.a. Danny Blue. The mystery is just what happened to the Capolavaro tapes? Some say lovely Lizzie Salt has them stashed away and just may turn them over to Daddy's network if Dannyboy gets tired of licking Salt's wounds or if Salt herself gets rid of that Blue feeling. Whatever, Nigel predicts a network special later in the season. . . . **RAINBOW IN THE GREEN SKY**: Though we might report that Enzo Carbonare's new movie may not in itself be great, its star, Maria Cortese, is. Her role is the kind that would do most actresses in, since she's on screen for 180 minutes straight, playing a wealthy woman who one day decides that her husband either is having an affair with the butler or is dead, and who retaliates either by having an affair with the gardener or by committing suicide. Carbonare leaves this ambiguous. But one thing is clear: Cortese herself is a genius and the epitome of femininity. She's one woman who looks better with her blouse off than on. . . . **AND SPEAKING OF MARIA**: Sad to say that she and debonair editor Richard Singer-Murray, one of Gotham's most beautiful couples, are no longer an item. Bye, bye, beautiful couple. . . . **STEERING YOU RIGHT**: Word is out that Becky Luna has been driving Gyorgii Gdansk to distraction. If Becky isn't careful, he'll be driving her into traction. Right, Googie? Nigel's got it all down, right here in his little black book. . . . ★

11

HEY, CONNELLY, what're you smiling about?" Sergeant O'Reilly looked up from his desk as Michael passed.

"The gorgeous morning," Michael returned, tipping an imaginary hat.

"Sure, sure. Just like you to notice the morning." O'Reilly grinned knowingly. "Brunette or blonde?"

"Redhead."

"Well, whoever she is, she's written all over you," O'Reilly observed before returning his attention to the pile of papers which were strewn messily across his desk.

Was she really? Well, it was no surprise, she was certainly on his mind. It was her spunk that really got to him. He wouldn't have missed last night for all the tea in China—or was it all the coke in Alan Savory's nose? Watching Sara stomp out of Fenton's after giving Singer-Murray a piece of her mind was really something. And he was glad, when they talked about it afterward, that she wasn't doing that article after all. She was a brainy girl, and she could spend her time better than writing some crap about what Nigel Whitty's death meant to the film community. Still, he knew that she'd never get movies completely out of her system. It was a disease that some people couldn't be cured of.

"Hey, Connelly, wait a minute!"

Michael wasn't even halfway down the corridor when he heard O'Reilly call him O'Reilly's burly form trudged toward him. "Damn, you had me so caught up in your love life that I forgot to tell you we put a twenty-four-hour guard on Elizabeth Salt. Like you asked. We tracked her down at the studio this A.M. Oh, boy, did Miss Big Mouth Television Star squawk like mad! She said our men were cramping her style and that she'd have it out with you later."

"When is later?"

O'Reilly ran a hand through his curly gray hair. "We set up an appointment for three o'clock. Over at her office."

"Good work, O'Reilly."

"Thanks."

Michael continued down the corridor to his office, glancing at his watch. Only eight o'clock. Elizabeth Salt may have been up and working at that hour, but surely not Richard Singer-Murray. Still, Michael had to talk to him as soon as he could about the Capolavaro stuff that had appeared in Whitty's column this morning. Sara had known nothing about it, except for what Nigel had written. What had bothered her was the mini-review of *The Green Sky*. Somehow, she'd said, it looked odd, not quite the way she recalled it. Probably, she'd suggested, Singer-Murray was allowing his power as editor and his fame as erstwhile lover of Maria Cortese to go to his head and was providing much of Nigel's recent material himself. Maybe. Michael couldn't be sure. Sara was not only a little disorganized, but she was also pretty forgetful at times.

The phone was ringing when Michael unlocked the door to his office. At eight in the morning, it could only be one person.

"Mick, is that you?" Bridget Connelly's voice greeted him when he picked up the receiver. "I've been trying to reach you on into the wee hours, you naughty boy," she went on, her usually soft Irish lilt touched with disapproval. "I only hope the good Lord was busy last night and didn't notice what you were doing."

Michael laughed in spite of himself. He really wanted to say, "It's none of your business, Ma." But since he'd said it a million times before, he didn't bother now. What was the point anyway?

"What's up, gorgeous?" He changed the subject.

"The gala tonight, the big festivities."

Michael drew a blank.

"Come now, Mick, don't you remember? Radio City. A Hollywood opening. With famous stars. The picture's called *The Green Emerald*?" Bridget Connelly's voice was developing an edge to it; she was beginning to sound crestfallen.

"Of course I remember, Ma. It's *The Green Sky*, and I'm expecting to take you and Father Fitzgerald for a night on the town."

He could hear her sigh with relief. "Well, that's what I was calling you about, Mick. Where do we meet you?"

Michael thought for a minute. What arrangements had Sara made again? Oh, yeah. "Look, Ma, the tickets will be at the box office under your name. I'll look for you in the lobby, but if we don't meet there, you and the Father will be sitting right next to me and Sara."

There was a pause.

"Sara?"

"Yeah, Sara. I'll introduce you tonight."

"Irish?"

"I don't think so, but she's got red hair."

"Like Maureen O'Hara!" Bridget Connelly's voice perked up. "And that reminds me, Mick. Shall I wear my black suit tonight? The one with the little white collar like Maureen O'Hara wore in *Dance, Girl, Dance*?"

Oh, Christ!

"How the hell do I know what Maureen O'Hara wore in *Dance, Girl, Dance*?" Was it his mother on the phone, or Fenton Farnabee? The world seemed to be closing in on him.

"Oh, Mick, don't blaspheme."

"Look, Ma, I'm sorry. Wear it—it sounds terrific."

"Maybe you're right," Bridget mused aloud. "If I wear

it, I'll be matching Father Fitzgerald. But then again,"—her tone shifted to one of gravity,—"maybe I'll be matching the Father too much."

"No, Ma. Nobody's gonna think you're Mother and Father, if that's what you mean."

Bridget Connelly giggled. "One last question, Mick. Who do you think will be there? Mia Farrow? Geraldine Fitzgerald? Phil Donahue? Maybe even Jimmy Cagney?"

"Look, Ma, it's the Italian-American Anti-Defamation League that's running this show, not the Sons of Ireland. Think you've a better chance for Sergio Franchi."

"Lord protect us."

As soon as Bridget Connelly had hung up, Michael dialed Richard Singer-Murray's home number. His service picked up, and the operator told him that Mr. Singer-Murray wouldn't be available until noon. Where was he, Michael asked. She wasn't permitted to say, the high-pitched voice announced. Pressed, however, she revealed that Mr. Singer-Murray was spending the morning at Georgette Klinger's salon having a facial. Probably, Michael thought with a smirk, in order to wash Maria Cortese right out of his pores.

"Well, tell good old S—M to give me a call when his pores are closed," Michael instructed the operator. "Tell him it's urgent."

Michael's intercom started buzzing just then, and he flipped it on.

"Hey, Lieutenant." It was Friedkin. "Emergency message for you—about Becky Luna. She's lying unconscious in Metropolitan Hospital. Just had her stomach pumped.

"What was it? What'd she take?"

"The report didn't say. Only that it was an O.D."

Poor, pathetic Becky. Michael felt a twinge of conscience. He should have seen this coming—and not just last night. Even at the Russian Tea Room, it was obvious that Becky had been climbing the stairway to drug heaven. And now she was almost there.

Tubes were everywhere: they were coming out of her nostrils, running into her mouth; they were attached to her wrists, her arms, and God knew where else. Her eyes weren't open. Although she'd been conscious earlier, Michael had been told, now she was asleep.

"And I wouldn't wake her, Lieutenant," the big coffee-colored nurse admonished in her most officious tone. "The poor thing has been through a great deal."

She did an about-face, started toward the door, and signaled to Michael to do the same.

What the hell, he thought. He didn't have to stand there watching Becky Luna sleep.

"She's going to be fine, Lieutenant," a middle-sized, middle-aged man in a white coat offered. Then he extended his hand. "Dr. Mahandru Gupta. Quite a scandal, hmmm?" Mahandru Gupta raised one of his dark eyebrows. "But we shall do our best to keep it out of the journals," the doctor went on. "Good thing they brought Miss Luna here. Nobody would think to look for a famous person in this kind of hospital."

Come to think of it, why had she been brought here to a city hospital, and one located all the way uptown on 97th Street and Third Avenue, right in the midst of *el barrio?* The last time Michael had seen Becky, she'd been on the West Side, way across town at Fenton's. And the apartment she was currently subletting was down in Gramercy Park. It was obvious that she's wound up somewhere in the neighborhood of Metropolitan last night, but where and with whom? Some Spanish Lothario who danced a mean *salsa*? Some street shark who dealt in dirty drugs? Whoever, it was someone who didn't know that when a star like Becky Luna O.D.'d, you took her to one of those private hospitals that looked and smelled like an elegant hotel and not to a public one where they wheeled you down vomit-green custodial corridors stinking of death and formaldehyde, weaving you in between shivering junkies, battered babies, and sliced-up storekeepers.

He turned to Dr. Gupta. "Who brought her in?"

"That Polish dancer. What is his name—Gdansk? And he was in quite a hurry. He just dropped her off, not even staying to find out how she was, whether she was going to live or die. With a friend like that, who needs an enemy?"

Well, that at least explained something. Gdansk's apartment was only a few blocks away, on Park and 91st. Of course, he could have taken her to Mount Sinai rather than Metropolitan, but who knew what went on in that crazy Pole's head. More important, how had she ended up with him last night? What happened to Monty and Marlon? And what in the hell happened to Becky?

"Can I use your phone, Doc?"

"Certainly, Lieutenant," Dr. Gupta said, leading the way down the hall to a small office, just slightly less grimy and depressing than the corridor itself. Dr. Gupta lit a pipe as Michael took out his notebook, checked Gyorgii Gdansk's number, and dialed.

The voice on the other end informed him that Gdansk was not available. It was his part-time secretary, a young ballet student, as Michael recalled from his records, who furthermore claimed he had no idea of Gdansk's whereabouts. Michael didn't believe him.

"Look, buddy, if you don't tell me right now just where I can find your boss, I'm gonna send two uniformed cops up there to ram your ballet slippers down your throat and book you for obstruction of justice."

Michael felt a little guilty, bullying the kid in this way. But he felt it was important to get to Gdansk immediately. What the hell was going on that he couldn't stay around to find out whether Becky lived or died? What kind of heel was that toe-dancer anyway?

The voice on the other end of the phone started to waver. "He'll kill me, Lieutenant," the thin male voice fluttered. "He'll absolutely kill me. I'm sworn to secrecy. I can't jeopardize my job. And if I tell you, I'll jeopardize his."

"I'm going to jeopardize your legs in a minute . . ."

"Oh, God," the voice whined, "why me?"

"Look, buster, I'm giving you thirty seconds."

"How do I know you're the police anyway?" The voice developed a bit of assertiveness.

"You don't know. Just stay put. In about five minutes, you'll see a man in blue . . ."

"Oh, no," the voice trembled. "All right, he's at Hightstown, New Jersey. At the Hightstown Raceway. But swear you won't tell him I told you."

Michael hung up the receiver.

"Thanks, Doc," Michael said. "Keep me posted, will you, as to how she's doing."

"Oh, no worry, she'll be fine," Dr. Gupta said. "She'll be out of here by tonight."

"If you say so," Michael said, hurrying down the hall toward the exit and passing the emergency room on his way. It was crowded with hysterical women, frightened men, and crying children. One boy's face was covered with blood, while another sat doubled over and screaming with pain. And there weren't enough ears to hear them or hands to care for them. Poor Becky. She hadn't made it to drug heaven. She'd made it to hell instead.

A cloud of dust rose in the air as one after another the sleek, shiny, low-slung racing cars took the curve. Now they were in the straight, the black in the lead, the blue close and coming fast, the others—some eight or ten of them—all grouped together several lengths behind. A small yellow car skidded and spun around the track in a wild 360-degree turn, narrowly missing first one head-on collision and then another.

What a way to go, Michael thought, as he stood at the guardrail of the sparsely populated track. Or better, what a way to get your kicks. He looked at his watch. It was after twelve—it had taken almost an hour and a half to get out here to Hightstown from Metropolitan Hospital. And

Gyorgii Gdansk was nowhere to be seen. No one had heard of him: not the guard at the entrance; not the secretary in the office; nor any of the several drivers who had come out today to qualify for the weekend race. And what would Gyorgii Gdansk be doing here in the first place? Did that item in Whitty's column this morning—the one about Gdansk "driving" Becky to distraction—have some literal meaning after all? Could Gdansk possibly be a racing buff rather than a movie buff like the rest of them? Or could he possibly be a racer himself? But would a ballet dancer actually dirty his little slippers in the dust and mud of this heavy macho sport? The whole thing didn't make sense. That goddamn secretary had probably thrown him a bum steer. Michael would throw the book at him in return.

The black car was braking at the finish line as Michael walked toward the exit. He looked back to see a stocky man in a yellow helmet and black nylon jacket leaping out of the car and bounding across the track, his arms raised over his head and his fists clenched together in a gesture of victory.

"Great time. Who's the driver?" Michael heard one of the racers—a tall, craggy-looking man—ask one of the fellows at the registration desk.

The man looked over the list before him. "Number forty-one," he squinted. "Name's Rhett Butler."

The racer knotted his forehead quizzically. "You mean Red Butler, don't you?"

"Nah, look here. It says Rhett Butler." The man held out the list for the other to see.

"Well, I'll be damned!"

Small world, Michael thought. Time to check out Number 41. He started to make his way toward the driver in the yellow helmet who now was walking toward the locker room, his arms still braced in their victory clench.

"Great time, Rhett," one of Rhett's colleagues called out. "How'd you do it?"

"You vant my secret? My secret is: fear of nothing," Rhett said, puffing out his chest and walking on.

"Congratulations, Rhett." Another driver tipped his helmet.

"I good, no?" Rhett smiled. "I fast. I beautiful. And I good."

That was some peculiar southern accent this Rhett had, Michael thought as he caught up with the proud winner. "Mr. Butler, I presume?" he said, placing his hand on Rhett's black nylon battle jacket.

Rhett turned around abruptly. "Don't I know your face somewhere?" He squinted.

"Yes, Mr. Butler, I'm Lieutenant Michael Connelly. We met on the set of *Brother, Can You Spare a Dance?*"

Gyorgii gasped. His already flushed face turned crimson. "How you found me? Who tell you my secret?" he whispered. "And how you know I Rhett Butler?"

"Lucky guess." Michael smiled. "How you choose that name?" Michael realized with a start that he had begun to speak pidgin English.

"Name most famous American man, except maybe John Wayne. And John Wayne I think too short."

"But why another name? Why all this secrecy?"

"First, because my contract with U.S. Ballet Theatre read, 'No racing.' And second, because my contract with Alan Savory read, 'No racing.' Two good reason, no?"

"Yes," Michael returned.

"You see, they want to make sissy out of me. And Googie Gdansk no sissy. I love danger. It make my heart beat. I love go fast. It make my pulse race."

"You certainly left Becky Luna pretty fast this morning."

"You know about that?"

Michael nodded. "Look, can we find some place to talk? There are a lot of things I'd like to clear up."

Gyorgii led Michael into the stands—higher and higher until they were as high as they could go.

"This is fine," Michael said, afraid that Gyorgii, with his passion for danger, was going to lead him up onto the roof.

"Now, vat you vant to know?" asked Gyorgii, taking off his helmet, shaking out his mane of blond hair, and then stretching his body as if in preparation for a set of ballet exercises.

"First, why did you run away so quickly this morning?"

"Aha! You think I run because I guilty!" Gdansk exclaimed, his deep blue eyes suddenly widening into twin pools of comprehension. "Guilty of vat? Of stuffing poor Becky with all those silly pills? Not Googie. No, no. Googie explain. Googie run because all this . . ." his arms gestured gracefully over all he surveyed, namely the flat, gray landscape and the dusty Hightstown Raceway, ". . . all this is vat I love most in this world. All this is closest to my heart, next to Googie's memory of Mother Poland."

Were those tears in Gdansk's eyes as he spoke, or was Michael just imagining it? "You mean, dirt racing?" Michael asked, incredulous.

Gyorgii nodded vigorously. His eyes blazed with excitement. "Ya, ya. The dirt. I love the good, clean, brown dirt against the face. I love go fast: one hundred, one hundred twenty, like a bird, like a plane. You think a little ballet leap or a perfect *plié*, they compare? You know how hot I feel when I hug track faster than wind? You know vat it like? It like giant come."

So that was Gdansk's story. Michael recalled the reference in Nigel's column to Gyorgii's insatiable appetites. It seemed that what Gdansk the great dancer couldn't satisfy with sex, he satisfied with speed; where he couldn't get off on people, he got off instead on cars; and that where he couldn't find release in bed, he found it instead on the track.

"Why don't you stop dancing then and just drive?" Michael couldn't resist asking.

"Googie no able to make living coming. That why."

"It's not that I'm uninterested in how you feel about racing," Michael went on, almost apologizing, "but let's get back to Becky. What happened last night?"

"You talk with Becky?" Gdansk asked, raising an eyebrow suspiciously.

"Yes," Michael lied.

"Vat she tell you?"

"You first," Michael said firmly. "Let me warn you, Gdansk, it's pointless to lie."

Gyorgii sighed as though the weight of the world had just been placed on his shoulders. "You right. Someone always find out. Lie always come back in face like dirt on track or words in 'What Nigel Knows.'"

Michael knew he was on the right track, dirt or not. This trip was going to turn out to be worth it, after all.

"All right," Michael encouraged, "as long as we're agreed on the value of truth, let's begin."

As if in some crazy response to his instruction, a roar came from the track as a dozen cars revved their motors and a new heat began. Gdansk's face brightened with excitement. He moved forward on his seat, his eyes following the motion of the cars.

"You like God. From your mouth to cars' ears," he smiled.

"I meant you, not the cars," Michael said. "Now tell me, what happened last night? Or this morning? Or whenever the hell it did happen?"

Gdansk drew his attention from the track reluctantly. He ran a delicate hand through his golden hair. "Aacchh! I sleeping to make ready for big heat today when doorbell ring. I look at fancy American digital clock. It four-thirty. 'Oh, shit,' I say. Must be Maria Cortese forget something. She at my apartment early in evening and we make a little zoom zoom together."

Maria Cortese! But she had been with Danny Blue last night, at least according to Richard Singer-Murray. Christ, the lives these people led! Michael couldn't keep up with their appetites.

"But not Maria Cortese," Googie went on. "I should

have think. Only person bother me at this hour is Becky Luna. And sure enough, that is what at door, surrounded by two queers. They are quick to throw her in my house like she was hot potato burning their fingers. They disappear before you can say Jackie Robinski, and they leave Becky standing there. She colder than a Polish winter and twice as angry."

"Angry at what?" Michael asked.

"She have newspaper in hand, shaking at me. 'What Nigel know?' she keep screaming at me. 'What Nigel know?' 'Beat it, Becky,' I say. 'You tell Nigel I driving you crazy,' she scream. 'You tell him that?' I say, 'What you talking about, crazy woman?' She say, 'Look at paper. Look at "What Nigel Knows."' I rather look at race," Gdansk suddenly interrupted himself. "Look at Number 26 go. Zoom, zoom," he called out, this time like a child playing with miniature cars.

"So what did you do then?" Michael asked, hoping to bring Gdansk back to his story.

"I look. I get crazy. That Nigel. That Whitty. I could kill him. I could run him over with my black race car, if he not already dead. Then Becky scream, 'You don't love me.' I scream back, 'You damn right.' 'But what about our wonderful nights together?' she say. 'Wonderful for you,' I say, 'but work for me.' 'Work,' she scream, 'what you mean?' And then I say vat I shouldn't say. Whitty on my nerve and she on my nerve, I open my mouth too big. I say, 'I nice to you because Alan Savory, he pay me to be nice to you. For sake of movie picture.' 'What you mean?' she shriek."

A huge screech from the track sent Gdansk flying to his feet.

"Look at that," he cried out, pointing to the small red car that had just gone out of control and, jumping over the inner guardrail, was now flipping to a standstill on the grassy center island.

"Fantastic. More beautiful than a grand *jeté* more sexy than a ballerina's split."

It had never struck Michael that a ballerina's split was particularly sexy. In fact, ballerinas themselves never struck him as particularly sexy. But maybe he'd been missing something.

In any case he turned to Gyorgii. "Let's get to Becky, okay?"

"Hokay," Gdansk said hesitantly. "Well, after she shriek, I tell her something I shouldn't tell her. I tell her, 'Every time I fock you, Alan Savory give me $1,000. Which mean I make $29,000 off you, tax free.'" Gdansk looked at Michael imploringly. "You no report this, Detective? Has nothing to do with case, my taxes, no?"

Michael shrugged. "I don't think so," he said. "But back to Becky."

"Aacchh, Becky! Soon as I say this, she run into bathroom and begin to cry. And I think, let her cry. I go sleep now and make ready for big heat. One hour later, I get up and go to make pee. And what I find in bathtub is no cockroach. It Becky. I risk hernia and end to whole dance career and carry her downstairs and into taxi. I tell driver, 'Nearest hospital, quick.' I drop her but cannot stay or be late for heat. And that, Detective Connelly, is whole story."

"Not quite," Michael advised. "Let's talk a little more about Whitty. And about that item."

Gyorgii's delicate features coarsened with fear. "Vat to say? Nothing. Just another item."

"I don't think so," Michael challenged him. Although Michael wasn't really sure, his instincts told him that there was something here worth pushing for. And the clue probably lay in the word "driving." Michael knew by now that Nigel Whitty never used any word lightly.

"Whitty knew about your driving, didn't he?"

"Vat you mean?" Gdansk asked sharply.

Too sharply, Michael thought. This guy was like a porch screen, you could see right through him.

"I mean exactly what I say. Whitty knew about your driving."

"And you know, too?" Gdansk gulped.

"I know, too," Michael confirmed. "But I want to hear it in your own words."

"How you find out? You have little black book, no?"

It was a risk, Michael knew, but Gdansk seemed so naïve, so simple, that he dared it and reached into his inside pocket for his own black leather address book. He waved it in front of him.

Gyorgii gasped. "Ay, ay, ay," he moaned. "You really vant me tell story, when you know already?"

"Yes."

"Aacchh! I wish I had glass of hot tea."

"Mr. Butler, Mr. Butler!" Two young girls, one in a pink T-shirt, the other in a blue one, came scrambling up the bleachers. "Could we have your autograph?" they panted in unison.

Michael suspected they weren't more than twelve.

"Your race was wonderful," the one in pink said excitedly.

"You go so fast," the one in blue giggled.

"Not so fast where it count." Gdansk winked and licked his lips. Then he scribbled his name twice.

"What's this?" the pink looked puzzled.

"Looks like Greek to me," said the blue.

"It Rhett Butler in Polish" said Gdansk proudly.

The girls giggled hysterically as they scampered away.

"You were saying, or about to say, something about your driving," Michael jolted Gdansk's memory.

"Ya," he began again. "It last summer, when company making guest performance at Jacob's Pillow in Massachusetts. Everyone know story how most promising ballerina and partner out on picnic in meadow get career ruined when crazy driver hit and run over all four legs and rosebush."

Michael recalled the story. It had made the front page of all the papers.

"You remember, too," Gdansk went on, "nobody see car, nobody see driver. But Nigel Whitty with eagle eye see piece of tutu on fender of Googie's yellow Porsche. I feel terrible enough United States Ballet Theatre lose two great dancers, and Googie lose sleep from guilt and tears. Ay, ay, ay. 'But should United States Ballet Theatre lose third great dancer?' I say to Nigel Whitty. And he say, 'Not if you pay me.' So you know what I do with $29,000 I get for focking Becky?"

"You gave it to Whitty?"

"Yes, I give to Whitty the buttinski. But that all I give. No typewriter ribbon, no hug round the neck, I swear."

At that moment, a purple car careened out of control. It spun across the track, hit the guardrail, flew in the air, and landed on top of a green one. In a moment, the two ignited, the flames rising high over Hightstown, licking the cloudy Jersey sky.

"Ohhh, that a marvel," Gdansk said, leaping out of his seat. "Look! look!" He grabbed Michael's arm and shook it madly. "You like, no? You have to like! It make you spin more than double pirouette. It have more leap and muscle than *entrechat-dix*. It make you hotter than warm pussy."

Elizabeth Salt's office was dynamite—worthy of the chairman of the board, or better, his daughter—which was fine because that was exactly what she was. Her corner office was on the forty-ninth floor of the new TCA building on Sixth and 55th; and its walls of windows faced both south and east. The view, Michael imagined, would have been spectacular had he been able to see it. However, thick drapes hung across the windows, keeping both New York and the daylight out. Too bad, he thought. From this height, the city really must've been something.

As for the office, itself, it didn't even need a view to be grand. It was so huge that Michael figured he could fit his own apartment in here three times over. But what got to him most was the plushness and femininity of the room. It reminded him of the ladies' powder room at the Waldorf where last month they'd closed in on a ring of prostitutes and found the madam hiding in one of the toilet stalls. All the colors were pastel: pale blues, pale pinks, pale greens, pale purples, like a package of Necco wafers. Except that here, all the colors were runny around the edges, the way ink gets when you spill water on the paper. At one end of the room sat a desk, a big pale purple enamel piece whose ends looked as if they were composed of two mammoth snail shells. Across from the desk was a matching conference table, around which were eight chairs carved out of ivory, each with more curves than the Cyclone at Coney Island. At the other end of the room, tucked in a small alcove, were two sofas upholstered in rainbow silk. It was here that Michael sat, sipping the coffee that Elizabeth Salt's secretary had prepared for him.

"She should be here in fifteen minutes," the fat, homely girl with frizzy hair and a bulbous nose honked at him. "Miss Salt is taping."

No surprise. Of all the suspects, Elizabeth Salt had been the hardest to get hold of. Michael should have grabbed her that very first day after the murder, or at least the very next. For since that Friday night when she'd collapsed on the table at Tavern-on-the-Green, she'd been in Teheran for an interview with the Ayatollah, in Cairo to chat with Sadat, at the Vatican for an audience with the Pope, and had stopped off in Havana to put the frosting on a television special about public ownership of sugar-cane factories, as narrated by Fidel.

"The name is Bonita. If you need anything, just call," the secretary said. "And you, too," she said, glancing behind her at the uniformed policeman whom Michael had assigned that morning to the task of guarding Elizabeth Salt's office. Then Bonita turned back to Michael. "We really are sorry," she said brightly. "Miss Salt is never late. Never."

Bonita waved an if-you-need-anything wave and shut the door behind her. Michael signaled the policeman to leave as well. He got up and walked to the window and tried to push the drapes aside. They wouldn't budge. Christ! He was pissed about everything. This case wouldn't budge either. Almost an entire week had gone by and he was nowhere. But when the man whom everybody loved to hate—"the meanest man in the world," according to Becky Luna—gets knocked off, how do you figure who hated him most?

But maybe, Michael sighed, he was just being impatient. He knew, after all, that these things sometimes took weeks, even months, now and then years, before you could crack them. He walked back to the sofa and sat down, turning his attention to the stack of giant volumes sitting on the pale pink marble coffee table in front of him. The light was so dim, he could hardly make out the titles. But then his eyes adjusted and he read: *Elizabeth Salt: The Woman Behind the Anchor* on the cover of one volume; *Elizabeth Salt: Superwoman (The Authorized Biography)* on the cover of another. *Sensational Salt: The Seven Wonders of the World, or Living with Lizzie Drove Me Crazy (Interviews with the Seven Husbands of Elizabeth Salt)* was the title of a third. And a fourth book, a thick scholarly looking volume, was called *Sanford Salt: Tycoon.* Michael picked it up and began thumbing through it.

Elizabeth Salt's life and times right here on the coffee table, he thought. And in four different versions. Well, why not? It was quite a life. Something out of the movies, he had to admit, and one he was sure his mother would have adored. Some of the story, Michael knew already. In fact, everybody knew. Some things about some people were just common knowledge. Everyone knew, for example, everything about Elizabeth Salt's father, the fabulous Sanford Salt, a radio engineer whose creative genius and business acumen had made him president of a growing broadcasting company by the time he was thirty-five.

Everyone also knew all about Elizabeth Salt's mother, the exquisite socialite and former Debutante of the Year, Gloria Frasier Salt, who suffocated to death when the steam room door accidentally locked on her at the elegant Frances Sherwood Beauty Salon where she usually went for her afternoon exercises. And everyone, of course,knew a lot about Elizabeth Salt herself. After all, she was the most famous woman in broadcasting, had anchored the top-rated television news show for years, and now was television's most famous interviewer. Everyone knew that it was Daddy who had started her in the business, but it wasn't Daddy who had kept her there. Rather, it was her own sharp wit and intelligence. And although the world couldn't keep track of all seven of her disastrous marriages, everyone was certainly aware that she was the Tommy Manville of the newsroom set.

What most people didn't know and what Michael surely hadn't known, until he'd done his research, was the story behind these marriages. Fenton Farnabee had been his most helpful source here and had suggested that the key to everything lay in Elizabeth Salt's obsession with beauty. Indeed, Fenton claimed, Elizabeth Salt, brilliant as she was, would have traded in every brain cell she had for just one day as Marilyn Monroe. For all she really wanted in this world was to be breathtakingly gorgeous. Like her mother and for her father.

And if she couldn't be that ravishing beauty herself, she'd do the next best thing—she'd marry one. Or, at least, that's the way Fenton had sized it all up. After all, each and every one of her husbands, whatever else they'd been—princes, peasants, or pro-athletes—had been beauties. They were also to a one dopes, but Lizzie must have liked the idea of playing Pygmalion with them. Why else, Fenton pointed out, would she have gone to the trouble of buying each and every one of them a set of leatherbound *Encyclopedia Britannica* as a wedding present and then inserting at the end of volume 24, an application for MENSA membership?

What was MENSA anyway? Michael had meant to ask Fenton, but somehow had never gotten around to it. And so, as Bonita stuck her frizzy head in the door to check if everything was still all right, he found himself saying, "Hey, do you know what MENSA is?"

"MENSA?" Bonita walked into the room and placed some mail on Elizabeth Salt's desk. "Maybe it's a Spanish dance?"

Michael shook his head.

"Or, maybe," she smiled, revealing a set of stained and crooked teeth, "it's a society for Druids?"

"MENSA? You want to know what MENSA is?" asked a resonant female voice.

Michael turned to see Elizabeth Salt poised in the doorway, several policemen behind her. She slammed the door in their faces and strode over to greet Michael as rapidly as her four-inch heels would allow.

"MENSA," she announced, "is an organization for very bright people, for people with high I.Q.'s. That is, for people who are gorgeous on the inside." Smiling, she extended her hand to Michael. "Well, what can I do for you, Lieutenant? I'll tell you what you can do for me: call off your damned policemen."

"After Whitty's item this morning about Caplovaro, the Mafia, and you, I'd be nuts to call them off," Michael said. "You're a sitting duck for a murder contract."

Elizabeth Salt threw back her head and laughed recklessly. As he watched her, Michael was struck by the extent to which she blended with the room, the way the room in turn matched her as if it were part of her outfit. For like the furnishings and draperies, her clothes—her unbelted shirtwaist, her long scarf, and her sweater that was now tossed over one shoulder—were multicolored and multitextured, in various pastel shades. Michael couldn't help but smile. Elizabeth Salt reminded him of a short, chubby Necco wafer.

"Look," she said, settling back into the rainbow sofa now, almost blending with it, "I've lived through husbands who've beaten me, lovers who've jilted me, and men who've poisoned me with their indifference. You think I need your policemen? You think I'm afraid of a few little bullets?"

She was funny—all this bravado coming from this little butterball who probably didn't stand very much higher than *his* shoulder when she took off those high spiked heels. Close to her now, he also found her obsession with beauty somehow ridiculous. Though the light was low and dim and, even Michael knew, rather flattering, he could still see that she was, despite her weight, an attractive woman and must—in the bloom of her youth, at any rate—have been fairly pretty. Not gorgeous, not breathtaking, but really nice looking. Her hair, which neatly framed her face, was blond and seemingly thick; her brown eyes were large and wide; her mouth was small and delicate. She was very feminine and warm, and he could see how she could get secretaries of state and premiers and deposed princes to spill their guts out to her.

"I'm sorry if those guards are bothering you, Miss Salt," Michael said, "but it's really for your own protection."

"Oh, come now, Lieutenant. I've been to the Mideast, the Far East, the Southeast. I've traveled in dirigibles, by kayak and water buffalo. I've been in the midst of coups and revolutions. You think I'm worried about a ridiculous item in Nigel Whitty's idiotic column! Ha!"

This was a good place to start, Michael thought. "Why don't you tell me about that Whitty item?" he asked.

"Surely, why not? It's all very simple. I interviewed Carmine Caplovaro and the tapes were stolen. Probably by the Bambino family."

"Why would the Bambino family want to steal the tapes?" Michael asked.

"How should I know?" She shrugged.

"You heard the tapes. And you knew what was on them. That's how."

"Are you investigating the Bambino family"—Elizabeth Salt's voice was sharp—"or the death of Nigel Whitty? Frankly, Lieutenant, I don't know what you're getting at."

She was smooth, Michael thought. Aloud, he said, "Let's just say I think there might be a connection between the Bambinos and Whitty and I'd like to hear one of those tapes."

"A lot of people would. But sorry, Lieutenant, I just don't have them."

"You know, Miss Salt, I don't believe you."

"You're calling me a liar then?"

"That isn't the point. And in this instance, Nigel Whitty's murder isn't really the point either. It's . . ."

"I know what you're going to tell me, Lieutenant," she interrupted. "Don't forget that I went through this six months ago when the tapes were first stolen, and the FBI conducted a hush-hush investigation. You're going to tell me . . ."

Michael felt uncomfortable. He should have assumed the FBI would have been in on this, and he should have checked it out.

". . . you're going to tell me," she went on, "that I'm fooling around with the U.S. Government on the one hand, and with gangland murderers on the other. That the public's interest is at stake, and so is my life."

"You took the words out of my mouth."

"Look, Lieutenant, you worry about Nigel Whitty's murder and I'll worry about mine. Okay?"

"Miss Salt," Michael smiled at her, "if you get murdered, it'll be my job."

"Well put. For a dumb cop you're not so dumb after all."

What crap! Michael was beginning to get annoyed. If she wanted to play little games, he'd give her little games all right.

"So, Miss Salt," he began, "you're one of those women willing to sacrifice all for love."

"How sweetly put, Lieutenant. My, you're not only not dumb, you even have a way with words."

Keep cool, Connelly, he told himself. This one's got a razor's edge and you don't want to get sliced.

"Miss Salt, it seems to me that you're willing to risk a lot just for a roll in the hay."

"I beg your pardon, Lieutenant?" Elizabeth Salt was sitting erect now, gritting her teeth.

Michael leaned forward and looked at her for a long time with what he hoped were sympathetic eyes. "Do you think all this is worth it?" he asked. "For the sake of Danny Blue? For the sake of a two-bit Hollywood heartthrob? For a raunchy Romeo who'll stick it into anything that walks?"

"Your vulgarity offends me, Lieutenant," Elizabeth Salt said sharply. Then, with dignity, she smoothed the pastel pleats of her skirt and announced coolly, "Danny Blue and I have an arrangement."

"And that arrangement includes Maria Cortese?"

Elizabeth Salt jerked her head forward. She dug her perfectly manicured nails into the arm of the sofa, so deeply and so hard that the rainbow cloth shredded beneath them. She got up and marched to her desk. Opening the top drawer, she removed a lavender dart, turned squarely to face what Michael had earlier assumed was a work of art, and sent the dart hurling to its bull's-eye center. "That Italian bitch! What are you talking about?" She turned to Michael. She had pretty good aim. Thinking about that dart, with its little purple feather, speeding toward the wall, Michael considered taking cover and dropping the whole matter. But, bravely, he decided to continue. "Remember that other little item in Whitty's column this morning? The one about Maria Cortese and Richard Singer-Murray?" he asked.

"Richard Singer-Murray? That four-eyed four-flusher? That two-faced twit who isn't worth two cents? What does he have to do with Danny Blue?" Elizabeth Salt sent another dart flying.

"Well, for whatever it's worth, Maria Cortese stood him up last night in order to spend a little time in her hotel room with Danny Blue. And from what I gather, I'm sure they weren't playing tiddlywinks."

"He was in her hotel room?" Elizabeth Salt opened another drawer, pulled out a small photograph, marched over to the work of art, and tacked it in the center. Then she picked up another dart and threw it. It landed right in Danny Blue's eye.

"Why, that two-timing louse! That lying bastard! I told him that if he so much as went to see her rotten film, I'd never speak to him again. Maria Cortese! I can't believe it." Elizabeth Salt took a long, deep breath. Her pale complexion pinked. "What do you want to know, Lieutenant?" she said in a sad, husky voice.

"What was on those tapes?"

"Nothing the FBI didn't know about already. We were only talking with Capolavoro for TV. It was a show—an entertainment—not an investigation. He said nothing."

"Nothing?"

"Well, nothing except one small thing. And the FBI didn't care about that."

"You mean the business about Danny Blue?"

"Yes."

"What about him?"

"Capolavoro was just talking about how Danny got started. About how, when he was up for his first big role, his Godfather, Rico Bambino, saw to it that the competition's nose was moved across his face and that his ear was ground up for pasta."

"And what happened to the tape?"

Elizabeth Salt didn't say anything.

"You made a tradeoff, didn't you?" Michael asked. "And with those tapes tucked safely away where only you had access to them, Danny Blue belonged to you, didn't he?"

She didn't have to take the Fifth. Elizabeth Salt was smart enough to know when to keep her mouth shut. She was the type, Michael could see, who kept all the angles covered. However, he'd have to notify the FBI. There was no doubt in his mind that Elizabeth Salt had suppressed evidence. The idea struck Michael that even if he never found Nigel Whitty's murderer, by the end of his search half the suspects would be in jail anyway: Biffy Adams for assault and battery; Gyorgii Gdansk for hit-and-run driving. Becky, maybe, would be up on drug charges. And now Elizabeth Salt. These people were unbelievable, mired in dirt up to their necks. He pressed further: "You also financed Danny Blue's movie, didn't you?"

Again, Elizabeth Salt said nothing. But the color that had faded from her face now crept back into it to tell him yes.

"You stand to lose a lot on it," he fished.

She threw her head back in the same gesture she had made earlier. But this time she didn't laugh. "More than you know," she said in a garbled voice.

Michael leapt at it. "You mean it wasn't your money?"

"Yes, it was," she said quickly. "TCA money is my money."

What was she telling him? That she took company funds to finance her boy friend's lousy home movie? Oh, Christ!

"But that's not the point," Elizabeth Salt went on, frantic now, very near tears. "The point is that Nigel Whitty told the whole world. And the whole goddamn world is going to say, 'Elizabeth Salt had to buy it again. Elizabeth Salt had to buy herself another pretty face. And another pretty face made an ugly fool out of her.' But then, Lieutenant, that's the story of my life."

She walked across the room to a wall on which were displayed dozens of framed photos, obviously mementoes from her checkered past. "Look at this wall! Look at this life!" she declared.

And then the buzzer rang. It was Bonita.

"No, no," Elizabeth chided with great agitation. "Tell Henry I can't talk to him now. Tell him we'll discuss his trip to Bonn later. And tell him I refuse to have dinner in that restaurant. The lighting is horrible!" She slammed down the phone and returned to her wall, her life.

"Look at this, Lieutenant," she said to Michael, flipping on a small lamp to illuminate her wall. "Come see the dunces and cretins and ninnies and morons I collected just because they were pretty. Just because I thought that somewhere behind those gorgeous eyes and thick lashes, there might be a single active brain cell. Take a look at this one!"

Elizabeth Salt was pointing to a photo of a couple in wetsuits. The man, muscular and handsome, smiled broadly as he held up a giant octopus which totally obscured the face of the woman beside him. "Jean-Jacques Dussault," Elizabeth Salt said, "and me. The sardine fisherman from Marseilles. My second husband. Now that's a *bête* for you. Even in a wetsuit, you can see he's a *bête*. And look at this one," she said, pointing to a picture of a couple on a tennis court. The man was wearing white shorts and a V-neck ribbed sweater. His thigh muscles bulged, and his toothsome smile signaled victory as did the tennis racket he held in front of him, totally blocking the face of his female companion.

"That's Ken Mulberry, the gorgeous tennis champ I picked up at the Sydney Open, and me. Hubby number three. Let me tell you, he not only ate and slept tennis, he also dreamed it, and every night he kept flinging his racket arm and slamming an imaginary ball right into my face. It was like sleeping with a kangaroo. In fact, it was like living with a kangaroo. Believe me, that Australian animal had a marsupial mind to match his marsupial fist."

Her hangup wasn't difficult to get, Michael thought. These pictures certainly were a record of her, a record of the pretty faces she chose to live with and the shadows she chose to live in.

"Beauty may know no pain," she was saying now, "but let me tell you, Lieutenant, living under the same roof with it can be absolutely agonizing."

Michael's eyes moved across the crowded wall and lighted on a small framed photo of two men and a woman who were standing beneath a huge, flowering tree, the woman's face hidden under its blossom-filled branches. The boy to her left was small and delicately featured, like a young Montgomery Clift. And the older one, the one on the right, reminded Michael of Sean Connery. Or was it Errol Flynn? My God, it was Whitty! Or was it?

"Is that who I think it is?" Michael asked Elizabeth Salt. "Where and when was that photograph taken?"

"Sicily. In 1959. It was during the Taormina Film Festival."

"That's right. You and Whitty do go back that far, don't you?"

Could this be a copy of that same picture Sara had told him was missing from Nigel's wall? It must have been—it fit Sara's description so exactly, right down to the hidden woman. But what did it all mean, he wondered.

Elizabeth Salt returned to her rainbow sofa and began to relate the story of her long and embittered friendship with Nigel Whitty, a friendship that went back, she told Michael, more than twenty years. In the beginning, when she was a young reporter and he was a young critic, both starting out on their careers, they had spent a lot of time together.

"What did we have in common? Our brains, of course. Nigel was the only truly intelligent man I ever knew. And back then, we were very good friends."

"How good?"

"Very good."

"*Very* good?"

"Yes, we went to bed together, if that's what you mean.

But we weren't really what I'd call lovers; we were very close friends."

The point was, Elizabeth Salt went on to explain, that they were bound together less by any physical intimacy than by a true intellectual kinship. Besides, Nigel proved to be truly sensitive, truly supportive somehow. He recognized that she was insecure and he tried to give her confidence, constantly assuring her that she was appealing. He'd tell her that men were staring at her, eating her up with their glances, devouring her in their imaginations, desiring her from afar. In return for this ego massage, she paid his way. She paid for his dinners, his taxis, his theater tickets, even his air fares. She introduced him to Daddy's friends.

"During all that time when you two were so close, did you ever find out where he came from, what his background was?" Michael interrupted.

"Haifa, I think. His parents had been among the first Zionists. What made them so special is that they weren't Jewish, he said."

Michael frowned. "Did you believe that Zionist story?"

"No, but back then who cared?" Elizabeth Salt smiled wistfully. "If it made Nigel happy, I went along with it."

She'd gone along with a great deal. Until Taormina, that is. It was one of the several stops the two of them had made on the grand tour of Europe they had taken together back in the late fifties—a trip that, naturally, Elizabeth had paid for.

She'd never minded footing the bill. Nigel had no money, and Daddy was loaded. But in Taormina, Nigel not only took from her, he took one step too far. She could put up with his roving eye, his expensive tastes, his temper tantrums, and even his mean-spiritedness toward others. But desertion was unforgivable. And in Taormina, Nigel had deserted her.

For it was there that Nigel had come out of the closet, or to be more precise, she said, had wandered into it. He had met a beautiful young thing—the boy, in fact, in the picture on the wall—and he'd fallen head over heels. It was the first time in his life—for love, and for a man.

"If you could call that creature male," Elizabeth Salt snorted. "He was the most feminine thing I'd ever seen. He was only seventeen, and his skin was as smooth as a girl's, his features as delicate. He was lovely looking—I have to give Nigel that. And I hear that he really made Nigel suffer when he left him." Her eyes were bright now as she looked up at Michael. "You know, Lieutenant, I'm certain that that boy was the only person who ever made Nigel suffer. The only person who ever touched Nigel at all. The only human being he ever loved."

Her voice cracked, and she took a deep breath before going on. Still, there had been no excuse for Nigel to do what he did to her—no matter how much in love he was. He simply had no right to up and disappear that way—to run away with that kid and leave her alone and dumped. Worse, he was a thief, making off with her wallet, her travelers' checks, her passport, her jade pendant and gold watch. Actually, she suspected that it wasn't Nigel who took all those things—the kid was no doubt responsible for the jewelry. He was probably still wearing her pendant, that crazy little beauty, Mario. Mario Malvolio, if she remembered right.

Mario! M-A-R-I-O. An easy clip to Rio, wasn't it? Of course. This must be the missing Rio—the Rio who'd given Nigel that leather music box. What was that tune it played?

What a cheap and rotten shot, Elizabeth Salt was saying. What humiliation! Alone and violated in Taormino. Alone and stranded. It was like being rolled by a trick, and she never forgave Nigel for it. In fact, she could have killed him. And she couldn't wait for the chance to get even.

As luck would have it, it didn't take too long. About a year after the Taormina business, Nigel was up for a job at TCA, hosting a weekly nationwide talk show on the arts in

America. Naturally, he asked her to put in a word with Daddy.

"I put in a word, all right," Elizabeth Salt said quietly. "I told Daddy that if he hired Whitty then or ever, that if his friends ever hired Nigel Whitty, I'd shoot them all and burn down TCA to boot. And you know what? For once Daddy did just as I asked. Believe me, Daddy didn't do favors very willingly. He didn't do anything willingly. He isn't a willing man. But then, you can see that for yourself, can't you?"

She walked back to the wall of photographs and pointed to one of a stern-looking man with even features, a stiff collar, and a three-piece suit on whose lap sat a little girl with corkscrew curls. Her face was obscured by the giant Shirley Temple doll she carried.

"Look at that frown! Look at that mean, disapproving face," said Elizabeth Salt. "Any other father with such a daughter would have been in heaven. But not Sanford Salt. Not Daddy. He didn't give a damn if his daughter was Madame Curie or Florence Nightingale. And if he'd had an Eleanor Roosevelt, he'd have thrown her back. All he wanted was a Garbo, a Crawford, a Lana Turner. 'They had faces then,' he kept telling me. What did he think was sitting on my neck, my rear end?"

"Can we come back to Whitty for a minute?" Michael interrupted. He was afraid that Elizabeth Salt was losing control and he didn't want to lose her before she finished telling him what he wanted to know. "Was that business with your father why Whitty had it in for you? Was that why he kept taking jabs at you in his column? Or was there something else down in his little black book?"

"His little black book!" Elizabeth Salt threw her head back and laughed. "His little black book! Lieutenant, you've got to be kidding!"

Michael felt himself blushing. "What do you mean, Miss Salt?"

"Nigel never had a little black book!"

"How do you know?"

"I told you, Lieutenant, we were very good friends. There were a lot of things about him I knew. And one thing is that Nigel never had a little black book. Just a black heart and an even blacker soul." She began to laugh hysterically. "You know, the happiest day of my life was the day Daddy blacklisted Nigel Whitty. Tit for tat, you might say. I was happy because Nigel was miserable. And I was even happier because Daddy finally did something for me."

She grew quiet for a moment, thoughtful. "You know what, Lieutenant?" she said. "Screwing Nigel Whitty was the only thing Daddy ever did for me. The only goddamn thing." She reached out and took her father's picture off its hook. "You know, Daddy was a shit! A real shit! And he still is!" she said as she cracked the frame over her knee.

"They're all shits," she screamed. "Beautiful, vain, selfish shits—" She grabbed another photo from the wall.

"—Dussault, the fisherman—" She flung his photo across the room.

"—Mulberry, the tennis player—" His picture shattered against the edge of the conference table.

"—Danny Blue, the whore—" A dart now pierced his other eye.

"—and, of course, Nigel Whitty, the fuck—" She cracked the frame, tore the photo from it, and started to shred it. Then, as Michael snatched the images of Rio and Elizabeth Salt from impending doom, she lit a match, and Nigel Whitty went up in flames.

"Get a move on, birdie," Michael called out. "You don't want to be late for this one, do you? Not for a star-studded bash at the Music Hall. You might miss out on a valuable autograph."

"Very funny—haha," Sara called out from her bathroom where she was putting the finishing touches to her makeup. "Don't worry, I'll be there quick as a flash."

Quick as a flash, my Irish ass, Michael thought. She hadn't ever been on time, much less quick as a flash, since the day he met her. He leaned back into the wicker chair and made himself comfortable.

Well, the day hadn't been a bad one. In fact, the interview with Elizabeth Salt had been very helpful. That lady may have been neurotic, but his instincts told him she was trustworthy. And she sure as hell was on the ball. She had gotten rid of one red herring for him—the little black book—even if she'd thrown in another complication altogether, that of Rio, the boy who'd broken Nigel's heart. Chances were he was still turning tricks and taking gold watches from the bureaus of unsuspecting tourists somewhere in Taormina, but why then had his picture been stolen from Nigel's wall? And it had been stolen, all right, because when Michael showed what was left of Elizabeth Salt's picture to Sara, she'd confirmed that, just as he'd suspected, it was an exact copy of Nigel's missing photo.

Michael shook his head. He wished he could put it all together in a more satisfying way. Perhaps Elizabeth Salt and not Rio was the clue. Maybe she was the one who had broken into Nigel's house and made off with the picture. Yet, that seemed like perfect nonsense. Why then would she have a duplicate hanging on her wall? On the other hand, what if there was no duplicate, simply an original. But then Elizabeth Salt would be advertising her guilt, and that certainly made no sense.

In any case, Michael was convinced that Nigel's murderer was the same person who had broken into Sara's apartment, tried to push her off the balcony at Studio 54, and tried to bean her with that heavy light. Somehow that put quite a few of the suspects out of the picture. Elizabeth Salt was eliminated, since she'd been out of the country while most of these events were taking place. Gyorgii

Gdansk was also out, since he had been standing a bit too dangerously close to the path of the falling light to make it reasonable that he was responsible; while Becky Luna, Lynn Ericson, and Maria Cortese never could have landed that right to the jaw. It had to have been a man. Or Beatrix Leakey.

Michael felt a little better than he had. He may not have come up with the answer yet, but he was making progress at last. He began to whistle while he waited.

"Hey, Detective," Sara called out from the bathroom. "Do you know what tune you're whistling?"

"An Oscar winner?" Michael ventured.

"Wrong again, pal," she returned. "It's 'Arrivederci Roma,' and it's the tune on Nigel's leather music box."

12

RADIO CITY MUSIC HALL.

The Taj Mahal of movie palaces. The most opulent of fantasy worlds to house the most extravagant of fantasies. With its great henna-marble lobby, its sweeping Art Deco staircase, its steel-and-brass doors, and 24-carat gold-leaf ceiling, the grand foyer of the Music Hall seemed a movie set itself—a fabulous and crowded soundstage for a Cecil B. DeMille epic. And never more so than tonight when the New York Film Festival and the Italian-American Anti-Defamation League had joined hands in co-sponsorship of the premiere of Enso Carbonare's comeback film, *The Green Sky*.

"Everyone's here tonight. Every star in the city of New York and, especially, every Italian one," Sara whispered to Michael as she slipped her hand in his and squeezed it excitedly, thinking of the De Niros and Pacinos and Stallones and Travoltas, of the Scorseses and De Palmas and Coppolas, who might be in the crowd.

Funny, she thought, as the rush of excitement came over her, she had been apprehensive about attending this opening and had almost canceled out entirely. All the events since Nigel's death, capped by what she now saw as the Great Betrayal of Richard Singer-Murray, had begun to disillusion her. The glamor of the movie world was tarnishing, or so she'd believed until this very moment when, looking about her, everything seemed to have suddenly regained its luster.

"Not only are all your stars out tonight, birdie, but so are all my suspects," Michael said. "There's Elizabeth Salt"—Sara followed his glance toward the corner of the lobby where, looking like a red ball of fire in a flame-colored dress, Elizabeth Salt stood with her TV crew, microphone in hand—"and even Becky Luna." Sara looked up at the busy, richly colored mural that ran along the staircase wall. There, in front of it, and leaning over the balustrade, was Becky, all in white: white organdy dress, white lace gloves, white face. Had she been prettier, Sara thought, she might have passed for Camille right before her tubercular end. As it was, she looked like a clown who hadn't yet added the red patches.

"What some people will go through just to be at a party," Michael observed dryly as he placed his hand on the small of Sara's back.

"I like the feel of your dress, birdie," he smiled. "Come to think of it, I like the feel of you."

"Smart man, good taste," Sara said, thinking that she had bought this dress—a soft, flowered chiffon in shades of beige, pink, and green—just for such a special occasion. She was glad now. She felt pretty, and Michael made her feel even prettier.

"Lieutenant! Lieutenant! I've been looking for you all over." It was Sammy Nachman, and right now, Sara noticed, his brow was furrowing with worry about his tiny raisin eyes. "You got my invitation, didn't you? To the party at Mamma Leone's later? The mail has been terrible. People have been calling right and left. You will come, won't you? The canneloni's terrific. Wait till you taste it. Paradise! Stuffed with meat from my own kosher butcher. Topped with a green sauce. Green Sky Sauce, we're calling it. Clever, huh? You're coming, aren't you, Lieutenant? And you, too, Sara."

"Sure." Sara nodded.

"I'll try to make it," Michael said.

"Try, really, try," Sammy pressed. After all, he reminded

them, Frankie was supposed to be there. And Dino. And Sergio. And Sophia and Gina and Lina. Sara smiled, imagining the Latin line-up gorging on kosher canneloni buried under Green Sky Sauce.

Then suddenly she remembered: she'd wanted to talk to Richard. Had Nachman seen him?

"Richard? He's not in town."

"He is so in town. He would have told me if he were leaving."

"He would have?" Sammy asked, incredulous. "You two good friends?"

"I wouldn't exactly say that. But we spend enough time together. Or at least we did."

"You did? Then how come you didn't know he's in Scotland shooting a movie?"

Sara laughed. She knew he had the wrong Richard. "That's not the Richard," she announced.

"Oh! You mean the other one. No, he wasn't invited. The I.A.A.D.L. specifically requested, no politicos here tonight."

These were the dangers, Sara thought, of living in a world where everyone was on a first-name basis with everyone else, and especially with kings, queens, and prime ministers. "I meant Richard Singer-Murray," she explained.

Sammy Nachman tapped his balding forehead with his palm.

"*Dummkopf!*" he said, and gestured over his shoulder. "Over there."

Sara looked at Michael. "I'm going over to talk to Richard."

"Can you manage alone," he asked, "I mean, after last night?"

"Of course."

"Then go on without me. I have to check in with the precinct before the movie starts. If you see a Father with my Mother, say hello."

Sara grinned and slipped through the crowd to find Richard Singer-Murray deep in conversation with the bandaged Biffy Adams and the swollen-faced Alan Savory. Totally inattentive to Richard, the two stood pawing each other shamelessly. From the passion in their black-and-blue eyes, not only was it clear that they had forgiven each other after their horrendous fight, but it seemed as if their desire for each other was so intense that they were going to fling themselves on top of each other and copulate right here and now. Richard Singer-Murray was droning on about the *coup* he had just carried out by hiring Fenton Farnabee away from the opposition: "'Fenny's from Heaven' is going to triple our circulation—an ex-astrologer friend of mine told me so," he was saying. "At any rate, Savory, I wanted you to be among the first to know."

"Thanks, Richard, I always appreciate a good tip," Savory replied as he chomped on the tip of Biffy Adams's ear. Biffy groaned and ran her fingers down Savory's neck. Savory, in turn, emitted a sigh.

Sara felt as though she were standing in the midst of a blue movie. She cleared her throat. "Excuse me, Richard, can I talk to you for a minute?"

"Can't you see I'm busy," Richard said coolly. Then his voice dropped what seemed like an octave, and he said out of the corner of his mouth, "Your timing is lousy, kid. I was just making contacts."

If he wasn't, Biffy Adams certainly was. And just as Richard Singer-Murray made his excuses and turned to Sara, she stuck her little pink tongue into Alan Savory's ready and waiting mouth.

"I'm sorry, Richard, but this is important." Sara's voice was sharp.

"Okay, what is it?" Richard asked impatiently.

"It's about Nigel's column. How come you changed the item on *The Green Sky?*"

"What are you talking about?" Richard peered at her with annoyance from behind his wire-rimmed glasses.

"The item with the slug, 'Rainbow in *The Green Sky*.' The rave on Maria Cortese."

Richard looked puzzled. "I didn't change anything," he said. "I want nothing further to do with Maria Cortese, the Italian slut. And I wouldn't expend the energy to pick up one little pencil and change even one tiny word concerning her."

"It wasn't one 'tiny' word, Richard, it was the whole piece. Nigel *hated* the picture," Sara explained. "He said Maria was grotesque, not great. That she was an idiot, not a genius. Look." Sara fished inside her small gold evening purse and brought forth a crumpled piece of yellow paper. Here's the carbon," she said. "Listen to this:

> *Fungus in The Green Sky:* Though we must report that Enzo Carbonare's new movie may not in itself be completely grotesque, its star, Maria Cortese, is. Her role is the kind that would do most actresses in, and does her, since she's on the screen for 180 revolting minutes, playing a wealthy woman who one day decides that her husband either is having an affair with the butler or is dead, and who retaliates either by having an affair with the gardener or committing suicide. Carbonare leaves this ambiguous. But one thing is clear: Cortese herself is idiotic and an insult to femininity. She's one woman who looks better with her blouse on rather than off.

"Whitty was a genius," Richard sighed. "Such pearls of truth! He knew an Italian slut when he saw one. He was a paragon of taste and esthetic judgment."

"That's not the point, Richard." It was Sara who was becoming impatient now. "The point is the difference between Nigel's copy and the copy that you ran."

"But Sara, what ran in the column this morning is

exactly what I received from Nigel"—his pale face looked at her accusingly—"or rather, from you."

"Even the bit about the 'debonair editor' and the 'aging sexpot'?" Sara had to admit that she loved putting her ex-boss on the spot. Still, she was genuinely confused. She didn't know how far the truth was stretched by Singer-Murray or how much to trust his perception of events. And she simply couldn't account for those two reviews. Could Richard have been persuaded to change the piece during the brief period when he and Maria were an item? She didn't know, but obviously anything was possible with someone who thought of himself as "dashing Dickie."

Richard flared his pale nostrils. "Some people," he said icily, removing his rimless glasses and peering at Sara through humorless eyes, "just don't know how to take a joke." And he stalked off into the crowd of potential contacts.

He was really no help whatsoever, Sara shrugged. He had in fact left her even more confused than she had been before. What had happened to that last column, that last "What Nigel Knows"? Had Nigel written a second review which she had overlooked? If so, why? Who had twisted his arm to change his mind? Or had Richard lied to her just now in order to protect his own foolishness and impetuosity from being discovered? But perhaps she was on the wrong track altogether. Perhaps neither Richard nor Nigel but someone else had tampered with the copy. The intruder the night of the break-in? Or the only two people who would have benefited from the changes: Enzo Carbonare and Maria Cortese? Then one of them was most likely the intruder. Unless . . . unless . . . unless someone wanted to frame them? But who? And why?

"Hi, there, sugar plum! Glad you dumped that Lieutenant of yours, that little piggy in blue. Or did he finally find the real woman in him, the little Miss Piggy, and dump you?" It was Fenton, all dolled up in a baby-blue velvet jacket. He either wanted something, or else he had a faulty recollection of last night and Sara's angry exit.

"You look stunning, Fenton. Good enough to eat."

"Oh, don't say that," he giggled as he moved closer. "Any news? Any hot ones for Fenny? Any Fenny-pennies?" His voice quivered with excitement.

"Not a red cent, Fenny."

"Too bad, because I've a rich one for you. What would you say to a remake of *Gone With the Wind*, starring Googie Gdansk as none other than Rhett Butler?"

"Butler? Butler?" a voice behind her thundered. "Who found me out of cognito?" Gyorgii Gdansk whirled into their little circle and brought his hands together in a resounding clap. He glared at Fenton. "You print one word about me and life as Rhett Butler, Farnabeet, and I run you over like skunk on country road, then I make tail for bicycle out of you. Get it?"

As Fenny began to offer an unctuous bit of assurance that of course he wouldn't print a thing, Sara looked around her and, spotting Michael in the crowd, edged away. She had nearly reached him when, suddenly, she was caught in a barrage of flashing bulbs and elbowing reporters. The stars of the evening—Enzo Carbonare, Maria Cortese, and her escort, Danny Blue—had arrived. Maria wore a scarlet smile and a gown of peacock feathers. Peacock feathers, Sara thought, were gorgeous—but only on peacocks.

At last, Sara felt Michael's hand reach out and pull her toward him. It was as if he were rescuing her from a bed of quicksand. He was standing with Lynn Ericson, who looked quite lovely to Sara in her black brocade evening suit, her dark shiny hair swept up in an intricate French knot.

"Lynn was just telling me," Michael said to Sara, "that Nigel was the chief opponent of the Committee to Save Radio City Music Hall. In fact, if I have it right, Lynn, didn't you just say he formed his own group, Friends for the Demolition of the Music Hall?"

Lynn nodded her head yes. "Isn't that incredible?" she remarked. "A film critic in this day and age attempting to destroy this architectural wonder?"

"What's even more incredible," Michael said, "is that this gives me about two thousand more suspects! Just what I need." His eyes skimmed the crowd. "I guess you didn't find my mother?" he asked Sara.

"Sorry, no."

"What about you, Lynn, you didn't happen to see a Father around, a priest, I mean?"

"Why? You want to take confession? Are things that bad?"

"No, an old friend of the family. He's here with my mother. He's her boyfriend, so to speak."

"Does he have any friends?" Lynn laughed. "I think I've finished with body and I've had it with heart and mind. I'd like to try a little soul for a change."

"Well, I'll say a prayer for you," Michael replied. "But right now, I think we'd better look for the divine couple." Taking Sara's hand, he guided her through the grand foyer and past the steel-and-bronze doors into the Music Hall's auditorium. "If I know Bridget Connelly," he said as they made their way down the aisle, "she made a beeline for those seats. Just to make sure nobody else grabbed them."

Sure enough, Sara thought, he was right. For there, stiff in their starched black suits and prim white collars, like two pilgrims in a time-warp, sat Michael's mother and the Father.

"Bridget Connelly, Father Fitzgerald. This is Sara Nightingale," Michael said, bending down and giving his mother a peck on the cheek.

Bridget Connelly took Sara's hand in hers. "Isn't it a glamorous evening here, dear?" she beamed. She craned her neck and twisted around in her seat. "Tell me, you haven't happened across Jimmy Cagney tonight, have you?"

Sara smiled.

"No, of course not," Michael said.

Bridget swallowed her disappointment and soon enough distracted herself with the other celebrities in the movie house. She confided to Sara and Michael that she had read in the *Star*, while waiting on line at Key Food, that Danny Blue was a real lady killer. Had they heard that too? She'd also read something about the daughter of Billie Glover—rest her soul—being mixed up with drugs. And now that she'd seen the poor girl, she was sure the awful story was true. That Becky Luna really should see a doctor at once—if not, in fact, a priest. As for Elizabeth Salt, she looked prettier in person than on TV.

"But not as pretty as you, Bridget," Father Fitzgerald said, leaning close to her and patting her hand.

"Oh, Father, be gone with you." Bridget Connelly blushed.

Sara liked her. She was funny and better still, enthusiastic—a quality, Sara thought, really rare in people her age. She couldn't help but be struck by the great difference between Bridget Connelly and her own unflappable, stuffy mother back in Grosse Pointe. Were Michael and she also so different? Perhaps it was true, after all, that opposites attract.

"Isn't this Radio City Music Hall really something?" Bridget Connelly was saying.

It certainly was. Sara looked up at the great sunburst arches and the massive organ sitting to the left of the stage. She recalled the first time she'd been here. It had been on her first visit to New York. She'd been eight, and her parents brought her here for a special treat. The movie had been *The Unsinkable Molly Brown*, and the stage show featured the Rockettes dancing in unison to Ravel's *Bolero*.

Sara couldn't get over so many people lifting their legs all at once. In her mind, it had been a miracle, and for the longest time after, she had wanted to be a Rockette. Even now the idea struck her as somehow appealing. Being a Rockette seemed an infinitely more significant occupation than being a gossip columnist.

Now the lights dimmed, interrupting her thoughts, and *The Green Sky* clouded the screen with a ten-minute shot of what looked like thick, boiling pea soup. Finally, the green sky faded and was transformed into a lush garden through which Maria Cortese, playing a bored, elegant contessa, ambled at a snail's pace. She paused and smelled the roses, then the daffodils and the pansies, and after what seemed an interminable amount of time, leaned toward the giant zinnias. A man appeared from nowhere. "The count is dead," he yawned.

"No," she said, crumpling a puffy white flower in her fist, then tossing its petals madly over her shoulder. "He is only dead to me. But he is very much alive to the butler."

"There is no butler," the man yawned.

Bridget Connelly yawned along with him. She leaned over to Sara and whispered, "I don't get these new kinds of movies, dear. I like a good old-fashioned story, don't you? A movie where something happens, where you know who to cheer for right from the beginning."

On screen, Maria Cortese had descended, slowly and carefully, into a bed of petunias. The camera, obviously infatuated with the image, repeated the same shot over and over again.

"Dear, is it possible the projector's stuck?" Bridget whispered to Sara.

If it had been, it was now unstuck. And Maria Cortese was rolling around in the bed of petunias like a ship in a storm. Back and forth, back and forth.

"I love you," the man yawned, clipping a nearby hedge. "You are beautiful as a hollyhock."

"Dear, do you think she's beautiful?" Bridget asked, placing her small plump hand on Sara's. "In the days of Maureen O'Hara, she would never have been a glamor girl."

Sara was amused since Bridget Connelly was probably right. In the golden past, Maria Cortese, with her aggressively female aura, her almost terrifyingly voluptuous looks, would never have been taken seriously. Maybe she would have played the comic vamp, maybe the second banana.

Maria Cortese groaned in the flower bed. The man put down his clippers and bent over her. Lovingly, he crushed a petunia into her gaping, impassioned mouth.

"Look!" Bridget Connelly pointed out; "her head is bigger than his?"

Now the man removed first one of Maria's shoes, then the other, and began massaging her feet.

"And look at that, dear, her feet are so big! Not ladylike at all," Bridget Connelly whispered. "Really now!" She leaned across Sara and tapped Michael. "Mick, what kind of moving picture is this you bring me to where the leading lady looks more like a man than the leading man?"

Oh, my God! Sara thought. Could it be? Oh, no. It was ridiculous, absurd. But she couldn't help flashing back to the photograph that had been stolen from Nigel's wall. What a weird connection, that faded photograph of Nigel and that young boy in Taormina and this movie. Oh, no, Sara told herself. It was too incredible, too coincidental. Still, as her eyes fixed on Maria Cortese's face, she couldn't get that boy out of her mind. The resemblance was there. Yes. The two people—the woman and the boy, the movie star and the young hustler. Could they be the same? The same, yet somehow different. Yes, of course. Maria—Mario—Rio. That was the connection. Maria Cortese was a man. Or had been one.

It was all falling into place. The review of *The Green Sky* with its snide innuendos—"an insult to femininity," Nigel had written. Then the blind items in his column, especially the one that appeared on the day of his death:

> What chic celebrity, having slowly chomped on the feminist chestnut that it's a woman's world, has decided with a vengeance to cut off all her old acquaintances?

Even the intruder with the sharp right jab. It could have been Maria. How easily she could have gotten all the information about Sara working on the columns at home from that idiot, Richard Singer-Murray. And certainly she had been at Studio 54 and on the set of *Brother, Can You Spare a Dance?* Sara laughed out loud. A strange shiver of delight ran down her spine. How perfect, she thought. What divine justice! If, in fact, Maria had once been a man, all the greatest studs in the world—the Danny Blues and Gyorgii Gdansks—couldn't tell the difference.

Sara's eyes searched the darkness. There, some four rows back, sat Richard Singer-Murray, his expression one of evident discomfort, his eyes turned not toward the screen, but toward Danny Blue whose arm was flung possessively around Maria's shoulder. Maria nuzzled him, then got up with a flourish.

"Watching such *splendore*, my heart beat like wild flower. I must take intermission in room of powder, she announced *ad alta voce*. Then, saying her "*prego, pregos,*" she quickly made her way through the row toward the aisle.

Sara stood up. She knew she had to follow her.

Michael grabbed her hand. "What are you doing, birdie?" he asked.

"Going to the ladies' room," she answered quickly. "If I'm not back in ten minutes, follow me—or call the police."

"How many times do I have to remind you, I *am* the police," Michael replied.

"And a mother couldn't be prouder," Bridget cooed happily.

Sara rushed up the aisle, into the lobby which was now devoid of revelers, and descended the grand staircase. Far down to the right, she saw Maria Cortese entering the ladies' lounge. Sara rushed after her, first into the anteroom, then into the mirrored beige and silver powder room. Maria Cortese was standing before a mirror brushing her thick black hair.

"You have lipstick, no?" she asked Sara. "To make lips like cherries?"

Sara shook her head. "Sorry." She studied Maria primping before the mirror, laying out an abundant supply of eye shadow, rouge, powder, mascara, and liner, and finally, delighting in her image like a spoiled child who not only knows she's beautiful but has fallen in love with that beauty. Sara felt a stitch in her side, suddenly wondering if she were about to overstep her bounds.

"You like the film?" Maria asked. "*Molto* sophisticated, no?"

"Yes." Sara was getting cold feet.

"You like me? I pretty, no?" Maria sat down in an upholstered green leather seat. She fluffed out her thick dark hair and stared, mesmerized, into the glass.

Sara braced herself. "I saw a picture of you today."

"Ah." Maria was pleased. "In *Time*? *Life*? *Newsweek*? Or *Playboy* centerfold?"

"No. In Taormina, 1959."

Maria gasped. "What you talking about?"

"You, Nigel Whitty, and Elizabeth Salt. In Taormina in 1959."

Maria threw her head back and laughed wildly. "That not me, *carissima*. That my twin brother, Mario."

Sara had never accounted for that possibility. But she just knew it was nonsense. "You're lying, Maria. That was you."

"How you know this?" Maria squinted suspiciously.

"Nigel," Sara gulped. "Nigel told me."

"What he tell you?"

"He told me about . . ." Sara hesitated, "about Taormina."

Maria drew herself up proudly. "Then he tell you how wonderful Mario be? He tell you how much he love me. Right?"

Sara nodded. "Right."

"He tell you how every man—and every woman—all want night of joy with Mario. How Elizabeth Salt want Mario, too, but how Mario no want her. Mario, you see, want only men. Always. From time he was little *bambino*—and felt like little *bambina.*"

Her voice became husky, almost forlorn, and then Maria launched into the sad, sad tale of a young boy too sensitive for his own good, and too beautiful for everyone's else's. From the age of three, he knew he was different. It was not only that he had no father, it was also that he lived together with his fifteen-year-old mother and her twelve female friends in a warm and busy household—commonly known in the village as the bordello. Ah, Mama! Maria recalled her fondly, Mama with the black silk stockings, the negligees with cut-outs in special places, and the sleek, long black whips. Mama smelling of Nina Ricci and cigars and what Rio later discovered was sperm. As a tiny *ragazzo*, he would follow Mama and her friends around, from room to room, from bed to bed. He loved to stroke their silky kimonos and polish their leather boots. How excited he was by the little tokens they received—the bottles of chianti, the boxes of pasta, the American cigarettes and chocolates that were left on their doorstep below the red light. And he knew he was like these women in his heart and in his soul. And soon, though his body was different in certain places, his smooth and delicate features were like theirs too. In fact, by the time he was fourteen, his beauty surpassed every one of theirs. Which is when Mama and all the rest of the girls threw him out.

"But Mario learn well. And from home in the street, Mario do as Mama did. But though he much desired by sailors and soldiers and thinkers like Nigel Whitty, he still feel something strange in his way. *Capisce,* Sara Reporter?"

Sara nodded. Somehow, despite the madness, she was touched. She couldn't quite grasp the feelings of this terrifying, yet pathetic creature, but she knew they were deep and painful.

"Yes, Mario feel something wrong," Maria went on. "So one day, when shooting star fall in Venus, Mario get sign. Sign to create a great woman, sign to re-create Mama . . ."

"So you had an operation," Sara interrupted. "A sex change . . ."

"Not just sex change," Maria thundered. "Not just sex change. No simple case of doctor's knife, cut-cut and bang-bang. I am woman from tip to top, from out to in, from eyelash to fingernail." Triumphantly, she held out her long, scarlet nails for Sara to examine.

"Very lovely," Sara murmured politely, not knowing what else was expected of her.

"Yes." Maria tossed her head back. "Everyone think so. Today, Maria Cortese most desired woman in world. Ask Danny Blue. Ask Googie Gdansk. Ask your own Ricardo Singer-Murray. Every man want Maria. Every man"—her voice suddenly broke—"but two."

Sara was about to ask which two, but before she could, Maria told her.

"One—Enzo. He so stupid. All he care about is his estates, his mother, his genius movie. He not interested in bed except to give rest, he say, to creative spark."

"And the other man?" Sara encouraged. "Nigel Whitty?"

"Yes." Maria nodded. "He love me so much as Mario. . . . He call me 'Bello Rio.' 'Mio Rio' he call me too. And when I surprise him as Maria, he cannot accept it. He a true Scorpio. Narrow mind. Cruel, evil. 'I never love a man before you,' he scream. 'What you do to me, you phony cunt? I get even with you,' he say. 'You live to regret you are woman. Every day of your life you be sorry.' But he say too, 'You owe me, Rio. You hurt me very much in my heart and you owe me.' Then he send me bill for two hundred thousand lire, he say, 'for suffering,' plus ten thousand lire for transportation and postage. That *bastardo,* you see, begin to blackmail me, to suck my blood, to threaten to ruin me."

Sara's heart began to pound. "And that's why you killed him," she gasped.

"Yes," Maria hissed. "That why I steal his filthy ribbon and squeeze it around his neck and pull tighter and tighter and tighter until the *bastardo* is dead. 'You Scorpio,' I whisper to him. "May you sizzle in the fires of hell, you prick.' That shut him up." She whipped around like a snake. "But not shut you up, Sara Reporter," she glared.

"Why you print all those terrible things, Sara Reporter?" she asked suddenly. "You want to hurt another woman, a sister, a human person of your own kind? What I do to you, *carissima*, that you want to harm Maria?" Her eyes began to blaze, her voice began to tremble. "You jealous. Maria know you jealous. But I find columns with help of Ricardo Singer-Murray. I say to him when we are in office, 'You big strong editor, so many papers on your handsome desk, what this one? What that one?' And he tell me, that *stupido* who so moron that he never notice I take Nigel Whitty's columns and when he on telephone, I make changes. He so deaf-dumb-blind that he even help. I say, 'Ricardo, *caro,* what is opposite of *idiot*?' And he say, '*genius,*' and I fix copy. And now, *carissima* Sara, "I fix you too."

Maria reached into her purse, and suddenly Sara saw the glint of steel. Was that a knife Maria held in her hand?

Sara took a deep breath. "Now, Maria," she began, "let's not do anything rash. Let's talk a little more."

"Maria talk too much already tonight," she said menacingly and took a step toward Sara.

Sara backed away. "Look," she said, "I think you should calm down. I can really help you. I . . ."

But before she could finish, Maria lunged at her. Sara screamed and started to run. But where to? Maria was blocking her way out of the powder room, and so the only direction to go in was toward the inside of the ladies' room. Sara was terrified of being trapped, but she had no choice. And besides, the thought flashed through her mind that she might be able to lock herself in a stall for some protection.

"Help!" she screamed as she ran, her heels clattering on the black tile floor.

Then she saw it: a door marked "Emergency Only" at the end of the row of stalls. If this wasn't an emergency, what was? Sara spun around, flung the door open, and found herself racing down a long narrow corridor. She could hear Maria behind her and she hoped behind Maria, Michael as well.

Michael hadn't taken his eyes off his digital watch since Sara left, and it wasn't only that he was worried about her. It was also that there was nothing whatever on the screen to distract him. Fifty minutes into the film and *The Green Sky* hadn't as yet gotten off the ground—not only figuratively but literally. Maria was still lolling about her garden. Things perked up a bit, however, when she rolled on to a thorny wild rosebush and began to cry out alternately, "Help," as she rolled to the left, and "I love it," as she rolled to the right. Then, she rolled too far, and with the rosebush at a distance, things quieted down again. Michael checked his watch. Ten minutes had passed. He glanced around the auditorium—no sign of Sara, no sign of Maria. It was time, he figured to go take a look. . . .

Sara ran down the long narrow corridor, wishing she hadn't been wearing such very high heels. Her pulse was racing and she was almost completely out of breath by the time she arrived at a narrow flight of stairs and began to take them, two steps at a time. There was no one around and, although she wanted to cry out for help, she knew it was pointless.

What was it Maria was screaming at her? Something in Italian? She couldn't make out the words, and perhaps it was for the best. Maria was probably threatening to do some unspeakable thing to her, and Sara preferred not to hear. Not to know. To be surprised. Very funny, Nightingale, she said to herself as she clambered to the top of the stairs, blood pounding in her temples. You picked a perfect time to be amused. Maria, she could feel, was barking at her heels. And Michael, nowhere in sight.

At the top of the steps, Sara turned and ran through a door. Please, she prayed, let it lead to people. Instead, it led to an empty, cavernous, and dimly lit space. Where was she? She wanted to stop and collect herself, but she could hear Maria gaining on her. She propelled herself forward. Move, Nightingale, she told herself, move. She was nearing collapse, but she had no choice other than to keep pressing onward.

Michael ran out into the lobby. His eye caught a woman in an elegantly beaded gown at the top of the stairs, evidently on her way to the powder room. He crossed the floor and, taking the steps two at a time, followed her along the balcony corridor to a small room at the far end. As he entered, his hand searched for his gun, which was secured comfortingly under his shoulder.

"Eech! Help! A man!" screamed the woman he'd followed, who was now powdering her nose in the dozen or so multiple mirrors lining the circular room.

Michael dashed past her and into the inner room lined with stalls. "Sara!" he shouted. "Sara? Are you here? Answer me." Frantically he began banging on the doors. "Sara? Sara?" But no answer. Goddamnit, where was she?

Suddenly one door swung open and practically smacked him in the face. "Get out, you pervert," ordered a large woman with short gray hair who began to beat him with her tiny gold-lame evening bag.

"Madame, I am no pervert; I am the police," Michael said with as much dignity as he could muster under the circumstances. And then he pushed past her and headed out of the room. . . .

Sara was disoriented. She tried to focus her eyes. Suddenly she felt herself running into the folds of a thick, heavy velvet curtain, and she realized that she must be on the stage. All she had to do was to get through that curtain—after all, on the other side of it were people, thousands of them. She began pushing, but the heavy drapes wouldn't separate. Perhaps, she could lift them—but no, they were of astonishing weight and simply too much for her. Frantically, she made her way along the velvet path. It seemed interminable. And where was Maria? Were those footsteps she was hearing? She couldn't tell.

Sara steeled herself and grabbed the drape for all she was worth, literally swinging on it. And suddenly, it began to move. As the two immense black panels parted, an eerie light permeated the cavernous space. What was it? Of course, the film itself, filtering its light through the huge wall of screen. Another barricade to that auditorium filled with people. How to get out from behind it? Where to go? Sara tried to adjust her eyes, and as she did, she saw Maria at the other end of the stage, poised like a tigress stalking her prey.

Panicked, Sara looked about her. She stepped back and bumped into a huge instrument panel. Perhaps the stage controls were here—perhaps a way to raise the screen? Madly, she began pressing buttons, flipping levers. Lights flickered on, then off. Maria was closer now, calling out something to her. Oh, where was Michael? Sara ran toward the back of the cavernous space. If she could get to the rear, there'd surely be a door, a stairwell, a way out.

Frantically, she ran across the huge stage, tripping against a raised step. She climbed up onto it, losing her balance once again and this time, falling. Somehow, she realized, she had ended up on a circular elevated platform—whose motion she must have started when working the instrument panel. It must have been ten, fifteen feet in diameter and was now ascending—two feet, three, four. . . . "Help!" she began to cry, but no one, she knew, could hear her above the din of the movie's soundtrack. The platform kept rising—seven feet, eight—and below, she could see Maria, her peacock feathers shimmering in the strange, unearthly light. She was at the instrument panel and pulling the levers like a madwoman.

Michael rushed down the steps and across the foyer to the uniformed usher who was lounging distractedly near the heavy brass front doors. "Look, I was just in the ladies' room upstairs. Where's another one?" he asked quickly.

"Busy fellow," the usher smirked, raising an eyebrow.

"Police," Michael answered and flashed his badge.

"Well, then, try the grand lounge. It's quite chi-chi."

"Where's the grand lounge?" Michael asked. His patience was wearing thin now.

"Down there." The usher pointed toward a staircase leading to a basement level. "Down, like the stock market, like the economy, like my spirits."

"Sorry to hear that, buddy," Michael said as he ran down the stairs.

"Anyone in there?" he called, standing now at the entrance to the ladies' lounge. No answer. "Police," he announced and charged in. The anteroom was empty. The powder room was empty. The washroom was empty. And so was the room that housed the stalls. "Sara!" he shouted out. No answer again. Then he saw that the "Emergency Only" exit door stood ajar. He raced toward it. . . .

The platform began to descend now, lower and lower. At floor level, Sara leapt off and scrambled across the stage. Her ankle twisted, and she fell to her knees, ripping her dress. Get up, Nightingale, she commanded herself, get up. Straining and breathless, she fought her way to her feet, but then faltered and stumbled. Just a few more steps, she reminded herself, keep going, girl. But suddenly the stage seemed like a mine field, full of holes, traps, and mysterious obstacles conspiring to do her in and beginning to move in slow motion—turning clockwise, counterclockwise, rising, and falling. Something—a huge rope perhaps—was swinging across the stage as well, and it was directly in her path. Sara ducked to miss it, but a sandbag hit her in the belly. Teetering, she caught herself once again. But now the floor beneath her began to turn, and she uttered a short, terrified scream as she found herself caught for a moment on a huge revolving turntable. She jumped off, her equilibrium shot. Dizzily, she spun about, then staggered, directionless, across the stage. Once again, the floor beneath her began to rise. She was on another elevated platform and this time, as a bloodcurdling laugh informed her, she was not alone. Maria and Maria's knife were going up with her.

Michael found himself in a small, tiled passageway with one path leading straight ahead and one forking directly to his left. He listened carefully for some sound, some clue, and hearing none, sprinted to his left. "Sara!" he called, but only the sound of his footsteps on the concrete floor answered him. "Sara?" After a few yards, he retraced his way to the main corridor and moved quickly along the mustard-colored tile walls toward a flight of stairs. Where was this passage leading? Where was he in relationship to the goddamned stage? And where in God's name was Sara?

As the platform rose, five, eight, then ten feet off the ground, Maria, wobbling unsteadily, took one step toward Sara and then another. Sara wanted to talk to her, to try to soothe her, to reason with her, but the woman looked too fierce, and Sara was too frightened to find her own voice. She opened her mouth to speak, but only a pathetic garbled squeak seemed to come forth. Meanwhile, Maria's face, distorted by strange harsh shadows, was looming larger as she moved closer now, suddenly flinging herself on Sara. Sara struggled for all she was worth, but she was no match for this Amazon. And where was the knife? Her eyes caught it, menacing her from above. She leaned over and bit Maria on the forearm, hard.

"*Squaldrina,*" Maria screamed, and the steel blade went flying thirteen feet to the floor below.

Suddenly, a burst of light, like a giant klieg, illuminated the stage. The heat was immense, and the brightness was blinding. It took Sara a moment to realize what was happening: the screen was rolling up, and the film was being projected onto the barren stage, onto Sara and Maria.

Maria seemed stunned. The light paralyzed her, and for a moment, Sara thought she could detect in Maria's face an expression not of fury, but of utter humiliation. The raised screen had exposed her—she was found out, publicly shamed—and her distorted features made clear her horror. But then, as if she had somehow suddenly decided to make the best of a rotten situation, she began to compose herself. She rose to her feet, turned toward the light like a moth, and faced her newfound audience with great dignity. Spreading her arms in a gesture of theatrical beneficence, she started to step forward on the elevator platform. Just then, the colors of the light changed—apparently, the screen image had returned to the soupy green sky. Maria's perception was obviously affected by the shift in color and the degree of light, for she misjudged her step, her foot tangling in the network of peacock feathers that was her dress.

"Ohhh, my focking feathers," she screamed, as she put her heel through her hem, then stumbled and fell off the elevator onto the revolving turntable thirteen feet below.

The audience shrieked, and Sara heard Michael call out, "Birdie, birdie, stay put—don't move. I'm here below, I'll get you down."

Sara peered over the edge of the platform in search of Michael. But all she could see was a mass of delicate feathers spinning on the turntable below, around and around and around. . . .

"Birdie, you're a genius," Michael said, walking into the upstairs ladies' lounge at the Music Hall. Sara was lying on a couch, covered with Father Fitzgerald's black coat. Bridget Connelly was fussing over her, alternately feeding her hot tea from a container and cold Irish whisky from a flask. Father Fitzgerald sat in a corner, rosary beads in his hands and a look of deep concern in his eyes. He had just administered the last rites to Maria Cortese.

"Oh, Michael," Sara sighed. "I'm so sorry about Maria. I'm so sorry about everything."

Why had she been so foolish? Why had she been so determined to confront Maria just when and where she did? Had she acted less hastily, Maria might still be alive at this moment. A great wave of sadness overcame her.

"Hey, birdie," Michael whispered, "it's tough sometimes, I know." He bent down and kissed her on the forehead.

She liked that kiss. Already, she felt a little better.

"Where were you when I needed you?" she asked.

"Well, this time, Nightingale, I was late. I waited just a little too long before crashing the ladies' room."

"Promise me," she smiled, "you'll never be late again."

"Never," he said.

Sara sighed. "What a crazy story. But it all fits together now, doesn't it?"

"Just about. Everything except maybe Nigel Whitty himself. I mean just who he was, where he really came from."

Sadly, the Father rolled his eyes downward. "But Michael," he said, "that doesn't really matter now, does it? What matters is where he is at this moment, Jesus be praised."

"What bothers me," Sara said, "is Elizabeth Salt. How is it that she never recognized Maria, especially since they almost pulled each other's hair out last week?"

"I asked her about it," Michael said. "She was really amazed that you were able to make the connection. She said you should come to see her when she gets back from Peking. Maybe she can get you a job in her photo research department. And Richard Singer-Murray also asked me to send his congratulations. He says he's making you a big item."

Sara burst out laughing. "Well, I've always wanted to play the Music Hall," she said, "but never in my wildest dreams did I aspire to be an item."

"And did you ever dream," Michael added, "that you'd be an item in 'Fenny's from Heaven'?"

"Oh, *Pennies from Heaven*!" Bridget Connelly exclaimed brightly. "Remember that, Father, with Bing Crosby? One of my favorite movies, one of my favorite Irish lads, and one of my favorite songs. I even have the record," she said, patting Sara's hand. "And," Bridget Connelly glanced up at Michael, "if Mick would bring you down tomorrow, I could cook up his favorite dish, my own corned beef and cabbage, play you some of my favorite records, and even show you my scrapbooks."

"Scrapbooks? Of Michael, when he was little?" Sara smiled.

"Goodness gracious, no," said Bridget Connelly, "of Jimmy Cagney."

Sara laughed and squeezed Bridget Connelly's hand. "You know, Mrs. Connelly, I think this is the beginning of a beautiful friendship."

Michael looked at the two of them, and his heart sank as he imagined them in days to come: the two women in his life forever exchanging movie-star stories, gushing over dashing heroes, and rushing off to every cockamamie movie in town while the corned beef and cabbage simmered on the stove. Oh, well, he thought, smiling. Small price to pay, small vice, too. And, ironically enough, a bit of movie trivia began to flash through his mind. . . . What was it? What was that line? He couldn't quite recall.

Oh, yeah, now he had it: "Nobody's perfect."